Why hadn't he just stayed away?

Because there had been no way in hell to predict Vanessa's murder. No way to know that deed would bring Julia back into his life, and, with her, the reminder of all he'd given up.

Julia, who made him want to make promises he couldn't keep. Julia, who wasn't just any woman. She was the *only* woman.

And now she knew the truth. Knew he'd loved her when he walked out, knew the real reason for his leaving. Sloan's mouth tightened as he pictured the mix of fire and challenge—and hurt—that had leaped into her eyes.

Maybe after all this time it was best. Maybe someday she would develop a grudging understanding of why he'd purposely destroyed her love for him.

Maybe she wouldn't hate him for the rest of her life....

Dear Reader,

They say all good things must end someday, and this month we bid a reluctant farewell to Nora Roberts' STARS OF MITHRA trilogy. *Secret Star* is a fitting windup to one of this *New York Times* bestselling author's most captivating miniseries ever. I don't want to give anything away, but I will say this: You're in for the ride of your life—and that's after one of the best openings ever. Enjoy!

Marilyn Pappano also wraps up a trilogy this month. *Knight Errant* is the last of her SOUTHERN KNIGHTS miniseries, the story of Nick Carlucci and the bodyguard he reluctantly accepts, then falls for—hook, line and sinker. Then say goodbye to MAXIMILLIAN'S CHILDREN, as reader favorite Alicia Scott offers *Brandon's Bride,* the book in which secrets are revealed and the last of the Ferringers finds love. Award-winning Maggie Price is back with her second book, *The Man She Almost Married,* and Christa Conan checks in with *One Night at a Time,* a sequel to *All I Need.* Finally, welcome new author Lauren Nichols, whose *Accidental Heiress* is a wonderful debut.

And then come back next month for more of the best romantic reading around—right here at Silhouette Intimate Moments.

Yours,

Leslie Wainger
Senior Editor and Editorial Coordinator

Please address questions and book requests to:
Silhouette Reader Service
U.S.: 3010 Walden Ave., P.O. Box 1325, Buffalo, NY 14269
Canadian: P.O. Box 609, Fort Erie, Ont. L2A 5X3

THE MAN SHE ALMOST MARRIED

MAGGIE PRICE

Silhouette®
INTIMATE™MOMENTS®
Published by Silhouette Books
America's Publisher of Contemporary Romance

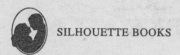

SILHOUETTE BOOKS

ISBN 0-373-07838-2

THE MAN SHE ALMOST MARRIED

Copyright © 1998 by Margaret Price

Printed in U.S.A.

Books by Maggie Price

Silhouette Intimate Moments

Prime Suspect #816
The Man She Almost Married #838

MAGGIE PRICE

turned to crime at the age of twenty-two. That's when she went to work at the Oklahoma City Police Department. As a civilian crime analyst, she evaluated suspects' methods of operation during the commission of robberies and sex crimes, and developed profiles on those suspects. During her tenure at OCPD, Maggie stood in lineups, worked on homicide task forces, established procedures for evidence submittal, even posed as the wife of an undercover officer in the investigation of a fortune-teller.

While at OCPD, Maggie stored up enough tales of intrigue, murder and mayhem to keep her at the keyboard for years. The first of those tales won the Romance Writers of America's Golden Heart Award for Romantic Suspense and was published by Silhouette Intimate Moments.

Maggie invites her readers to contact her at 5208 W. Reno, Suite 350, Oklahoma City, OK 73127-6317.

To my very fantastic critique partners, Nancy Berland and Merline Lovelace. Thank you for taking time on that wickedly cold January day to meet over brunch and weave your magic. You make the bad times better, and the good times fantastic. When it comes to support, you guys put an orthopedic mattress to shame.

Chapter 1

"A corpse awaits us."

With her cell phone crammed between her cheek and shoulder, Sergeant Julia Cruze checked the clock on her car's dashboard. Their shift didn't kick in for fifteen minutes, and already her partner was on the line to her.

She let out a weighty sigh as she glanced at her leather tote on the passenger seat, the morning newspaper bulging out its unzipped top. Inside was the case file on the unsolved homicide that had plagued her for the past month. She'd planned to spend part of the day reinterviewing the victim's neighbors and family. Now, unless they got lucky—real lucky—she'd have another case file to add to the one in her tote.

"What have we got?" Julia asked, slowing the unmarked cruiser to legal speed in case a change of direction was in her future.

"A woman bought it in the parking garage of her office building," her partner replied cheerfully. "I'm just leaving the station, so I don't have any specifics. But I imagine there's blood, gore and mayhem involved. The perfect welcome back after our days off.''

Rolling her eyes, Julia sipped the steaming coffee she'd purchased at the minimarket around the corner from her apartment. Sergeant Travis Halliday, her rookie partner of six months, had jumped into the fray of the Oklahoma City Police Department's Homicide detail with the gusto of a kid attacking Christmas presents. In a contest between Halliday and the medical examiner, it would be nose-to-nose who had a keener interest in viewing dead bodies.

''Here's an idea, Halliday,'' Julia began dryly. ''Instead of me driving around all morning looking for the scene, why don't you give me the address?''

''The deceased awaits us at Remington Aerospace's corporate office. Address is—''

''I know it,'' Julia shot back, and set her teeth against the quick, instinctive lurch of her stomach. Two years, and the name still had the impact of a bare-fisted punch.

''Ouch. What's the matter? Did you and Bill go a few rounds last night?''

''We never fight,'' Julia said, then blared her horn at a dented taxi that had cut in front of her. ''Does Lieutenant Ryan know we're on this?''

''He wasn't in the office when the call came in,'' Halliday answered. ''Anyway, you and I are first on the schedule so I—''

''Forget it. I'll meet you there,'' Julia said, then ended the connection.

She dragged in air between her teeth and waited for the tightness in her chest to ease. When it didn't, her temper stirred. ''Can the emotions, Cruze,'' she muttered. ''You got over Sloan Remington a long time ago.''

Punching the gas pedal, she lightened her mood with a neat, illegal U-turn against traffic.

It was barely eight o'clock, yet heat hung in humid waves in the still July air. Julia stood at the entrance to

Remington Aerospace's belowground parking garage, slid the holster that held her 9 mm Smith & Wesson onto her belt, then shrugged into the black pin-striped jacket that matched her slacks. After clipping her gold badge onto the breast pocket, she retrieved her coffee cup and recorder off the top of her cruiser. She glanced across her shoulder toward the street and scanned the continuous line of rush-hour traffic. If Halliday didn't show in the next few minutes, she'd go in without him and let him catch up.

Looking back toward the building, she took a sip of coffee, her gaze drifting upward like slow smoke. The sleek structure of glass and polished metal jutted fifteen floors from the concrete and surrounding pristine flower beds. When Julia realized her gaze had stopped its slow rise just short of the top floor, she expelled an oath. "Get a grip," she said in disgust. "Sloan's not there. Hasn't been for two years."

And even if the man who once occupied the CEO's expansive top-floor office was to stride out the revolving door this instant, it would mean nothing to her. Because *he* meant nothing to her. As if to lend credence to her thoughts, Julia glanced at the diamond engagement ring glittering on her left hand. She'd put her life back together, moved on.

The shout of her name coming from behind dispersed the ghosts. Turning, she watched Travis Halliday sprint toward her on short, stocky legs, his striped tie fluttering against the lapel of his suit coat.

"'Morning, partner." Grinning broadly, he tipped a bag sporting a bakery shop logo her way. "Chocolate chip heads today's menu."

Julia waved the bag away. "Keep eating cookies for breakfast, Halliday, and you'll have twenty pounds of lard on you before that baby gets here."

"What can I say?" he asked good-naturedly. "Pam gets a craving, I share the bounty." He sent a disparaging look at the foam cup in Julia's hand. "At least I don't expose my stomach lining to convenience store coffee. That stuff'll kill you.''

"My stomach," she commented as they ducked beneath a stretch of yellow crime scene tape.

Halliday glanced up at the towering glass structure and emitted a low whistle between his teeth. "Impressive. Must be good money in the aerospace business these days."

"If you call nineteen billion dollars in annual sales impressive."

He slanted her a look. "How the hell do you know that?"

"I read the paper," Julia answered, then nodded at the ebony-skinned uniformed officer who approached, notepad in hand. She was glad to see Roosevelt O'Shea on the scene. They'd worked the same shift in Patrol before her promotion to Homicide, and she knew he'd make sure things ran by the book.

"What have we got, O'Shea?" she asked while anchoring her recorder to the strap of her purse.

"Victim's a Vanessa West," the officer stated. "White female, early twenties. M.E.'s with her now."

"How'd she die?" Halliday asked.

"Bullet in the back."

Before them, the barred gate at the head of the ramp leading down to the parking garage stood open. Julia looked up, taking in the surveillance camera with its dark lens tilted at the security card scanner.

"Is the gate working?" she asked.

"Was when I got here," O'Shea answered. "The lab boys had them open it so they could move their equipment in and out."

"Are there cameras in the garage?"

"Just one, on the door that leads into the building," O'Shea said. "The door's secured like the gate—you have to scan a card to get in." The officer sent her a knowing smile. "Sorry, Sarge, the homicide occurred out of range of the camera. Guess you'll have to solve it the old-fashioned way."

Julia's mouth curved. "One can hope." As a concession to the heat, she slid a hand behind her neck and lifted her dark hair. "We need the tapes off both cameras."

"Already done," O'Shea said. "I turned them over to the lab."

"Who found the body?" Halliday asked as he and Julia fell in step with the officer. They headed down the ramp into the parking garage's welcome coolness.

O'Shea checked his notes. "Guy by the name of Smithson. Don Smithson. Says he drove in, parked and nearly tripped over her on his way to the door. He's shook up, lost his breakfast before he went in to report what he'd found."

"Where is he now?"

"Over there with one of my men. I put him out of sight of the body. Figured that'd be best."

Julia glanced across the garage. A uniformed officer stood beside a man hunched in a metal chair. The man had his elbows on his knees, his face buried in his hands. "Let's look at the victim before we talk to him," she said.

Their footsteps echoing hollowly off the concrete floor, they passed rows of parking spaces lit by bright overhead lights. "Someday I'm going to own one of these babies," Halliday commented as they passed an assortment of BMWs, several Mercedes and a sleek, black Jaguar.

O'Shea snorted. "Yeah, on a cop's salary?" He tilted his head toward the cars. "A few of these arrived between the time Smithson found the body and the first uniforms got here."

Julia looked at Halliday. "We need a list of who drove in each car, and what time."

"Right," he said, then popped the last bite of chocolate chip cookie into his mouth. "O'Shea, who's head of security around here?"

The officer frowned as he flipped through his notes with thick, impatient fingers. "I've got the name somewhere...."

"Rick Fox?" Julia asked.

"That's it," O'Shea commented. He met her gaze, and she saw the sudden realization settle in his dark eyes. "I guess you know a few people around here."

"Some."

He gave an uneasy shrug before looking back at his notes.

Fighting irritation, Julia downed the remains of her coffee, crushed the cup beneath her fingers and jammed it into her purse. What happened between her and Sloan Remington two years ago had cemented itself in the minds of the people she'd been working with at the time. People hadn't forgotten—*wouldn't* forget. That was a fact she'd grown to accept...and live with. What she couldn't stomach was the occasional look of pity that came her way.

"Is Forensics done with the scene?" she asked, her voice sharp enough to garner a curious look from her partner.

"They should finish soon," O'Shea advised. As if to verify his comment, a lab tech in a blue jumpsuit stepped around a concrete pillar.

"Scene's photographed and vacuumed, except the area beneath the body," he said, hiking the strap on his evidence kit higher on his shoulder. "After the M.E. finishes his prelim and moves her, I'll go back in and sweep that. The victim's briefcase needs dusting, but it's next to the body—didn't want to disturb anything."

Julia nodded. "Find anything we need to know about right now?"

"Maybe," the tech said, pulling a small, plastic evidence bag out of his kit. "Looks like some sort of service pin."

With Halliday and O'Shea leaning over her shoulders, Julia peered through the plastic at the gold "R" with a small diamond set into its center. She recognized it as the pin presented to Remington employees who hit the twenty-year mark with the company. "Where'd you find it?"

"A few feet from the passenger door of the victim's car," the tech said, as Julia returned the bag. "There's no way of knowing if it's connected to the homicide."

Julia expelled a slow breath. "All right, Halliday, let's make your day and look at the victim."

Death had not diminished Vanessa West's beauty. She lay on her back like a broken doll, her bloodless skin looking like porcelain over sculpted cheekbones. Subtle hues of smoke and teal emphasized eyes that stared glassily upward; gloss the color of rich rubies slicked her ripe, slack mouth. A cascade of blond hair fell softly over one cheek, then pooled in a golden frame around her shoulders. Her power-red suit was an expensive one, the snug jacket buttoned over a slim skirt that rode up, exposing sculpted thighs and the clasp of a black lace garter belt.

"Sweet Jesus," Halliday commented softly. "What a looker."

The M.E. glanced up from the long chemical thermometer in his hand. "Cruze, Halliday," he said, then rose, careful to avoid the pool of congealing blood that blossomed from beneath the victim's right shoulder.

Julia nodded to the small, trim man with graying hair. "What have you got for us?"

"She took a bullet in the back. Looks like small caliber—a .22 or maybe .25. There's no trace of gunpowder on her jacket around the wound."

"So she was shot at a distance," Julia stated.

"Over five feet away, I'd say." He slid the thermometer into his black medical bag. "Judging by the body temp, she's been dead an hour...two at the most."

Julia glanced at her watch, noted it was eight-fifteen. She looked at O'Shea. "Do we have the weapon?"

"Nowhere in sight," the officer answered. "I was waiting for the lab to clear out before the uniforms started looking down here."

"Bring them in now," she said. "If the gun doesn't turn up, do a grid search of the grounds."

While O'Shea unhooked his radio from his Sam Browne belt to issue the order, Julia turned to Halliday. "We'll need each owner's permission to search inside their car. If anyone balks, get a warrant. A car doesn't leave here until it's checked."

"Right."

She glanced back at Vanessa West, regarding the black leather briefcase that lay beside her left, red spiked heel. Julia's brows knitted and she took a step closer, her eyes narrowing at what she'd first taken as a shadow across one side of the woman's skirt. "Is that a stain?" she asked, crouching beside the body.

"Looks like it," the M.E. said, leaning in. "Not blood. That's for sure."

Gathering her long hair in one hand to keep it out of her face, Julia lowered her head and caught a whiff of expensive perfume mixed with a familiar scent. "Carrots," she said as she rose.

"Carrots?" Halliday asked, giving her a blank look.

"Carrot juice," Julia amended. "O'Shea, was there a cup anywhere around here? Any sign of spilled juice?"

The officer shook his head. "Didn't see anything."

"Which of these cars is hers?"

"The Jaguar."

"Check inside, Halliday. Maybe she brought juice for the drive to work and spilled it in the car."

He walked the few steps to the shiny, black car, pulled open the door and bent out of sight. "Smells like a salad bar inside," he said as his head reappeared over the Jag's gleaming top. "One side of the driver's seat is soaked. So's part of the carpet."

"What about a cup?"

"There's an empty one sitting on the console," he said as he rejoined her.

Julia looked back at O'Shea. "Do you have the victim's address?"

"Not yet. The security chief's getting it for me now."

"Okay. The minute we have it, send a patrol unit to check the place. If there's no sign of forced entry, keep a uniform on the door until either Halliday or I can break loose and get there."

"You got it, Sarge."

She shook her head, grateful for O'Shea's efficiency. "Now, let's talk to the guy who found her."

At normal times, Don Smithson would be considered distinguished, Julia decided—maybe even handsome with his carefully brushed iron-gray hair and strong, square jaw. Now, sitting hunched over on the metal chair with a greenish tint to his complexion and sweat on his brow, he looked distinctly ill and helpless.

"Mr. Smithson, I'm Sergeant Cruze. This is my partner, Sergeant Halliday. Are you feeling up to answering some questions?" Julia noted the man's slight nod, then gestured at the recorder clipped to her purse strap. "I'm taping our conversation, Mr. Smithson. I understand you found Ms. West's body."

With obvious effort, he straightened in the chair and clasped his well-molded hands in a tight grip. "It was awful...awful."

"Did you see the victim when you drove in?"

"Not until I got out of my car. I was preoccupied, thinking about the dinner party my wife and I are giving tonight. Dear Lord, I nearly stepped on poor Vanessa."

"What time did you arrive?"

"Seven...a little after. I used my ID card to open the gate. You can check the records to get the exact time."

"I will," Julia said matter-of-factly. "Was this your usual time to arrive for work?"

"Around seven, yes."

"Did you see anyone in the garage when you pulled in?"

"No. Well, except Vanessa."

"What did you do when you saw her?"

"I thought for a minute she'd slipped on some oil, fallen on her back and hit her head." He wiped an unsteady hand across his forehead. "I bent down, touched her. I think I said her name."

"You touched the body?"

"Her shoulder. That's when I saw her eyes…the blood."

"What did you do after that?"

"Stumbled into a corner and got sick." He shuddered visibly. "I know you people are used to this, but I… My stomach just turned over."

"You saw no one else in the garage between the time you found the body and you went in to notify security?"

"That's right. No one."

Julia nodded. "What is your job here?"

"Personnel. I head the Personnel Division. Remington has over forty-three thousand employees nationwide—"

"How well did you know the victim?"

"We…not well. We worked together on a project about a month ago. Ms. West was brilliant. She had a remarkable understanding of risk management principles."

Smithson propped his elbows on his knees and dropped his face in his hands. "This is terrible. Terrible. I don't feel well. All I see is Vanessa's face…her eyes. I'm going home."

Julia glanced at Halliday, then looked back at the man who seemed to be coming apart in front of her. If anything, his skin had gotten greener as they'd talked. "Okay, Mr. Smithson, that's all for now. We may want to talk to you again."

Nodding, he slowly lifted his head and blinked. A network of lines pulled at the flesh around his eyes.

"Two more quick things," Julia added as he rose unsteadily. She took in the dark suit tailored to fit his lanky frame, and realized he was taller than she'd first thought. "Do you own a gun?"

His eyes widened. "Surely you don't think I had anything to do with Vanessa's death."

"It's a routine question."

"I hunt quail. I own several shotguns."

"Any handguns?"

"No." He jerked at his tie, fumbled with the top button of his starched shirt. "Can I go now?"

"After we check your car."

"My car?"

"This entire garage is a crime scene. We have to search all vehicles."

"Fine." He took a deep, unsteady breath. "Fine."

Julia extended her hand. "Thank you, Mr. Smithson."

He hesitated only a second, then returned her handshake.

O'Shea stepped forward. "Here's a standard release form for you to sign," he said as he ushered the man away. "If you'll give this officer your keys, he'll check your car and then you can leave."

Julia waited until they were out of earshot, then turned to Halliday. "What do you think?"

"That O'Shea better keep his distance, or the guy might upchuck on his shoes," Halliday commented while nudging his glasses up the bridge of his nose. "Smithson's upset. Scared."

Julia pulled a tissue out of her purse and scrubbed her palm. "He's also sweating like a hooker in church."

"Well, he just stumbled across a dead body. Not the normal routine for a guy used to cozying up with risk management stats."

"Yeah." Julia pursed her lips.

"By the way, what did O'Shea mean when he said he guessed you knew a few people around here? You used to work here or something?"

"Or something," Julia said under her breath. She turned at the hollow echo of footsteps coming from behind, and felt an instant tightening in her shoulders.

Fair-haired, with appealing blue eyes in a weather-beaten face, Rick Fox walked toward her, his tall, burly frame clad in gray slacks and a dark blazer that sported Remington Aerospace's logo on the breast pocket.

"Julia, if this isn't one hell of a way to get old friends

together, I don't know what is.'' His lips curved, but his eyes remained sober as he reached for her hand. ''How are you?''

The fingers that curled around hers were as hard as marble. ''I'm fine,'' Julia said, and frowned at the thickness that had settled in her voice. The last time she'd seen the security director she'd wept like a baby while pleading that he tell her Sloan Remington's whereabouts. Hell, she thought with derision, she hadn't pleaded—she'd begged.

And accomplished nothing. Rick had patiently lent his sturdy shoulder to cry on, poured her an ocean of coffee, then driven her home. But he'd remained loyally silent regarding the man who was both his best friend and boss.

Thinking again of how she'd demeaned herself in those first grief-stricken days after Sloan walked out on her brought the old hurt—the bitterness—crashing in on Julia. *That was then,* she reminded herself. *It doesn't matter now.*

Rick cocked his head. ''I have to say I'm surprised you're on this call.''

''Luck of the draw,'' she said evenly, and nodded in Halliday's direction. ''Rick Fox, meet my partner, Sergeant Halliday.''

Rick shook Halliday's hand, nodding when the detective requested a printout of everyone who'd scanned an ID card at both the gate and the door that led into the building.

''I've got the one from the gate with me,'' Rick said as he pulled a folded paper from the inside pocket of his blazer. ''This shows everyone who used their ID card to enter this garage beginning at midnight until we opened the gate for your lab people. The names are in order by time of arrival.''

''What about the printout from the door into the building?'' Halliday asked.

''I'll have that for you before you leave.''

''Rick, what was Vanessa West's job?'' Julia asked while her partner unfolded the paper.

''Executive assistant to the CEO.''

Julia held his gaze. "She worked directly for Sloan?"

"Yeah." Rick shoved his thick hands into the pockets of his slacks, looking distinctly uncomfortable.

"She worked out of this office?" Julia persisted.

"Has, for the past three months."

"Before that?"

His eyes cut to the recorder clipped to her purse strap. "I'll have to check her personnel file."

"We'll need a copy of everything you've got on her."

When he frowned, Julia added, "I can get a warrant, if it's necessary."

He held up a palm. "It's not. We'll cooperate fully."

"I hope so," she said evenly, then paused. "Rick, I need to know if you're armed."

"I'm an ex-cop, Julia. Old habits die hard."

"Is your permit to carry current?"

"You bet." He shoved back one flap of his blazer to reveal a holstered automatic. "Glock, 9 mm," he added.

"Draw the weapon," Julia said. "We need to record the serial number."

Rick nodded. The sound of steel withdrawing from the leather holster hung in the garage's cool air.

The automatic felt cool and heavy in her palm as she recited the serial number into her recorder.

"We may need to run a test on it," she said, handing the Glock back to Rick.

"Just let me know."

She tilted her head. "Is that the only gun you're carrying?"

A slow grin crossed his face as he spread his arms. "You can search me, darlin'," he drawled in a voice heavy with the thick tones of his native Louisiana.

In a brief flash of memory, Julia recalled the comfort she'd derived from the soft words spoken in slow, Southern cadences while she cried on Rick's shoulder. Kind words. Words meant to soothe, but couldn't.

Her spine went as stiff as a nail. *Damn,* she thought, and

mentally shoved the past back to the dark recesses of her heart, where it belonged.

"Why don't you give me a rundown on the victim," she suggested. "What kind of person was Vanessa West?"

"The best at her job."

Julia narrowed her eyes at Rick's avoidance of an answer. "Did she have enemies?"

"Vanessa liked to roll over people who got in her way. You make enemies when you do that."

"Roll over them how?"

"Whatever way was most advantageous to her."

"Did she ever roll over you?"

"No. I guess I didn't have anything she wanted."

Julia gave a slow, assessing nod. "Officer O'Shea said he asked you to get Miss West's address."

"Right." Rick slid an index card out of his pocket and handed it over. "I had one of my men call personnel to get it."

"Any idea if she has a roommate?" Julia asked, noting the address on the card was in an upscale part of the city.

Rick shrugged. "I don't know for sure, but I doubt it. Having a roommate means you share. Vanessa didn't share. Not her space, not anything."

"Something tells me you weren't in the running for president of her fan club."

"Hardly."

O'Shea stepped to her side and Julia handed him the index card. He checked the address, then walked discreetly away, pulling the radio off his belt.

Halliday looked up from the list. "We need to interview everyone on here. Can you set us up in a room where we can talk to them one at a time?"

"This garage is reserved for executive-level staff, so everyone on that list works on the upper floors," Rick advised. "I'll clear you to use the CEO's conference room. Let me know in what order you want to talk to them, and I'll have a secretary arrange things."

"We'll start with whoever logged in just after the victim," Julia said, peering at the printout in her partner's hand. "That'll be..."

"Sloan Remington," Halliday finished.

Julia looked up slowly. A dull roar started at the base of her skull. She met Rick's gaze. It took everything she had, but she met his gaze. "He's on-site? Sloan's here?"

Rick's mouth settled in a hard, tight line. "He's back, Julia. Has been for three months."

The comment hit her like a slap in the face. Legs weak with reaction, she bit down on a curse, telling herself she'd deal with the storm inside later. "We'll finish down here, then talk to Mr. Remington," she said without inflection.

"Okay, Julia, we've got a few minutes alone," Halliday said as the elevator soundlessly whisked them toward the fifteenth floor. "What's the deal? How do you know so many people around here?"

She glanced up at the gleaming ceiling, saw no sign of a microphone or surveillance camera. Still, either one could be hidden between the polished aluminum panels. "We'll talk later."

"Julia——"

"Later!"

Eyes narrowing behind his wire-rim glasses, Halliday opened his mouth to speak, then shut it when the doors slid apart.

"Sloan's between appointments," Rick said, striding across the carpeted reception area to meet them. "He can see you now."

Julia raised her chin. "If we're putting a chink in the CEO's schedule, we'll be happy to talk to him downtown."

Rick's mouth kicked up on one side. "Just some standard office lingo on my part, Julia. We're all at your disposal." He swept a hand toward the towering paneled doors on the far wall. "I'll show you in."

A sense of déjà vu settled around her as her gaze swept

the reception area. The heavy English motif with its polished brasses and pewters looked unchanged. The paneled walls gleamed with the same rich luster. The heady, aged scent of leather furniture hung familiarly on the air.

Her throat tightened as memories closed in, hovering just at the edge of her consciousness. With great effort, she pushed them away. God, if she'd known Sloan was back, she would have passed the call to another Homicide team. But she hadn't known. Hadn't thought she would ever see him again. Sure as hell hadn't wanted to.

Halliday touched her shoulder, nodding at the oil portrait of a silver-haired man with kind eyes and a shrewd face, which hung on one of the paneled walls. "That the CEO?" he asked quietly.

"His father."

Rick slowed his steps as they approached the U-shaped mahogany desk rising from a great span of sand-colored carpet. The white-haired woman whose fingers raced across the computer's keyboard looked up, a smile crinkling the corners of her eyes.

"Hello, Miss Cruze."

"Elizabeth. How are you?"

"Very well, except for what happened downstairs. Mr. Remington has asked me to bring in juice for him, and coffee for yourself. Do you still take yours with cream?"

"Yes." Julia ignored the look Halliday sliced her way.

"And you, sir?" Elizabeth asked, turning her efficient attention to him. "Would you care for something?"

"I'll pass." The hard edge in Halliday's voice made Julia regret not briefing him on her history with Sloan Remington. Because of that, her partner was going into this interview cold, and that put him at a disadvantage.

"Rick will show you into the office," Elizabeth said, then turned back to her computer.

With her insides twisted into a knot, Julia followed the head of security through the paneled doors. She paused, standing motionless as she took in the lush office with its deep chairs, sofas and antique rug.

As if cold air had seeped through her, she felt the man's presence before she saw him.

Sloan stood with his back toward them on the far side of the vast office, his gaze focused out the wall of windows on a point somewhere off on the horizon. Julia stared at the thick, black hair, remembering the touch of it against her hands, knew too well the firmness of the broad shoulders beneath the dark, tailored suit.

Her hands began to tremble.

Rick remained just inside the door. "Sloan, Sergeants Cruze and Halliday," he said, then stepped out, closing the door behind him.

After a moment's hesitation, Sloan turned. His gaze locked with Julia's, and he slanted her a smile in an intensely handsome face that had changed little in two years.

"Hello, Jules," he said softly.

Chapter 2

"It's *Sergeant* Cruze now." Despite the blood pounding in her cheeks from Sloan's use of his private nickname for her, Julia kept her voice carefully void of emotion.

"Sergeant, then," he said, his gaze holding hers steadily. "Do you know who killed my assistant?"

"The investigation's ongoing," Julia said, tightening her fingers on the strap of her purse.

He lifted a dark brow. "Is that police jargon for no?"

"We haven't made an arrest. Yet." Julia felt as if a stone had lodged in her chest. How could she have forgotten Sloan's startling sense of presence? The hard impact of his dark, good looks. The eyes the color of melt-in-your-mouth chocolate.

No, she hadn't forgotten, she corrected herself as realization swept through her. She'd blocked those pulse-stirring details, built a wall against the gut-wrenching memories. But she hadn't forgotten or blocked what this man who looked so coolly refined in the dark suit and knotted silk tie had done to her. Remembered well the relentless pain she had sometimes thought she would die of.

Stiffening her shoulders, she took a firm grip on her composure and got down to business. "This is Sergeant Halliday. We need to ask you some questions about Vanessa West."

Sloan nodded, then gestured toward the pair of leather chairs positioned in front of the desk. "Have a seat."

Halliday slid his hands into the pockets of his slacks. "I'll stand."

The soft click of the door sounded from behind. Julia glanced around, her gaze tracking Elizabeth's smooth glide across the plush rug, silver tray in hand. Wearing a classy gray suit that made her look cool and capable, the woman bristled with efficiency.

"Can I bring anything else?" the secretary asked after settling the tray on the mahogany credenza behind Sloan's massive desk.

Sloan gave her a brief smile. "I'll let you know." He picked up the silver coffeepot and began pouring. As he moved, gold cuff links peeked out of his coat sleeves.

Edgy, Julia slid onto a chair and looked at Halliday. He roamed the length of the far wall, conducting a random study of the leather books on the shelves of the floor-to-ceiling built-ins.

"Julia."

Her head jerked up at the nearness of Sloan's voice. She swiveled, and found him standing so close she could see the fine weave of his silk tie. Sitting as rigid as cold steel, she accepted the cup and saucer he offered, careful to avoid contact with his fingers. Agitation stirred in her when she saw he'd added the exact amount of cream she preferred to the steaming brew. China rattled against china when she abruptly set the cup and saucer on the small table beside her chair.

Sloan regarded her with interest as he settled into the

high-backed leather chair behind his desk. "Something wrong with the coffee?"

"No."

He leaned, lifted a glass off the silver tray. "There's orange juice if you'd prefer—"

"I'd prefer to get started." She jerked the recorder off her purse strap, clicked on the Play button and placed the device on the edge of his desk.

He gave the machine a quick assessment. "Why the recorder?"

"I need your statement on record," Julia explained.

"I wasn't aware I was about to make a statement."

"Your response to our questions, then."

He shrugged his acquiescence.

"Mr. Remington," she began, "what time did you arrive here this morning?"

"I'm not sure." He looked at Halliday. "But since my head of security gave you the printout from the scanner in the garage, you already have that information."

"Yeah," Halliday said, leaning a shoulder against the bookcase. "You get to the office about the same time each morning?"

"Earlier. I usually work out here."

"Work out?" Julia asked blankly.

Sloan's gaze ranged casually back to where she sat. "In the gym." His lips curved with the hint of a smile. "I exercise."

She dropped her gaze. The Sloan Remington she'd known was the last person who would flex a muscle to exercise. Yet, despite a love of fried foods and desserts, he'd had the physique of an athlete. Her eyes lifted for an instant to skim across the broad chest beneath the tailored suit. It appeared his body was as rock solid as ever. The fact that she'd looked had Julia's mouth tightening.

Halliday spoke from across the room. "Why didn't you work out this morning?"

"I did. I swam laps in my pool at home."

"All right," Halliday said, crossing his arms over his chest. "You took a dip in your pool, got cleaned up and came to work. Did you see Vanessa West in the garage when you drove in?"

"No."

"Did you see her car?" Julia asked.

"No, but then, I didn't look for it. When I drove in, I was talking on the phone—a call to D.C. I parked in my slot and stayed in my car until I completed my business."

"How long was that?" Julia asked.

"Five minutes—could have been more."

The phone on Sloan's desk buzzed. He pressed a button on the intercom. "Yes, Elizabeth?"

"I have a call holding on my line from a Lieutenant Ryan. He'd like to speak with either Sergeant Halliday or Cruze."

Travis pushed off the bookcase. "I'll take it."

Sloan nodded. "Elizabeth, show Sergeant Halliday into my conference room, then transfer the call there."

"Yes, sir."

When the door closed behind Halliday, Julia felt her skin prick with the uncomfortable knowledge that she and Sloan were alone. As if pulled by a magnet, her gaze went to the vast desk, swept across the leather blotter, then settled on the ebony pen set positioned at exact angles on the polished surface. The remembered feel of the cool, smooth wood against her bare flesh snuck up like a phantom, tossing her back to the night of the Christmas party when she and Sloan had barricaded themselves into this very room, so damned hungry for each other that they'd rolled onto the desk, tearing at clothes, yielding to the fast, molten ride of urgent sex for which their bodies clamored. Later, after they'd moved across the room to the leather couch and she lay in his arms, all sated and warm and drowsy, he'd proposed.

"It's good to see you again, Julia," Sloan said quietly. "How are you?"

A slash of temper followed on the heels of the sudden

jump of her pulse. She grabbed the recorder and snapped it off. "I'm here as a cop, Sloan, not an old acquaintance wanting to play catch-up. Let me explain how a homicide investigation works. We ask the questions. You answer them. Period. Is that clear?"

His dark eyes stayed steady on hers, betraying nothing. "Crystal."

She switched on the recorder and replaced it on the desk, pleased to see that her hand was steadier than her heartbeat. "Mr. Remington, how long have you known Vanessa West?"

He settled back in his chair, watching her over his steepled fingers. "A couple of years. She first worked at our West Coast facility, then transferred to Houston. She came here a few months ago."

"A few months?" Julia asked. "You need to be more specific with the time frame."

He sipped his orange juice before answering. "Three months."

"About the same time you came back to Oklahoma?"

"About."

"How would you define your relationship with the victim?"

"I was her employer, she my employee."

"That's it?"

Sloan leaned forward, propping his forearms on the desk. "You need to be more specific with your question, Sergeant Cruze. I'm not exactly sure what you're asking."

Julia narrowed her eyes at his carelessly polite tone. "Did you ever have, or were you having, a physical relationship with Vanessa West?"

"You mean were we lovers?" He paused, letting the question hover on the still air. "No, Sergeant. As I've already stated, our relationship was platonic. Strictly business."

The inner swing of the door pulled Julia's eyes from the

dark ones that bored into her. Halliday stepped in, his mouth set in a tight, thin line.

Taking a deep breath, she looked back at Sloan. Whatever had Halliday hot under the collar would have to wait. "Was your assistant involved in a relationship with someone else?"

"I have no idea."

"Can you give us the name of someone who might know?"

"Her secretary, Eve Nelson, might have some idea. Eve's off today, having minor foot surgery. I'll have Elizabeth give you her phone number." Sloan jotted a note with the ebony pen. He paused and looked up. "I understand Rick is getting Vanessa's personnel file for you."

"Yes."

"Do you need anything else?"

"I'll let you know." Julia waited a moment, then asked, "What kind of person was Vanessa West?"

Saying nothing, Sloan turned his head toward the window, but not before Julia spied the jump of a muscle in his jaw.

"She was your assistant," she persisted when he remained silent. "You must have had a close working relationship. Surely you have an opinion of her character."

"Vanessa wasn't a nice person," Sloan said bluntly, re-meeting her gaze.

"How so?"

"She was beautiful, and she knew it. She could knock a man over with just a glance. Then she'd laugh when he couldn't get up. Not nice at all."

His frank assessment caught Julia off guard. "You thought that about her, yet you had her working directly for you?"

"Considering her skills, having her work for me was much preferable than her working for a competitor," Sloan answered. "Despite Vanessa's...personal faults, she had a brilliant mind for business. Assign her a project and she gave five hundred percent of herself. Her work ethic might sometimes have been questionable, but never her work product. Replacing her won't be easy.''

Julia rose, walked to the wall of windows and stared out. Traffic had thinned; the sun beat down with such intensity that she could see heat rising off the pavement. Her brows slid together, and she wondered if she felt hesitant about asking the next question because she already knew the answer.

She straightened her shoulders and turned. It didn't matter what she knew. She needed Sloan's verification on record. ''Do you own a gun, Mr. Remington?''

He sat silent, his eyes so cool and unblinking that she shifted her stance. ''Shall I repeat the question?'' she asked.

''No. I'm wondering why you asked it, since you know the answer.''

Her hands curled against her thighs. ''I need your answer on record.''

''Yes, I own a gun…more than two hundred to be exact. I inherited my father's collection when he died.'' Sloan flicked a glance at the recorder. ''For the record, Sergeant Cruze, you and I have taken several of my handguns to the range and fired them. Since I haven't sold or bought any during the past two years, you're as familiar as I with the weapons I own.''

Julia fought to stay calm. ''We need a copy of the inventory.''

His dark eyes narrowed. ''You think one of my guns might have killed Vanessa?''

''It's a possibility.''

''Hardly. My collection is kept under lock and key, remember?''

What Julia remembered was that only Sloan had the key to the fireproof room off what had been his father's study. ''Do you have a copy of the inventory here?'' she asked.

Keeping his eyes locked with hers, Sloan picked up the phone and issued orders for Elizabeth to print the list. He hung up, then stood, an obvious sign that they'd worn out their welcome.

"I understand you'll be using my conference room to interview my staff."

"That's the plan," Halliday said.

"There's one other thing." Julia walked to the desk and retrieved her recorder. She didn't have to look at Sloan to feel his eyes tracking her movements.

"What's that?"

She raised her gaze and met dark eyes that looked as hard as iron. "Don't leave town, Mr. Remington."

Halliday exploded before they got halfway to the conference room. "Dammit, Cruze, I want an explanation."

Seeing Sloan had left Julia with weak knees and damp palms. Her stomach was in knots. The last thing she wanted to do right now was explain.

"Later—"

"Like hell."

Her gaze darted down the length of the paneled corridor, lined with glowing light fixtures and discreetly closed doors. The hallway was empty except for the two of them, but it wouldn't be that way long. Elizabeth had already summoned the first staff member to the conference room.

"Halliday, give me a break. I've got interviews to conduct, and you need to meet a lab unit at Vanessa West's apartment. I'll run everything down to you when we meet back at the station."

"I already gave you a break," he shot back. "I didn't drag you out of Remington's office in the middle of the interview."

Julia heard the familiar buzz in her head seconds before her temper snapped. "Look, pal," she said, poking her index finger against his chest. "I'm lead investigator on this team. You don't tell me what to do, and you sure as hell don't drag me anywhere."

"Fine. You're in charge. You've got more experience at this than me. Maybe that's why I'm missing something."

She gave him a wary look. "Like what?"

"Like why you left me open to explain to the lieutenant why we're here."

"That's what Ryan called about?"

"Yeah. My explanation of 'to investigate a homicide' didn't exactly sit too well. When I inquired if there was a reason we shouldn't be on this case, he said to ask you. So, Cruze, I'm asking. Why are you so chummy with the head of security? How does the secretary know you like cream in your coffee? And what the hell were you doing hanging out at a pistol range with Remington?"

"Lord!" Julia grabbed the nearest doorknob, twisted it and dragged her partner into what turned out to be a mirror-walled bathroom with gleaming brass fixtures. As she moved, her purse slid down her arm and landed with a thud on the pristine marble floor. She shoved the door closed, then stepped to the sink and turned on the water full blast.

"What are you doing?"

"Interference," she said, glancing at his reflection in the mirrored wall. "Rick Fox has a talent for hiding microphones in all sorts of places."

"Another fact I would have liked to know before I took Ryan's call," Halliday rasped, anger seething in his voice. His hands curled against his sides. "Cruze, what the hell was—or is—going on between you and Remington?"

"Nothing!" she snapped, and whirled to face him. "There's nothing going on between Sloan and me."

"*Sloan.*" Giving her a smug look, Halliday leaned against the door and crossed his arms. "Well, *Jules,* I don't exactly buy that."

Julia blew air between her clenched teeth. Shifting her gaze to the small chandelier that hung over the marble vanity, she waited for her anger to subside.

Halliday glanced at his watch. "I've got all day—"

"You're right," she shot back. "There *is* something between Sloan and me. It's called dislike. I dislike the man."

"Why?"

"Because two days before our wedding was to take place he decided he'd made a mistake." Her voice shook and she took a deep breath. "It hit him that he didn't love me."

Halliday gaped. "You and the silk suit were engaged?"

"That's usually the next step after two people decide to get married," she said, shoving her hand through her hair.

"Damn." The rush of angry emotion had disappeared from Halliday's face, and in its place was quiet assessment. "Damn," he repeated softly.

"I know the director of security because he's Sloan's best friend. I actually spent a few days crying on Rick's shoulder. And if you think Elizabeth is efficient with coffee, you should see how capably she handles sending five hundred telegrams that regrettably inform people the wedding is off," Julia continued, her body trembling with the words. "She didn't miss notifying anyone on the guest list, not the governor, the four senators...she even remembered my Aunt Tilly in Woonsocket, South Dakota."

"Julia—"

"Then there was the matter of returning all those gifts."

Halliday held up a hand. "Okay, I get the idea." He frowned, his voice softening. "So when I told you the location of the homicide, why didn't you hand it to another team? I'd think Remington would be the last person you'd want to deal with."

"He is." For the first time Julia glanced at her reflection in the mirrored wall directly in front of her. Her cheeks and lips were pale, her eyes glassy. "I didn't know he was back."

"Back from where?"

"I don't know. Right after Sloan called things off, he left the state. At first I was fool enough to think he'd just gotten cold feet and I could make him see...." She shrugged. "Anyway, I tried to find out where he'd gone.

Rick was the only one who knew, but he's as loyal to Sloan as a pet dog and he refused to tell me anything. After a while, I came to my senses and stopped asking. When a man tells you he never loved you, it makes a big dent in your pride." She raised her chin. "Overall, it was a very humbling experience."

"I can imagine."

The sympathy that settled in Halliday's eyes fired Julia's temper. "I got over it," she said through her teeth. "Three weeks after Sloan walked out, my promotion to Homicide came through. I had plenty of dead bodies to keep my mind occupied. Later, I met Bill." She held up her left hand, the diamond sparking beneath the chandelier's brilliant rays. "My life is exactly what I want it to be. I'm exactly where I want to be. End of story."

"Julia…"

She leaned and snatched her purse off the floor. "Did Lieutenant Ryan pull us off this case?"

"No. But he wants you in his office the minute you hit the station."

"Fine," she said, cringing on the inside at the prospect of facing her steely eyed boss. "We've got an investigation to conduct, Halliday. Let's stop wasting time."

He remained unmoving, blocking the door while he gave her a long stare.

"What?" she asked with impatience. "Did my nose suddenly fall off or something?"

"What if Remington turns out to be our guy?" he asked quietly. "How are you going to handle it if he's the one who pumped that bullet into Vanessa West?"

"If he did it, I'll arrest him and lock him in a cage," Julia said, then reached past him and jerked open the door.

"Thought you might want this." Rick Fox tapped an envelope against his palm as he strode across the office.

Sloan looked up from the financial report he'd stared at the past half hour. He'd opened the file right after Julia and her partner left his office. Right after she'd looked at him as if he were a murderer on the prowl.

Expelling a slow breath, he closed the folder, having no idea what the report said. "What is it?" Sloan asked as Rick handed the envelope across the desk.

"A photograph. I printed it off the tape from the camera at the entrance to the garage."

Sloan pulled out the photo, his gut tightening at the image of Julia's grave, beautiful face staring up into the camera's lens. She looked controlled and efficient, like a tough little gangster in her pin-striped suit.

How little she'd changed in appearance, he thought, his gaze tracing the hair that spilled across her shoulders like a dark shaft of silk. The same crimson gloss slicked the mouth that in another lifetime had marked his flesh with kisses, sighs and soft words. Sloan dragged in air to loosen the knots in his stomach, and only proceeded in filling his lungs with the familiar scent of her that still lingered in the air. A warm, soft scent that aroused a million memories he'd vowed to keep buried.

His fingers tightened on the photo. Dammit, why the hell had fate thrown them together again? He didn't want Julia Cruze in his life. *Couldn't* want her.

"You're wrong, Rick," Sloan said, crumpling the photo in his fist. "I don't want it." He didn't need a photo to remind him of how her face looked in morning sunlight, of the arc of those sculpted cheekbones, of the sensual set of the mouth that had taken him to heaven countless times. Those images were branded on his soul.

Rick lifted a shoulder. "My mistake."

"You've kept tabs on her for me for two years," Sloan said with disdain. "You know as well as I do that she's gotten on with her life. She's engaged to the first assistant district attorney." Sloan tossed the wadded photo into the trash. "I doubt he'd appreciate my pinning her picture on the wall."

"I see your point. You know, Sloan, all you have to do

is call the mayor and Julia's off the investigation. That way you won't have to deal with her.''

"The thought crossed my mind." When he'd stood beside her chair with her coffee cup, he'd wanted to reach out and skim his fingertips across her hair. One touch. One touch he'd denied himself because he couldn't have stood to watch her cringe away.

"You going to make the call?"

"No. For two reasons. An innocent person shouldn't care what cop shows up to investigate. I'm innocent."

"The second reason?"

Sloan's gaze drifted to the chair where Julia had sat. After her partner left to take the phone call, there had been an instant when her gaze dropped to his desk, and she'd fallen silent. When she looked up, he'd seen a flash of vulnerability in her face before her eyes went cool and remote. Had she been remembering that long-ago Christmas Eve? The night he'd made promises to her, had told her he wanted her for a lifetime. Forever. And he had. He just hadn't known then how tenuous a lifetime could be.

"Sloan?"

He looked up. "What?"

"What's the second reason you won't call the mayor?"

"It wouldn't be fair to Julia," he said quietly as he leaned back in his chair. "She's doing her job. Who the hell am I to get her kicked off an assignment?"

Rick's mouth tightened. "Well, that's your call."

"That's right, it is."

"So, what are you going to do?"

"Ask my head of security what steps he's taking to find out who killed my assistant."

"I'm working on it." Rick slid a thigh onto the edge of the desk. "Vanessa worked out of this office barely three months, but I'm hard-pressed to find someone whose toes she hasn't stepped on. That leaves a lot of people with a motive."

"She didn't care what anyone thought about her," Sloan agreed. "Including me."

Rick frowned. "Let's hope the police don't hear about what happened between the two of you last night."

Sloan cocked his head. "It was a museum fund-raiser. Over two hundred people were there. What are the odds that no one heard?"

"Not good," Rick said matter-of-factly. "At this point, all we can do is keep our fingers crossed."

"Julia thinks I killed her," Sloan said as he ran a finger absently across a gold-plated letter opener. "She didn't come right out and say it, but it was in her eyes." He shook his head. "She believes I'm capable of murder."

Rick's voice went quiet. "It wasn't your shoulder she cried her eyes out on, Sloan. It was mine. I think she felt like you'd killed her."

Sloan's hand fisted around the letter opener. Julia had bound herself to him, given him all that was in her heart. And with purposeful determination he'd walked away. *Had* to walk away.

"I did what was best," he hissed through his teeth.

Rick stood and dipped his hands into the pockets of his slacks. "You having second thoughts?"

"Hell no." The letter opener slipped from Sloan's hand, thudding hollowly against the desk's leather blotter. "She's alive, isn't she?"

"Yeah. The problem is, old buddy, so are you."

Chapter 3

Julia stood under the shower's pelting rays while the heat of the water seeped into her tired bones. Her numbed brain pounded with the headache that had settled behind her eyes after about the twentieth interview she'd conducted. She had asked the same questions of so many people since leaving the murder site that morning that if someone had admitted killing Vanessa West, Julia wasn't sure she'd have noticed right off.

The minute she got back to the station, she'd had a session with her boss. It had taken the better part of an hour to explain to Lieutenant Ryan why, in view of her past relationship with the CEO of Remington Aerospace, she'd taken the call. She'd then outlined the reasons she and Halliday should remain on the case, finishing with a firm, "It makes no difference whether the janitor offed her or Sloan Remington, I'll handle it by the book."

"All right, Cruze," Ryan had finally said, giving her his infamous arctic-blue stare. "The investigation's yours...for now. Don't let personal feelings screw it up."

"Personal feelings," she muttered as she stepped out of the shower and toweled off. If she was going to let a little thing like personal feelings rule her actions, she'd have hunted Sloan down two years ago and shot him square between the eyes.

She dug her hair dryer out of a drawer and clicked it on. As she raked her fingers through her thick, damp hair, the logical part of her mind sent a firm reminder that Sloan had been right to call off their wedding. As hard as it had been to accept his explanation that he'd suddenly realized his feelings for her didn't extend beyond blood-stirring lust, it would have been much harder on her heart if he'd gone through with the wedding, then asked for a divorce sometime down the line.

But she had loved him, and logic hadn't eased the relentless, wearing grief and pain she'd suffered. Thank God her promotion had come so close on the heels of Sloan's leaving. Thank God the intense nature of homicide investigations, combined with the unending pressure to clear each case, had been all-consuming.

And thank God for Bill, Julia silently added, her lips curving as she glanced down at the counter where her diamond ring lay. Over time, Bill Taylor had filled the void Sloan had left, bringing to her tormented heart some modicum of peace. She loved him, was going to marry him, make him a good wife. The fact that Sloan had reentered her life—even for a brief time—didn't matter. His presence was simply business. Julia's smile transformed into an ironic arch. She couldn't count the times she'd heard Sloan say the key to successful business was to deal with whatever came one's way on a cool, unemotional basis, then move on. He had extended that philosophy to their relationship. There was no reason she couldn't do the same.

Fifteen minutes later, Julia fastened the hook on her wraparound halter dress of starched white cotton, then slid her feet into a pair of strappy white sandals. As a concession to the pounding July heat, she'd left her panty hose in her lingerie drawer.

She checked her reflection in a gilded mirror festooned with garlands of dried flowers that added the crisp scent of lavender to the air. Behind her sat the brass bed with its white mesh-draped canopy. The bed reminded Julia of a hulking, white ghost. It, and the rest of the apartment's decor, had come compliments of her mother, an interior decorator with a flair for the eccentric. Georgia Cruze had goaded and prodded until Julia gave her free reign to decorate when she'd signed the lease two years ago. Numb from having her life turned upside down, Julia hadn't cared if the place had curtains, much less wallpaper. Had she paid attention, she would have called a halt to Georgia's project. But she hadn't paid attention, and months later when equilibrium returned and Julia noticed her surroundings, she realized she had a tufted, white satin, pillow-heaped bedroom straight out of the *Arabian Nights*. In her typical whimsical fashion, Georgia had waved away her daughter's protests, claiming she was busy with other jobs and would change things later.

She'd never gotten around to it, and Julia knew why. A tireless romantic, Georgia had created a sensual place of refuge for her daughter to heal in. Heal she had. She and Bill had become lovers in the big, fairy-tale bed.

The sharp ring of the doorbell jerked Julia out of her thoughts. On the way through the living room she checked her watch, and saw she had only a few minutes before she had to leave to meet Bill.

"Mother?" Julia pulled the door wide to avoid a collision with Georgia as she swept into the apartment. Along with her mother's talent for interior design came a flair for the dramatic. "What are you doing here?"

Georgia raised her hand to pat Julia's cheek, the gesture accompanied by the clatter of gold bracelets. "It's nice to see you, too, dear."

Julia smiled and placed a kiss on her mother's fine-boned

cheek, which remained soft and unlined thanks to a religious pampering regime. Dressed in a stylish daffodil-yellow suit with red lapels, Georgia looked as flamboyant and memorable as the settings she created.

"Have you seen this morning's paper?"

Julia flicked a look at the button-tufted sofa where she'd dumped her leather portfolio. The unopened newspaper still stuck out of its top. "No. I've been…busy."

"So have I, dealing all day with the Hendersons' contractor on their remodeling project. That's why I didn't get your father's message until late. I have to say, I'm beside myself."

Julia scrunched her nose. "Over what?"

Georgia plucked a folded newspaper out of her oversize cherry-red leather tote. "You'd better have some wine before you see this."

"I don't really want any wine—"

"Well, I do."

Sighing, Julia trailed her mother into the kitchen, where Georgia had created a cheerful, ice-cream-parlor look with stark-white appliances, sparkling ceramic tiles and countertops. A green-and-white striped curtain that matched the wallpaper covered the window.

Georgia swung open the refrigerator, clucking as she regarded its meager contents. "Wine, a block of cheese that needs a shave and a few bottles of soda don't evidence a well-stocked kitchen, Julia."

"Doesn't matter if you don't know how to cook," Julia countered easily, and watched her mother's fine-plucked brow arch. Georgia created gourmet meals with the same ease that Julia combined cereal and milk.

"I worry that you're not eating right."

"You shouldn't worry. Mother, I have to meet Bill for dinner—"

"Bill. You should be thankful for Bill," Georgia said as she whisked two stemmed glasses from a cabinet.

"I am."

Georgia pursed her glossed lips and gestured toward the white cane stool that nestled below the counter. "Sit."

Julia accepted the glass from her mother's manicured hand, settled onto the stool and took a sip. "Okay, I'm sitting. I've had some wine. The ball's in your court, Mother."

"The art museum held a fund-raiser last night," Georgia said as she slid the half-folded newspaper onto the counter. "Your father and I had other plans, so we couldn't attend. Thank God. It would have been so...strained."

Julia glanced down at the society page, her gaze scanning the pictures of the city's elite who'd attended the fund-raiser.

"I just couldn't believe it when your father told me," Georgia added as she reached out, flipped the page over and pointed a bloodred nail. "Just couldn't believe Sloan Remington came back here after what he did to you...to us."

Julia froze, wineglass suspended halfway to her mouth as her eyes settled on the picture. Her breathing shallowed. Fire settled in her cheeks...then a string of firecrackers exploded in her head.

She rose slowly, her body vibrating with fury. "Sloan Remington, you're a lying bastard," she said through her teeth.

"Well, we already knew that, didn't we?" Georgia asked as Julia grabbed her purse and headed out the door.

Sloan dived into the water with the precision of an Olympic athlete, his powerful strokes propelling him swiftly toward the far side of the pool. The heated water surrounded his tense body like a warm glove, easing the stress of the day from his muscles.

Stress of the day, he thought cynically as his fingers grazed the pool's tiled side. Without surfacing for air, he pushed off again, ignoring the burning in his lungs. The day had consisted of the murder of his assistant, ongoing sensitive negotiations of a final agreement with the military that could net Remington Aerospace millions...and Julia.

Julia, who for the past two years had remained lodged inside him, like a splinter beneath his flesh, festering and painful.

During his absence, thinking about her had been too easy. Now that he'd seen her again, to not think about her was impossible.

But thinking about Julia Cruze was all he could do, all he ever intended to do. Walking away from her had left a dark, unfillable void in his life, but he felt no remorse about the action he'd taken. He'd done the right thing then, just as he'd made the proper decision when he'd told Elizabeth before he left the office that if either Sergeants Cruze or Halliday phoned or showed up, to refer them to the legal department. Sloan had faith that the scores of lawyers on his company's payroll could keep the entire police force at bay for years.

But it wasn't the whole police department he was determined to banish from his sight...and mind. It was a dark-eyed, willowy sergeant with a soft, lean body that had joined so intimately with his own.

Lungs on fire, he pushed upward toward daylight, gulping air as he burst through the water's calm surface. He swam to the pool's edge and heaved himself up into a sitting position, his legs dangling in the warm water.

With the late-afternoon sun beating against his damp flesh, he stared across the pool at the wide, inviting terrace, the base of its slender columns accented with hydrangeas heavy with pink, blue and violet blossoms. He pictured his mother crouched on her knees, carefully setting each bush in place while their gardener stood by, anxious to do the job himself.

"We'll have blooms in two years, then every summer there after," she'd announced when her teenage son and daughter took a break from half-drowning each other in the pool. Sloan hadn't paid much attention at the time. It was years later—when he'd suffered the jarring, devastating loss of both his parents within months of each other—that he began to notice the flowers, bushes and plants that his mother had tended with such devotion.

Sloan dragged in a deep breath, pulling into his lungs the scent of the roses that clambered up the brick fences surrounding the perfectly mowed and raked lawn. He would miss living here, this place where he'd grown up.

His gaze shifted past the terrace to the stately three-story stone house, filled with aging wood and leather and silver. Everything quietly elegant, and getting slowly better and better with time.

True, he'd been gone for two years, he acknowledged as he used his forearm to swipe his wet brow. Nevertheless, he always knew the house was here, waiting. That wouldn't be the case when he left this time.

After the phenomenal success of the new-wing-design tests and the military's enthusiastic response, he'd decided to build a state-of-the-art production facility near D.C. and move there. Selling the house would be a natural result of that decision. His sister didn't want the house—she was married to a film producer, had two children and a life firmly ensconced on the West Coast. The family home was just another part of the past that needed letting go.

"Lord almighty!" His housekeeper's voice, raised to eardrum-rattling volume, split the air, snapping Sloan from his quiet thoughts. "Miss Cruze, if you'll just wait in the study, I'll announce you—"

"Not necessary, Hattie, I'll announce myself."

Eyes narrowed against the glaring sun, Sloan tracked Julia's determined march across the terrace, the hem of her white dress swirling around her calves like storm clouds. As she rounded the corner of the pool, he recognized the signs of boiling fury—the flashing of her dark eyes, the flush of her cheeks, her shoulders as stiff as wire.

"Have pity on an old lady, Miss Cruze, I can't keep up in this heat." When the housekeeper's gnarled hand settled on Julia's arm, Sloan saw the instant softening at the corners of her mouth. Her steps faltered and she turned.

"Hattie, I'm sorry. I...didn't mean to fluster you."

The woman patted at the gray tendrils that sprang from the tight bun at her nape. "Well, the way you came through the front door without knocking had me jumping out of my skin."

"I..." Biting her lip, Julia shoved her dark, tumbled hair behind her shoulders. "I forgot to knock. Didn't think..."

The sharp blade of regret pierced through Sloan when he saw the flush deepen in her cheeks. Not since the day they met had Julia ever had to knock on the front door of his home.

Her hands clenched, then unclenched. Standing there in a white halter dress that caressed her tan shoulders and cinched her waist to impossible thinness, she looked embarrassed...and gorgeous.

The sight of her made him want to forget all about blockading lawyers. Sloan pulled one leg out of the water and propped a forearm negligently across his knee. "Hattie, the heat's getting to all of us. Why don't you bring Julia and me something to drink?"

"Yes, sir."

His voice had Julia whipping around to face him. "You and I need to talk."

"Fine. We can talk while we drink—"

"I don't want a drink. I want to talk. Whether it happens here or downtown is up to you."

He shifted his gaze back to Hattie, whose eyes had gone saucer wide. "Bring a pitcher and two glasses. And my dinner, when it's ready. I'll eat on the terrace."

"Yes, sir." Hattie shot Julia a wary look before bustling off.

Making no move to stand, Sloan sat staring up, remembering how he used to enjoy watching Julia's temper take hold, then crack like lightning. Another memory that belonged to the past.

He cocked his head. "What can I do for you, Jules?"

"Like I said, we need to talk."

"Have you found out who killed Vanessa?"

She took a step toward him. "I think I'm getting close," she said evenly. "We need to talk. Now."

He flicked a glance toward the house. "Where's your partner?"

"Busy." She took another step forward. "*Now,* Sloan."

He shrugged and rose, a pool of dripping water forming at his bare feet. "All right, Julia, talk...." His voice caught when her gaze veered to the point just below his sternum. Damn, how the hell had he forgotten the scar?

He felt the intensity of her eyes as her gaze traced the line the scalpel had taken across his flesh.

Slowly, her eyes rose to meet his. "What happened?"

He forced a shrug. "Exploratory surgery. No big deal."

Her eyes narrowed and he saw the silent questions forming.

Later, he would excuse his actions by telling himself he could feel the damnable scar heat beneath her gaze. But at this instant, his only thought was to divert her eyes, erase from her mind the questions he could never answer. His hand shot out, cupping her nape, and he closed the distance between them.

"Why don't you peel off that fine white dress and slide into the hot tub with me, Jules?"

Her lips parted and he saw the stark surprise in her eyes that rendered her motionless.

The familiar warm scent of *Obsession* pulsed off her in little waves, sending the low, drugging ache of need to his gut. Beneath his hand he felt the tenseness in her spine...and the gratifying hard, quick stutter of her pulse.

Reason told him to stop, to slide his fingers from that soft, heated flesh, step back and rid his lungs of air that so maddeningly smelled only of her. He would have...God, he would have, if he hadn't seen the flutter of her lashes, heard the soft hitch of her breath that had him wanting to pick her up, crush her to him.

Thought left him, as did sound judgment. He dipped his head, his mouth hovering inches from her ripe, glossed lips. "You and me, Jules," he suggested softly, meaning it, wanting it. "Like old times. You remember—"

She moved so fast, it was all he could do to keep his balance when she whacked his hand away, clamped onto his arm and twisted it like a pretzel against his spine.

"You're right, I remember." The same bitterness he heard in her voice flashed in her eyes. "*Everything*. Touch me again and I'll have you flat on your back before you can draw your next breath."

He tightened his jaw to hide a wince. "As I recall," he said in a smooth voice, "you having me on my back can be an exceptional experience."

She jerked back, almost pulling his arm out of the socket before she released her hold. "The days are gone when your smooth lines work on me, Sloan. I have no desire to jump into a hot tub, much less a bed, with you."

He cocked his head and resisted rubbing at the ache in his arm. "I didn't say anything about a bed, Jules, but I'm flattered you're thinking about it."

"Go to hell! And stop calling me *Jules!*"

His lips curved. Time had not dulled the fiery passion that simmered just beneath her controlled-cop exterior. Three years ago he'd walked into the governor's inaugural ball and seen not only a sharp-eyed uniformed officer with an automatic holstered at her waist, but the gorgeous woman behind the tough, aloof shell. And though he'd been mad with desire for her, he'd taken great pleasure in slowly, methodically, breaking through that shell, peeling away the layers of controlled resistance until, weeks later when she came to him, all that remained was drugging softness and heat.

Softness and heat that he suddenly found himself desperate to have again.

His hands fisted at his sides to keep from reaching for her. It was no surprise that his desire for her was as sharp as ever. What surprised him was that for a fleeting instant, he'd felt his resolve waiver.

Pulling in a deep breath, he took in the woman standing before him, her dark hair a ravishing frame around her face, her eyes sparking like hot, black coals. He was tempted, very tempted, to forget every gut-wrenching decision he'd made…but he had no intention of forgetting. He'd returned to Oklahoma City solely because of business, and he'd leave when he had things finalized. Julia Cruze represented the life he could not have. And he was damn sure going to remember that.

He crossed his arms over his bare chest and flicked her a mild look. "Interesting, isn't it, how fate has entwined our lives again?"

"Not fate, Sloan. Murder. If you refuse to talk to me, I'll cuff you and haul you in on a material-witness charge. It's up to you."

She might be bluffing, but the hard line of her mouth told him to take her seriously. "The handcuff part sounds intriguing," he drawled. "But in a few hours I have to dedicate a hospital wing in my parents' memory, so going to jail this evening would be a real inconvenience. If you'll make yourself comfortable on the terrace, I'll get out of these wet trunks, then we can talk. Does that suit you?"

"*Talking* to you will never 'suit' me, Sloan, but I do whatever it takes to put a murderer behind bars." Turning, she hiked the strap of her purse up on her shoulder and walked the length of the pool to the wrought-iron table that sat in the shadows of the flower-laden terrace.

Watching her, Sloan expelled a resigned breath. For the second time that day she had as good as accused him of murder, yet foremost in his mind was the alluring way her hips swung beneath the white dress.

Five minutes later, Sloan stepped onto the shaded terrace wearing a pair of white shorts and a faded denim shirt.

Halfway through a glass of lemonade, Julia looked coolly elegant sitting beneath the breeze-stirring ceiling fan, while magnolia boughs spilled from a Lallique vase on the table before her. The hem of her white dress had fallen back from her bare knees, revealing those long, lean calves so beautifully shaped.

The serene picture didn't fool him. She wasn't any less angry than she'd been when she crashed through his front door in rage-boiling fury. The brooding agitation was there, hidden behind that idle brown stare.

Sloan settled into the chair opposite hers, poured a glass of lemonade and took a sip. "Well, Jules, as you've so aptly shown, it's not my charm that brought you here. I assume it's business—yours, not mine."

"You assume right." She set her glass aside, slid her recorder out of her pocket and snapped it on.

He flicked the machine a look. He was beginning to dislike the damned thing.

"Mr. Remington," she began in a crisp voice, "you're entitled to have counsel present during this interview."

His brows rose. "Am I under arrest?"

"Not yet."

"Yet?"

The slight breeze from the ceiling fan fluttered wisps of dark hair against her cheek. "You're not under arrest at this time," she said, tucking the errant tendrils behind her ear.

"Then we'll leave the lawyers out of it for now."

Uncrossing her legs, she leaned forward, her eyes intent. "Why did you lie to me?"

He felt the hard kick of his heart. What had she found out? "Lie to you?"

"About your relationship with Vanessa West."

"I didn't lie."

She pulled a folded page of newsprint from her purse. "Explain this."

The paper landed on the table before him. Sloan stared down at the picture of himself and Vanessa West taken the previous night—had it only been last night?—at the museum fund-raiser. He vaguely remembered the scurrying photographer who'd asked him to pose beside the prized Remington bronze he'd donated to the museum, indistinctly recalled Vanessa stepping up before the shutter clicked to slip her arm through his while nudging her breast against his sleeve. Sloan studied the beautiful, flawless face that gazed up at him with a sultry mix of desire and ownership. Ten minutes after the photographer had clicked the camera's shutter, the look on Vanessa's face had transformed to iced fury.

"Want to change your statement?" Julia asked quietly.

He looked up. "What part of my statement are you referring to?"

"The part where you claimed your relationship with Vanessa West was strictly business."

"It was."

"She's looking at you like she's planning on having you for dessert."

"Plans change."

"Are you telling me there *had* been something other than business between you?"

"I'm telling you there wasn't."

"The victim desired you." Julia leaned in, her painted fingernail tapping against the photograph. "From the look on her face you could have had her without breaking a sweat."

"Nevertheless, I didn't have her. It would have been unprofessional for us to become sexually involved."

"Did you go to the museum alone?"

Sloan lifted a hand, rubbed his forehead. "Technically, no."

"Technically?"

"I didn't have a date. Vanessa called while I was on my way out the door. She said her Jaguar wouldn't start, and asked if I'd swing by and pick her up. I did."

"What was wrong with her car?"

"She didn't say."

"She drove it to work this morning."

Sloan nodded. "I'm aware of that."

"So, *technically,* you attended the fund-raiser together," Julia mused, her gaze flicking to the newspaper. "There, the two of you posed for a photograph. One might think it's unprofessional to behave in public as intimate friends when that's not the case."

She was good at this, Sloan realized, matching Julia's even stare. Cool and calm...and deadly.

"Most photographs are posed, as was that one," he noted. "Vanessa was into control. She liked power."

"Sex is one way to gain control and power."

"True, but if you can't achieve them by that means, there are others. Vanessa knew people would see us arrive together, see that photograph in the paper and read into it the same thing you have. If you think someone is sleeping with your boss, what do you do? You avoid conflict with them. You go along rather than cause waves. That gives a person power, control."

Julia leaned back, her tanned skin luminous against the chair's pale upholstered cushions. "Must have been maddening," she said coolly.

Sloan cocked his head. "What?"

"To have a beautiful woman throwing herself at you, and all that kept you from taking her was your strong sense of professionalism."

Sloan took a long draw of lemonade. "You're good."

Her eyes narrowed. "What are you talking about?"

"The way you conform things to fit into the puzzle you're trying to piece together." He smiled. "If I didn't kill Vanessa over some torrid affair, then I killed her due to the lack of one."

"I'm glad you're amused, Mr. Remington. Maybe you'll take me seriously when I charge you with murder."

"What makes you think you'll do that?"

"The records from your own security equipment show you arrived in the garage right after Vanessa. The person who drove in next says he found her dead."

"Who was that?"

She picked up her glass, drank. "Don Smithson."

Sloan shrugged. "You can believe him. Don's one of the most honest men I know."

"And I can attest that you're an excellent marksman. You had both the opportunity and the means to kill her."

"What about motive, Julia? Why would I kill Vanessa?"

She scowled as her long, slender fingers tightened on her glass. "I'm working on it."

"I didn't do it," he said quietly.

Saying nothing, she studied him across the table with such absorbed intensity that Sloan fought the urge to shift in his chair.

He dropped his gaze to her left hand, forcing himself to examine the ring that circled her finger. In size, the stone couldn't touch the diamond he'd given her, but it was just as much a symbol that a claim had been staked.

How much easier it would be to accept that she belonged to another man if the memory of her soft laughter wasn't branded in his brain. If he'd never felt her gentle touch against his flesh. If he didn't know that her smiles were breathtaking in their warmth. If she hadn't been everything he'd ever wanted…and the one thing he could never have.

A tightness settled in his chest, curled into a hard fist of regret. Because he couldn't help himself, he asked, "What's he like, Jules?"

A crease formed between her brows. "What's who like?"

"Your fiancé."

She set the glass down with ice-rattling force and hit the

recorder's Stop button. "I'm not going to discuss my private life with you."

Sloan reached out and settled his hand over hers, over the ring. When she tried to jerk away, he tightened his fingers on hers. "I'm asking because I'd like to know if you're happy. That he makes you happy."

Time inched its way forward while she stared down at their linked hands. Above them, the ceiling fan stirred the heated air. The magnolia's sweet fragrance drifted across the terrace. Water lapped softly against the sides of the pool.

Slowly, Julia's eyes rose. "People who meet Bill like him immediately. I was no exception. He's kind and caring. Full of confidence and strength." She paused. "Yes, he makes me happy."

Sloan nodded and said nothing—he couldn't have gotten any words past the lump in his throat if he'd wanted to. Damn, why the hell had he asked?

Across the terrace, a door slid open. Tray in hand, Hattie stepped into view and made her way toward the table. "Here's your salad, sir."

Sloan nodded. "Just leave it, Hattie. And you can call it quits for the day. I'll bring the tray in when I'm done."

He caught the rise of the housekeeper's brows when Julia jerked her hand from beneath his, the diamond scraping his palm.

Hattie picked up the pitcher and refilled his glass, then turned to Julia. "More lemonade, Miss Cruze?"

Julia moved her clearly perplexed gaze from the heaping green salad Hattie had delivered. "No...I'm leaving soon."

"Yes, ma'am. Well, you come back and visit anytime."

Julia reached out, squeezed the woman's sinewy hand. "Thank you, Hattie. It was good to see you again."

As Hattie disappeared into the house, Julia shifted her gaze back to the tray, and scowled.

"Something wrong, Jules?"

"I'm just wondering what you're planning on doing with that salad."

Sloan reached out, grabbed a radish and popped it into his mouth. "I cleaned up my act. No more French fries and greasy hamburgers. I even quit drinking."

"I see."

He watched her rise and slip the recorder into her purse. "I take it you're not going to put a chink in my evening by tossing me in jail."

"Not this evening."

He stood, wishing he could touch her. Wishing he had the right to do a lot more than just that.

"Julia, I didn't kill Vanessa. I give you my word."

She lifted her chin, bitterness sliding into her eyes. "Your word doesn't hold much weight with me, Sloan. I'm sure you understand."

He had told her he loved her, then two days before their wedding, he'd told her he lied. "Yes. I understand."

"Like I said this morning, don't take any trips." Instead of going through the house, she headed across the terrace toward the side gate, her sandaled heels tapping against the granite tiles.

Sloan shoved an unsteady hand through his hair. He knew she'd been unaware of how her voice had softened when she talked about her fiancé, but *he'd* been aware, and it had hit him with the force of a speeding truck.

He grabbed her glass off the table, stared broodingly at the half-moon lipstick kiss on its crystal rim. He'd known, of course, that she would find someone else. Someone who could keep the promises he made her. But it had never occurred to him, not for one instant, that any man could ever possess her as he once had.

He'd been wrong. Dead wrong.

Muttering a raw curse, Sloan raised the glass, then deliberately set his mouth over the place hers had been.

Chapter 4

Hoping speed would ease the tension from her meeting with Sloan, Julia stepped on the gas and steered toward the interstate.

She attributed the knot that had settled in her belly to her cop instincts. Sloan, after all, was a suspect. Interviewing suspects always shot adrenaline through her veins. Gunning the car's engine, she rolled through a yellow light, her knuckles bone-white on the steering wheel.

"Who are you trying to fool, Cruze?" she muttered, acknowledging it was not the interview that had left her nerves as taut as a bowstring. It was the sight of that scar.

What sort of surgery had left it? What had happened to Sloan?

Why the hell do you care?

"I don't!" she shot back, then felt like an idiot for yelling at herself. Flipping a lever on the dash, she turned the air on full blast and positioned the vents so the cold hit her heated face.

She had stopped caring about Sloan Remington a long

time ago. He was just another suspect now. She had a job to do—bring Vanessa West's killer to justice. If that was Sloan, so be it. With determination setting her jaw, Julia focused on the case, clicking off a mental list of everyone who had access to the parking garage where the woman died.

"Damn," she whispered after a few minutes when her thoughts drifted back to an area that had nothing to do with murder. Blowing out a resigned breath, she let her mind go.

The scar originated just below Sloan's breastbone and extended down the center of his abdomen. *Exploratory surgery. No big deal.*

A scar that resembled a long zipper with a slight pucker here and there looked like a big deal, Julia thought as she squinted out the windshield against the long rays of the setting sun. A very big deal.

The incision had been there long enough to heal. Long enough to lose all postsurgical redness and fade to a pale flesh tone.

Had the cause of the surgery been Sloan's incentive toward a healthier lifestyle?

He'd once been as much a coffee freak as she, but now he drank orange juice and lemonade—*fresh* lemonade. He worked out in a gym, swam laps. The man ate salads. Two years ago, he wouldn't have known endive from a nosedive. Now he ate the stuff.

Julia exited the interstate, veered through an alley and half a dozen side streets to avoid traffic, then pulled into an unloading zone at the back of the county courthouse. The clock on the dash served as a glaring reminder that her stop at Sloan's house had made her over an hour late to meet Bill. Yet she remained in her car with the motor idling and air conditioner blasting while her thoughts remained maddeningly on Sloan.

Judging from the looks of him, his fitness regime was nothing new. When she and Halliday interviewed him in his office that morning, Sloan's dark, tailored suit had been deceiving. But the sight of him in his bathing trunks revealed rock-solid muscles and powerful calves—not overdeveloped, but impressive all the same. Sloan's body looked harder, tougher, his muscles more distinctly defined than before.

His body not only looked that way, it felt that way, too. Heat pooled in her cheeks at the memory of the latent strength in the hand that had curved with familiar intimacy on the back of her neck. And when she shoved from his touch, she'd had the quick impression of pressing against steel.

Julia shifted her gaze and stared idly out the windshield at a bony black cat that slunk along the curb. There had been moments over the past two years when she thought she'd die of the need to feel Sloan's touch. She'd grieved with the knowledge that her flesh would never again ignite from the heady feel of his mouth slicking down her throat, her shoulder, then settling onto her breast to nip, suckle....

She closed her eyes on a groan. The first time he'd taken her in his arms, an instant, electric connection had hummed through her body. She'd felt it every time they'd touched, and today had been no exception. The moment Sloan's palm pressed against her flesh, a searing longing slammed into her like a fist. A longing as intense as it was unexpected.

Propping her elbows against the steering wheel, Julia pressed the heels of her palms against her eyes. Her reaction to Sloan's touch had been merely that—a knee-jerk response that meant nothing. *Nothing.* She couldn't let it affect the investigation, couldn't let it affect *her.*

With her next breath, anger stirred inside her as she acknowledged that was exactly what had happened. Otherwise, why had some reckless part of her wanted to lift a hand and touch that scar? Trace her fingers along the length of it? And why the hell was she allowing the aftermath of some unknown surgery to trail through her thoughts in an endless loop when she needed to concentrate on the case?

Killing the engine, she shoved open the door and stepped outside. The oppressive heat nearly took her breath away. She slammed the door, sending the scrawny black cat skittering beneath a graffiti-painted dumpster.

It was close to seven, and the only public access into the courthouse was through the sheriff's office. Julia checked in with a sleepy-eyed deputy who buzzed her through the security door. She cut across the dim rotunda, the marble halls echoing with the hollow clicking of her sandals as she made her way to the district attorney's office. There, the reception area was dark, the hallway filled with gray shadows. The wedge of light jutting from the office at the end of the corridor drew her like a divining rod to water.

She paused just outside the door, unobserved by the man sitting in his shirtsleeves behind a desk inch deep with file folders, legal documents and general clutter. At the front edge of the blotter sat a nameplate that read *Bill Taylor, First Assistant District Attorney.*

The office was simple, the furniture sturdy but utilitarian. Untidy piles of file folders sat on top of bookcases and beneath the two leather visitors' chairs at the front of the desk.

Julia shifted her gaze. While her fiancé concentrated on the contents of a legal pad, she concentrated on him. The glare of fluorescent lights emphasized the blond highlights in his thick, sandy hair; accentuated the firmness of his generous mouth, the awareness in his blue eyes. Those handsome, fine-honed features belonged to a man with a cool, purposeful temperament that Julia held in awe. Things that shot her blood pressure into the red zone often drew only a shrug from Bill.

They'd met a year ago when the first homicide case she'd handled went to trial. Over time, Bill's open expression and blue eyes that invited trust had pulled her from the alienated, cold existence that settled over her when Sloan left.

Thinking of the gentle tenderness and compassion Bill had shown her sent a wave of gratitude through Julia. What would she have done without him?

As if sensing her presence, Bill lifted his gaze. A tired smile flashed across his tanned face.

"Sorry I'm late," she said as she stepped into the office. "I got tied up. I hope you got the message I left on your voice mail."

"I did." He rose, came around the desk and dropped a kiss on her cheek. His white shirt was open at the collar; wrinkles gathered around his woven leather suspenders. "And it's just as well you got held up. A problem's come up with a key witness in the murder trial I start in the morning. I've got two clerks in the conference room researching case law and making calls to try to get things straightened out." He checked his watch. "I thought I'd have things wrapped in a couple of hours. Now it looks like it'll be an all-nighter."

"I can pick something up for dinner," Julia offered. "Bring it back here."

"Thanks, but the clerks ordered pizzas. I'll scavenge off them." He cocked his head, his appreciative gaze moving down the length of her halter dress. "You look great," he said softly.

Why don't you peel off that fine white dress and slide into the hot tub with me, Jules?

Spine going stiff, Julia closed her eyes on the sudden, unwanted intrusion of Sloan's words.

"Something wrong?" Bill asked as he curled his hand around hers.

"No," she managed around the knot in her throat. "Nothing."

She stared down at the large, firm hand that held hers. The gesture was typical of their relationship, Julia thought. Bill reaching for her, instead of her for him. Sloan had taught her well. Taught her that wanting something too much could rip you to shreds when you lost it. With Sloan, loving had mattered too much. It had ground her down, nearly destroyed her. And so, her relationship with Bill was different. She loved him in a quiet, calm way that allowed her to hold back. She seldom reached out. Never let herself want too much.

"I...my mind's on the case I got today," she added.

"So, tell me about it."

"Shouldn't you concentrate on your murder trial?"

He rolled his shoulders beneath his starched shirt. "To tell you the truth, I need a break." Keeping his fingers linked with hers, Bill gestured for her to sit in one of the visitors' chairs, then he settled into the other.

The warm, masculine scent of his cologne drifted into Julia's lungs, conjuring feelings of contentment. Peace. With Bill, she felt as if she'd pulled on a comfortable sweater.

"What about your case?" he prodded.

"Halliday and I answered a call this morning at Remington Aerospace."

"I heard about the homicide," Bill said after a moment. "I didn't know you took the call."

She nodded, not surprised Bill knew about the murder. Cops regularly visited the D.A.'s office throughout the day and mentioned whatever new cases were working.

"I would have passed the call to another team if I'd known what I do now," she said.

"What's that?"

"Sloan's back." When Bill remained silent, she shifted her gaze to his face, saw the awareness in his blue eyes. "Did you know?" she asked. "Did you know he's back?"

"I saw his picture in this morning's paper."

"So did Mother," Julia said dryly. "She showed up on my doorstep this evening, spouting fire." Julia lifted a brow as she regarded the man beside her. "Did you plan to mention the picture to me?"

"I'd have maybe gotten around to it...in about a hundred years." With his long legs stretched out in front of him,

Bill stared straight ahead, as if examining the framed law degree hanging on the wall behind his desk. "Sloan Remington's not exactly my choice topic of conversation."

"Nor mine." Julia tightened her fingers around the solid, firm hand that held hers. "I want you to know that I'll have to deal with Sloan awhile. He's a suspect."

Bill's fingers flinched. "Damn," he said softly, meeting her gaze. "Who got killed?"

"Vanessa West, Sloan's executive assistant." Julia raked her fingers through her hair. "Judging from what I heard in the interviews I conducted, the woman's unofficial title was 'Head Bitch.'"

"Wouldn't win Miss Congeniality?"

"Not even close. That was her with Sloan in the newspaper photo."

"I remember thinking how...involved they looked."

"I thought that, too. He swears the only relationship they had was the job."

"Do you believe him?"

"I don't know," she said in a quiet voice. "But I have an idea how to find out."

"I'm listening."

"While Halliday gets his jollies attending the autopsy in the morning, I'll pay the art museum a visit. I want to talk to people who saw Sloan and Vanessa together. I need to find out how they acted toward each other before and after they posed for the photo."

Bill cocked his head. "Don't expect the museum to willingly hand over its guest list. They don't want donors to come there one night, then get questioned by the police the next day."

"It's not the guests I intend to talk to, not now anyway. It's the people who worked the night of the fund-raiser. Museum staffers, catering crew, the parking-valet employees. Service people blend into the background, get overlooked. But they listen and they hear things."

"Good idea," Bill said, then fell silent. When he spoke

again, his voice had taken on a somber tone. "What will you do if Remington killed her?"

"Book him."

He raised their joined hands, pressed a soft kiss against her knuckles. "Maybe what I should ask is what's going to happen if he isn't the murderer?"

Julia's breathing shallowed. "The logical answer is that I'll arrest whoever is. But I don't think that's what you're asking."

"It's not." Bill stared gravely back at her. "Julia, I know how much you loved him. I know how much he hurt you." He paused. "I'm not sure you've ever gotten over that—"

"I did."

"Over him—"

"I did," she insisted, then dropped her gaze. The thought of the quick, instinctive wave of longing that had lurched through her when Sloan's hand settled against her flesh tugged at her conscience. *Knee-jerk reaction,* she reminded herself.

Taking firm hold of her emotions, she shifted to face Bill. "I wasn't over Sloan when you and I started seeing each other. But I got over him, and I did it with your help."

Mouth curving, Bill squeezed her hand, then leaned and settled a whisper-light kiss on her lips. "It was a pleasure," he murmured.

Eyes closed, Julia waited for the stirring of her pulse, the heated lurch of longing.

Neither came.

"Must be gratifying to have both the mayor and governor show up for your party," Rick Fox observed as he handed his boss a refill of club soda.

"It's not exactly my party."

Sloan's gaze swept across the tuxedoed and gowned bodies crowded into the hospital's formal reception room. The low hum of conversation drifted on the air, accompanied by the occasional clink of ice in glasses. The short speech he'd made from the dais, followed by the ribbon cutting, had officially dedicated the new oncology wing in his parents' memory. Following the ceremony, he'd made his way through the crush of guests, shaking more hands than a politician on the campaign trail. Now Sloan found himself fighting the need to leave, to rid himself of the damn place where the sterile-scented air flung him back to a world of grim, dark memories.

"Hell if it isn't your party," Rick observed. "If it wasn't for Remington money, the very spot we're standing on would still be a vacant lot."

"I suppose."

Rick unbuttoned the jacket of his tux, slid a hand into his trouser pocket and downed a hefty swallow of Scotch. "Since you chose to drift over here behind a potted palm, I gather you've got things on your mind other than this to-do. Like Julia's impromptu visit."

Sloan studied his security chief over the wedge of lime bestriding the rim of his glass. He and Rick Fox had been best friends since they'd roomed together at college. That Rick could read his thoughts was no surprise.

Sloan wasn't sure what darkened his mood more—the cool suspicion he'd seen in Julia's eyes when she accused him of murder, or the aching longing that her presence instilled in him. A longing that made him want to take, to reach out for the one thing he'd forbidden himself.

The one thing he no longer had the right to want.

"Vanessa's dead," Sloan said, aware of the edge that had settled in his voice. "The police think I killed her. What the hell do you expect I'm thinking about?"

"Julia," Rick repeated. "Correct me if I'm wrong, boss."

Sloan exhaled a slow breath through his teeth and said nothing.

"You nixed my suggestion this morning about asking the mayor to pull her off the investigation," Rick continued. "I think you ought to reconsider."

"Why?"

"She's too close to this. There's no way she can work the case without emotion having some influence."

"Trust me," Sloan began, his mouth taking on a sardonic arch. "Julia did a fine job of grilling me this evening." He took another sip of club soda, and found he no longer had a taste for it. Eyeing Rick's glass, he considered changing to Scotch, then decided against it. There wasn't enough whiskey in the world to ease the knot in his gut.

A man's loud, booming laugh sounded from somewhere across the crowded room. Sloan glanced up, saw the governor deep in conversation with the mayor and the hospital's administrator.

"Julia's having no problem doing her job," Sloan said, returning his attention to Rick. "I got the distinct impression she'd like nothing better than to slap a pair of handcuffs on me and haul me to jail."

"And why is that?" Rick asked quietly. "Because she thinks you're guilty, or because it's her chance to even the score? You walk out on her, she busts you for murder. You're tied."

"Revenge is not Julia's style."

"Maybe not. But it's damn foolish to leave a thing like your freedom to chance." Rick downed the remainder of his drink, then shoved his glass onto the tray of a scurrying waiter. "And you're no fool."

Sloan cocked his head. "I remember one time you called me a fool. You meant it."

"Yeah, well, it's still my opinion you made a mistake when you left Julia. But you did what you believed was right, and what I think doesn't matter. What matters is how you handle things from this point on. There are defense contracts pending for the new wing design that'll mean millions to Remington Aerospace. The whole thing could fall through if you're locked up just because some cop decides revenge is sweet."

"Julia might have a lot against me, but she wouldn't take things that far—"

"There's no way you can be sure. Two years have

passed since you had anything to do with her. People change, Sloan. Just because you had me keep tabs on her while you were gone doesn't mean you still know her—not in the sense you're talking about. You can't have any idea what she's thinking, what she feels.''

The persistent hum of conversation that filled the air faded from Sloan's hearing as he conjured up the image of Julia, her tanned skin dark against the white halter dress. She *had* changed, he silently conceded. He'd sensed an edge to her that had not existed before. Her body language was part of it, but mostly it was her eyes, the wariness in them, the hardness. Maybe some of that came naturally, considering the daily misery and violence she surely dealt with working in Homicide. But he had no doubt he'd had a part in putting the wary look in those dark eyes. The bitterness.

His jaw tightened. He remembered all too well the feel of her soft, luscious body quivering beneath his, her dark hair a wild cloud of tangles against the sheets while those same eyes gazed up at him, smoky with desire.

As much as he'd wanted her physically, he had wanted the woman more. Theirs had been a joining of the soul as well as the body. He had needed *her* in his life. But it was a life filled with uncertainty. He hadn't been willing two years ago to pull that dark, smothering cloud of uncertainty around her. Nor was he willing now when so much gray smoke remained.

"I agree...Julia's a good cop," Rick continued. "But there's no way in hell she should get within a mile of this case. The mayor's right over there, Sloan. All it'll take is a phone call from him to Chief McMillan, and you won't have to deal with Julia and all that emotional baggage."

"I have no intention of getting her tossed off the investigation, so forget it. Since you've been keeping up with her you know she worked hard to get that gold sergeant's badge."

"Sloan—"

"Do you know what my going to the mayor would do to her career?"

"Yeah, I know," Rick said through his teeth. He stared at the milling crowd for a long moment. "What about her fiancé?"

Sloan sliced his friend a narrow look. "What about him?"

"Bill Taylor's on the second rung of the ladder at the D.A.'s office. He usually tries high-profile cases. God forbid you'd have to face him from the defense table—"

"Dammit, I didn't kill Vanessa!"

"I know that, but—"

"Which means there's no evidence against me for Julia—or any other cop—to find. Stop predicting gloom and doom for me, Rick, and concentrate on finding who the hell shot Vanessa in the back!"

"Look, Sloan, I'm sorry." Mouth hard and unsmiling, Rick shoved a thick hand through his unruly, corn-colored hair. "I think the cards are stacked against you and there's no reason to let them stay that way."

"Let me worry about that."

Rick stood silent, his sharp gaze shifting from point to point across the crowded room. Finally he asked, "Did you know that Don Smithson found Vanessa's body?"

"Julia mentioned it."

"I think he and Vanessa had a thing going."

The statement brought Sloan's chin up. "Vanessa and Don?"

"Yep."

Sloan groaned as he pictured his silver-haired personnel director working at his desk, a photograph of his wife and three children smiling from the credenza behind him. "What makes you think they were involved?"

"I walked in his office without knocking one day. Vanessa was there. Neither of them heard me come in. She was sitting on the corner of his desk, smiling that pouty smile, her skirt hiked halfway up her thighs. Smithson had the look of a starving man who had a strawberry sundae in his sights.''

"If you thought they were involved, why didn't you tell me?"

"You expected me to pick up the phone every time I suspected Vanessa of sleeping with some guy?" Rick asked with derision. "Hell, Sloan, we'd have been on the phone more than we'd have been off.''

Sloan raised a hand, rubbed his forehead.

"There's something else," Rick went on. "One of my men overheard the cops talking. They found one of our employee service pins a few feet from Vanessa's body.''

"Those pins come from personnel," Sloan said.

"Right. Smithson's division.''

"Has anyone reported their pin lost?"

"Not to my people.''

Sloan's brows furrowed in thought. "All right. It's possible Don and Vanessa were involved. The police found an employee service pin near her body. In themselves, those two facts prove nothing.''

"I agree. But they suggest quite a lot.''

"Did you tell Julia your suspicions about Don and Vanessa?"

"No. It's only my guess they were involved." Rick shook his head. "One thing about having Julia on the case is she's as relentless as a jackhammer. If Smithson's the killer, she'll figure it out.''

Sloan glanced at the now dispersing crowd and set his glass aside. "I need to mingle, thank people again for coming.''

He made his way through the mass of bodies, shaking hands. At one point, he paused to listen with attentive interest while his father's longtime golf partner reminisced.

Later, Sloan shifted his gaze to the dais, where a portrait of his parents rested on a spotlighted easel. He expelled a slow breath, hoping like hell the name of Vanessa's killer was all that Julia figured out.

Chapter 5

Julia wanted coffee. Real coffee. Not the hideous *caffè latte* she'd forced down between interviews at the art museum.

She wanted a quick, humming hit of caffeine. Then she'd huddle with Halliday to compare notes. After that, they'd go through the manila evidence envelopes she'd checked out from the lab on her way upstairs.

Her thoughts churning with the results of that morning's interviews, she walked into the squad room, where every desk was occupied and the coffeepot empty.

"Damn." Scowling, she tossed her leather portfolio beside the stack of phone messages that had collected on her desk since the previous evening. "Where's Lonnie?" she asked while craning her neck to catch a glimpse of the Homicide detail's longtime secretary.

"Sick," Detective Sam Rogers said from his desk behind Julia's.

"Great."

She glanced at Halliday's empty chair. "Any sign of my partner?"

"Called from the M.E.'s office," Sam replied around the stub of a cigar. "He said not to expect him for a while." The veteran detective's loose jowls and protruding paunch lent him a harmless look, but he'd long maintained the division's highest clearance rate. "A family of four was found in their home last night, dead of who knows what," Sam continued as he reached for his ringing phone. "Your victim's autopsy got pushed back."

"Wonderful," Julia muttered, then grabbed the empty coffeepot and headed down the hallway. She had her own strong blend brewing in less than five minutes.

Adjusting the holster that held her 9 mm Smith & Wesson on the waistband of her slim, black skirt, she slid into her chair. Questions burned in her mind; foremost was whether Sloan would admit to the argument that had taken place between him and Vanessa West only hours before she'd died.

Julia had interviewed two museum staffers, then gone by the home of a catering employee who'd served champagne during the fund-raiser. They'd all overheard the "furious threats" flung at Mr. Remington by the stunning blonde who moments before had smiled at his side for the newspaper photographer. Mr. Remington, from all accounts, had shown no outward response to the woman's fury.

Classic Sloan, Julia thought. Cool under fire. Circumspect. Unshakable dignity. Didn't even flinch when accused of murder.

She checked her phone messages. Eve Nelson, Vanessa's secretary who'd had minor foot surgery the previous day, had returned the message Julia had left on her answering machine. She dialed the woman's number and scheduled an appointment to see her that afternoon.

After making several more case-related calls, Julia pushed away from her desk, drawn by the heady scent of real coffee. She wove her way through the maze of battleship gray, city-issue desks, passing by the doorway where a stuffed vulture perched on a dead tree limb. The Homicide Division's mascot glared at her, its oversize beak lending it a slightly cross-eyed look.

She filled a mug, blew across the coffee's steaming surface and decided to give up waiting for Halliday. Back at her desk she slit the top of the manila envelope and dumped the contents of Vanessa West's briefcase onto her desk. A black leather appointment book revealed that the victim typically filled her days with business meetings and corporate lunches. Every morning, she'd worked out in the gym. *With Sloan?* Julia wondered.

Sipping coffee, she continued flipping through pages, her fingers faltering when she saw the first of many evening entries that included the initial *S*. Dinner with *S*. Drinks with *S*. Spend night with *S*.

The lurch of her stomach had Julia gritting her teeth. *Don't jump to conclusions,* she cautioned herself. The entries could mean Sloan. But he wasn't the only man at Remington Aerospace whose initial was *S*.

Ignoring the thick feeling in her chest, Julia continued scanning the pages from which a faint drift of sweet, expensive perfume rose. *Vanessa's scent,* she realized. Her lips curved into an ironic arch. The woman who so often bared her fangs went around smelling as sweet as spun sugar.

Hundreds of names filled the book's address section, written in an all-business methodical script that Julia assumed belonged to the deceased. Most of the names had Houston addresses and phone numbers. Houston, Julia knew from the personnel file Rick Fox had supplied, was where Vanessa had worked prior to transferring to Remington's Oklahoma City office.

Julia set the book aside, reached into the evidence envelope and slid out a thick printout. Across the front page, the same precise, angular letters labeled the contents: *"HELD Wing—Test Stats."* Nose scrunched, she thumbed through the unending pages of charts and formulas, finally deciding Chinese algebra would be easier to figure out. A tape recorder with working batteries and blank cassette, and a file folder labeled *"Wind Tunnel Test No. 33"* summed up the remainder of the briefcase's contents.

The second evidence envelope Julia opened contained a receipt found in Vanessa's black Jaguar for a cup of carrot juice purchased the morning of the murder from a trendy health food store. A sack from an office supply store containing a box of unused computer disks had been found on the Jag's back seat. The three-line lab report taped to the envelope reported that the empty paper cup found inside the vehicle had a dozen latent prints on its surface, all too smudged for ID. The only prints found inside the Jaguar belonged to the victim.

Julia tipped the envelope upside down; the gold twenty-year Remington service pin, now officially sealed in plastic, slid out. She nibbled her bottom lip. Did the killer drop the pin before fleeing the scene, or had it lain on the garage floor for some time, lost by some loyal Remington employee who had nothing to do with the murder? She frowned. The city also issued service pins to its employees—pins that came from the Personnel Department. Don Smithson, the man who found Vanessa's body, headed Remington's Personnel division. Julia added the service pin to her growing list of items to check.

She glanced at the clock above the assignment board, where red grease-pencil letters displayed each team's unsolved cases. She scowled at the reminder of the still-open case that had plagued her and Halliday for the past month.

"One thing at a time," she mumbled, and decided to check Halliday's progress at the M.E.'s office. Grabbing her phone, she punched in a number every OCPD Homicide detective knew by heart.

"Oklahoma State Medical Examiner," a cheery-voiced receptionist answered.

Julia gave her name and asked the woman to page Sergeant Halliday.

"I think he's gone," the receptionist commented. "But I'm not sure—it's been a zoo here this morning. Dr. McClandess performed the autopsy on your case. I'll transfer you to his office."

Sipping coffee, Julia waited through a series of buzzes and clicks. Her brows shot up when the doctor himself answered. She identified herself and asked for Halliday.

"He left fifteen minutes ago, took his sack of apple turnovers with him," the doctor said, the deep timbre of his voice booming across the line. Julia pictured the man eternally garbed in a white lab coat, his gaunt face sharpened to the bone, black eyes unnaturally vibrant, gray hair combed back from the temples.

"Your partner consumed two turnovers during the autopsy."

Julia rolled her eyes. "He has an iron stomach."

"No doubt," the doctor agreed. "When Sergeant Halliday left, he said he was on his way to the station."

"Thanks," Julia said, then hesitated. She glanced around the busy office, making sure no one was within eavesdropping distance. "Dr. McClandess, do you have time to answer a question?"

"If it's about your victim, Sergeant Halliday has all the information."

"It's not." Julia knew she was about to blur the fine line between professional and personal interest, but it didn't seem to matter. "The question does relate to the case, though."

"Go ahead."

"I need to know what type of surgery leaves a certain incision." She then described the scar that extended downward from the base of Sloan's sternum. The scar that had kept her tossing and turning for hours in her *Arabian Nights* bed.

"A midline scar of that length could represent removal

of an organ, or exploratory surgery, or both. Does that answer your question, Sergeant?"

"Yes. One more thing," Julia said. "How long does it take an incision to heal?"

"On average a scar will lose its redness and begin to fade in about six months. After a year, it generally appears paler than the surrounding flesh."

Julia thanked the man, then slowly replaced the phone on its cradle, while Sloan's words replayed in her head.

Exploratory surgery. No big deal.

Julia closed her eyes, then took a deep breath. *What did it matter?* she asked herself.

Her fingers tightened on her coffee mug. The fact that Sloan had undergone surgery didn't mean a thing. Not a thing.

"'Morning, partner." Grinning, Halliday dropped into the chair at the desk that butted against the front of hers.

Julia gave the crumpled bakery sack he tossed at her fingertips a disdainful look. "Don't tell me. Apple turnovers. Bet you managed to choke down a couple during the autopsy."

His eyes widened behind his wire-rim glasses. "That," he said, "is why you're the lead detective on this team."

"And don't forget it." She pitched the sack behind her onto Sam Roger's desk.

"Thanks, sweetheart," he said, saluting her with his stubby cigar.

She looked back at Halliday. "What did the M.E. say?"

He pulled a small plastic evidence bag out of the inside pocket of his suit coat. "Vanessa died from one shot from a .22."

Julia nodded and kept her expression neutral. She knew without checking the inventory of Sloan's weapons that he owned both .22 revolvers and automatics. Her mind went to the parking garage, conjuring up the image of a shadowy killer squeezing the trigger of a .22, Vanessa's red power suit an ideal target. Julia's breath stilled. Try as she might, she couldn't put Sloan's face on that dark figure.

"You still with me?" Halliday asked.

Her gaze slid back to meet his. "Go on."

"The M.E. confirmed the shooter stood about five to eight feet from the victim."

"So it was a lucky shot," Julia said, aware of the slow velocity of a .22 slug. To kill at a distance, the small shell had to hit the right spot.

"Lucky, or our killer's a damn good shot." Halliday cocked his head. "How good is Remington?"

"As good as me," she said quietly.

"That good?" Halliday asked, his eyes narrowing with suspicious concentration.

"Anything else from the M.E.?"

"Just one minor detail. The bullet's mangled."

"Mangled?"

Halliday tossed the plastic bag onto her desk. "A .22 loses its form when it hits something solid. The slug that killed Vanessa smashed into her spine before hitting her heart. The bullet's deformed."

"Too deformed for testing?"

"I checked with Gomez in Ballistics on my way in. There are a few striations visible on the bullet. He can probably match them with the murder weapon...if we find it." Halliday dug through the clutter on his desk until he unearthed the printout Sloan's secretary had given him the previous day.

"Remington has two .22 revolvers...a Smith & Wesson and a Colt." Paper crinkled as Halliday flipped to the next page. "He's also got automatics—one competition-grade High Standard, a Colt and a Baretta. All have four-inch barrels or shorter. Easy to conceal." His mouth curved as he tossed the printout aside. "Remington's an excellent shot. He owns the right type weapon. He arrived in the garage just after Vanessa. There's a good chance he's our man."

Julia stared at the plastic-encased bullet. Halliday wasn't theorizing about some unknown person; he was talking about Sloan. Sloan as a killer. A man she had once loved. The man with whom she'd felt a closeness she'd never before, or since, experienced.

Her hand drifted up to rub at the pain that had settled in her right temple. For the past twenty-four hours, her thoughts of Sloan as a suspect had been vague, abstract. Now, as she stared down at the deformed bullet, realization hit. Could she do it? Could she coolly read Sloan his rights, then lock him in a cage and walk away without a backward glance?

Wasn't that, essentially, what he'd done to her? Plunged her into a world of grief, then walked away with no remorse, no regret?

She set her teeth. She was doing exactly what she'd assured her boss and her partner she wouldn't do. She was letting emotion seep in, color her thinking. She had to get a grip, had to maintain control.

"Julia?" Halliday asked softly.

She met his intense gaze. "What?"

"You have a problem dealing with Remington as a suspect?"

"No."

"Ryan can assign someone else to work with me on this case."

She leaned forward, her hand balled around the plastic bag. "Don't ever imply I can't do my job, Halliday," she said, her voice vibrating with temper.

"That's not what I said," he countered evenly. "You almost married Remington. The idea of hauling him in on a murder charge has to stir up a hell of a lot of emotion—"

"If we arrest him, it will be because he killed Vanessa West," Julia said. "The only emotion that's likely to '*stir up*' is satisfaction."

"Okay." Halliday leaned back in his chair and regarded

her while thumping a pencil against a stack of file folders. "If you say you can handle it, I'll take your word for it."

"You do that." She tossed the bag onto his desk. "If you're finished analyzing me, I'll tell you what I found out at the art museum."

"Tell away."

"They fought," she said.

"Remington and Vanessa?"

"Yes. After posing for the newspaper picture, they wound up in a display room that wasn't in use that night. But it's between the exhibit hall and the kitchen, where the caterer had set up, so a lot of service people and museum staff passed by. I interviewed three of them. They all overheard Vanessa threatening Sloan."

Halliday's pencil went still. "What sort of threats?"

"That he'd be sorry. That she'd expose him for what he was, make him and Remington Aerospace pay for what he'd done."

"Anyone hear what that was?"

"No."

"Too bad."

"When Vanessa left, she stalked into the hallway and crashed into a waiter with a tray loaded with champagne glasses. The poor guy lost his footing—champagne and glass went everywhere."

"Let me guess," Halliday began with a wry look. "Our Miss West had a man lying at her feet, and she left him there."

Julia nodded. "Cussed him for good measure, then stalked out."

Halliday stroked his chin. "When you called me last night, you said Remington told you Vanessa had car trouble and hitched a ride with him to the museum."

"Right," Julia confirmed.

"So how'd she get home?"

"I don't know. One of the museum staffers saw Vanessa storm out the front entrance. She was alone. The staffer remembers seeing Sloan leave about an hour after Vanessa. Could be, Vanessa had a phone in her purse and called a cab."

"Or she could have hitched a ride with another guest."

"I asked for a copy of the guest list. The only way the museum will release it is with a warrant." Julia shoved her dark hair across her shoulders and leaned in. "The catering employee let it slip that the mayor attended the fund-raiser. We also know about the guests whose pictures showed up in the paper—all of them are high-steppers when it comes to the social scene in this town. This case could turn political fast, Halliday. Before we go for the warrant and start questioning these people, let's check with the cab companies to see if Vanessa called. If she didn't, that probably means she hitched a ride with another guest. She was furious. She could have vented her anger on whoever drove her home, told them what happened between her and Sloan."

Julia paused, took a deep breath, then handed Halliday the leather appointment book. "Check how she spent most of her evenings."

"'Dinner with *S*,'" Halliday read, then turned a page. "'Drinks with *S*. Spend night with *S*.'" He looked up. "So, Remington lied about their relationship."

"Maybe. A couple of male Remington staffers I interviewed yesterday have the initial S in their name. Don Smithson, for one."

"What time did Smithson get to work yesterday?"

"Seven-oh-nine," Julia said after checking the printout. "That's when he scanned his card at the entrance to the parking garage."

"Have we confirmed that?"

Julia nodded. "After I finished the staff interviews yesterday, I went to Rick Fox's office and viewed the tapes."

Halliday picked up a rubber band, stretched it and relaxed it repeatedly. "I thought the lab confiscated the tapes."

"The cassettes out of the security cameras," she confirmed as she held up an evidence envelope. "The cassettes are in here. Rick showed me the master off their network system. The times on the printout agree with what's on the tapes."

Halliday's forehead creased as he worked the rubber band. "Fox said he's an ex-cop. What's the story on him?"

"He and Sloan met at college. After graduation, Rick went back home and signed on with the New Orleans PD. After about ten years, a back injury forced him to take a medical retirement. Around that same time, Sloan had an opening for head of security. He offered Rick the job."

Halliday tossed the rubber band away and prodded his glasses up the bridge of his nose. "I'll start the ball rolling on getting a warrant to seize Remington's .22s. If I keep on top of things, I should have the paperwork this afternoon."

"Before you start on the warrant, let's go over what you found at Vanessa's apartment."

"Like I said on the phone last night, the word 'apartment' doesn't do the place justice. 'Suite at the Ritz' is more like it." He leaned forward. "The landlord said the rent on a place the size of Vanessa's starts at fifteen hundred a month. *Fifteen hundred.* I'm telling you, Cruze, you and I ought to ditch this place and become corporate executives."

"And give up the glamour of our jobs?" Julia asked, her voice as dry as the Sahara. "How many corporate executives get to view dead bodies on an almost daily basis?"

"There is that," Halliday said, grinning. "Anyway, we found no signs of forced entry at Vanessa's place. Nothing disturbed or rummaged through. What Rick Fox said about her living alone rang true. There was no sign of men's clothing in any of the closets or drawers. The only messages on the answering machine were unimportant, all for Vanessa. The stereo was tuned to the same station as the radio in her Jaguar." He paused for a moment, his expression thoughtful. "I showed the picture from Vanessa's personnel file to a few of her neighbors. In the three months she lived there, she'd never spoken a word to any of them, just passed them in the hall without even a glance."

"Miss Warmth."

"Yeah. None of the neighbors ever saw her bring anybody into the apartment with her."

"What about the files you got off her computer?"

Halliday checked the time. "I'll call Kelly in the lab—he's the one who copied them. He's probably got a hard copy of everything for us by now."

Thoughtfully, Julia tapped an index finger against her coffee mug. "Did he access every program, every file?"

"Everything," Halliday confirmed. "The computer didn't even ask once for a password." He opened a file folder, checked his notes. "Did you get hold of NOK?"

"Yes. Next of kin is Vanessa's mother. She lives in Houston. I tried to call her yesterday between interviews, finally reached her when I got back here."

"So, how'd she take the news?"

"Not good. She and her husband, who is Vanessa's stepfather, are flying in sometime today."

Halliday nodded. "Well, it looks like we've got all the bases covered so far."

"I'll check the cab companies," Julia said, then dug into the evidence envelope for the health food store receipt. "While I'm out, I'll drop by *Here's to Your Health*."

"Where?"

"The place Vanessa bought the carrot juice she spilled in her Jag. Maybe she stopped there every morning. Maybe she wasn't always alone."

Julia stuck the receipt in her portfolio, then rose. "I've got a two o'clock appointment to interview Vanessa's secretary. Call me when you have the warrant for Sloan's weapons. I'll meet you at his house."

"I can handle this," Halliday said. "It'd be no big deal

to take a couple of extra uniforms to help with the search. You don't have to be there.''

"This is our case, Halliday," she snapped. "*Our* case."

Technically, her partner was right—she didn't need to be there. But she was lead on the investigation and she had a duty to perform. They needed to search a suspect's residence, so she'd be there. Period. Just because Sloan's home held a million memories didn't mean she'd allow emotion to figure into the equation.

"Get the warrant, Halliday," she said. "And let me know what time to meet you there."

Jaw set, Sloan sat on the leather couch in the study, while his anger built. He kept his hot gaze on the massive antique mahogany desk where Julia sat, her efficient fingers searching through a stack of papers she'd pulled from the bottom drawer. Finding nothing of apparent interest, she refiled the papers, closed the drawer, then opened another. On the far side of the paneled, book-filled study, a uniformed officer with a flat, masked expression peered into a brass urn that held an arrangement of dried eucalypti. Finding no murder weapon or other sinister object hidden inside, he moved to the huge, fieldstone fireplace, crouched and aimed the beam of a flashlight up the chimney.

"For crying out loud," Sloan muttered, and tightened his fingers on the couch's rolled arm. He looked away, fighting for control. It would do no one any good if he lost his temper.

A flash of movement in the marbled entry hall caught his attention. Through narrowed eyes he watched Julia's partner confer with a pair of uniformed officers. They nodded in unison at something the sergeant said, then turned and headed up the winding staircase. Sloan's mood darkened.

He detested this police-sponsored home invasion, resented his lack of control over the situation. He'd tried blocking the search after Halliday appeared at his office. It had taken a brief call to his humorless, dour-faced attorney for Sloan to learn that he was powerless against a properly executed search warrant. So, two hours ago, he'd arrived home to find several patrol cars in his driveway and an outraged Hattie barring the front door. A group of officers bristled with impatience while he tucked his indignant housekeeper into a cab and sent her home. That done, he settled onto the leather couch while the police searched every square inch of his house and grounds.

Rolling his knotted shoulders beneath his starched dress shirt, Sloan reminded himself that having some stranger rifle through his underwear drawer was just a minor annoyance. The police would find nothing, because there was nothing to find. Compared with other events he'd endured, this was small stuff.

Would be small stuff, if not for Julia, he amended, slicing his gaze back to her.

Both the desk and its tufted leather chair in which she sat had a dwarfing effect, as did the man's tie knotted at her throat and the white shirt tucked into her slim, black skirt. The whole effect seemed childlike, as if a little girl were playing "office" at the big mahogany desk.

Sloan tightened his jaw. In truth, he didn't give a damn about the rest of the people searching his house, but he minded like hell that Julia was a part of it. It was *her* presence that coiled his muscles. *Her* taste he remembered all too well on his tongue. *Her* he couldn't forget.

God knows he'd tried.

A thousand times he had attempted to blot out his physical and emotional need for her. His attempts had resulted in utter failure. So he'd continued to torment himself with thoughts of her over days, weeks, months. Years.

Sloan closed his eyes for an instant, then focused his gaze on her hand. The diamond ring glittered in the afternoon sunlight that slanted through the tall windows. Even now, when she so clearly belonged to someone else, he felt a powerful surge of need. To touch. To absorb. To just be with her.

It took a moment for Sloan to realize that all movement on Julia's part had ceased. She sat as still as stone, staring down into the desk's lap drawer, her thick lashes black as midnight against cheeks that had gone pale.

He leaned forward, the leather couch cushions shifting with his weight. "Something wrong—"

"Julia, we're done searching the house and grounds," Halliday said as he strode through the doorway. "All that's left is the gun collection."

Sloan rose, watching as her gaze slowly lifted to meet her partner's. "Fine." Emotion flashed in her eyes, but was swiftly controlled.

Halliday sliced Sloan a guarded look, then stepped to Julia's side. "You okay?"

"Yes."

He gestured at the open drawer. "Find something?"

"No." She shoved the drawer shut and stood. Eyes a cool blank, she turned to Sloan. "Please unlock the gun room, Mr. Remington."

Her cheeks were colorless, her eyes too dark. Tension betrayed itself in the hand she kept fisted against the gold badge and holstered automatic at her waist.

Sloan frowned. He had no idea what was in that drawer, hadn't looked inside the desk since his return three months ago. What the hell had Hattie put in there?

Shoulders squared, Julia led the way across the study; her heels snapped against the oak floor, then went silent when she stepped onto the thick Oriental rug. She reached a section of polished paneled wall, then paused and turned.

Halliday stopped beside her, looking blank. "The gun room's around here?" he asked.

She nodded. "In front of you."

Adjusting his glasses, he peered at the wall. "Fooled me." Shrugging, he slid a hand into his suit coat, pulled out a folded paper and looked at Sloan. "According to the inventory your secretary gave us, you own two .22 revolvers. A Smith & Wesson and a Colt.''

"So, someone shot Vanessa with a .22," Sloan said quietly.

Not waiting for verification, he stepped to the wall and pushed inward. A faint click sounded, then the panel swung outward to reveal a steel door. Out of the corner of his eye, he caught the impressed arch of Halliday's brows.

"Damn," the man said softly. "Any other hidden rooms around here?"

Sloan's eyes narrowed when Julia snapped on the tape recorder hooked to her waistband beside the badge. Color had seeped back into her cheeks; hardness had settled in her eyes.

"Sergeant Cruze knows this house," he said, his voice raised for the tape recorder's benefit. For some perverse reason that machine riled the hell out of him. "She can verify this is the only hidden room."

Julia shot him a dark look. "This is the only hidden room I *know* of."

Sloan slid a key out of his pocket, made quick work of the dead-bolt lock, then pulled the heavy door open. Movement activated a sensor. Lights winked on, revealing a small room where chrome and blue steel glinted behind glass-fronted cases.

Halliday peered in, remained silent for a moment before checking his list. "You also have three .22 automatics—a High Standard, a Colt and a Baretta."

Sloan stepped across the threshold onto the uncarpeted floor. Cool, still air settled around him. "The inventory's correct. I own five .22s. *Only* five. Do you want them all?"

"Yes," Julia said. "The lab will check them. We'll return them in a day or two if they're not booked into evidence."

"They won't be." Sloan met her gaze. "This is a waste of time, you know."

"This is a homicide investigation, Mr. Remington. We

go by hard evidence, not someone's opinion." She turned toward the shoulder-high series of drawers used to hold boxes of shells. "We need all your .22 ammunition."

"I don't own any ammo. I gave it all away two years ago."

She cocked her head. "Mind if we look?"

"You've checked every other drawer in the house," he said evenly. "Why should I care about some empty ones?"

He kept his eyes on Julia while Halliday slid each drawer open, then closed. How could he have forgotten the intriguing quality of the sharp angles and shadows of her face when determination set in?

"Empty," Halliday confirmed, his knees cracking as he stood.

"What a surprise," Sloan said mildly. He turned and opened a display case, took out the sleek blue-steel Smith & Wesson, then the Colt. "You should take my word for things."

Halliday eyed him with silent assessment as he accepted the revolvers. After checking the serial number against the inventory list, the detective slid the weapons into plastic bags he pulled from his suit pocket.

"Take your word for what, Mr. Remington?" Julia asked.

"Those drawers, for example. I told you they were empty, and they are."

He secured the door, then moved across the room to another glass-fronted case. The High Standard he retrieved felt cool and sturdy against his palm.

Julia stepped to his side. The room's close confines gathered in the warm scent of *Obsession*. He thought of long, endless nights of lovemaking when that scent had mixed with the heady fragrance of hot sex. Dammit, it had been two years—why the hell did she have to wear that same perfume?

"What else should we take your word for, Mr. Remington?'' she persisted, while her sharp cop's gaze took in the array of revolvers and automatics inside the case.

"That I haven't fired these guns recently. But you won't accept that as truth until the results of your tests prove it.''

"What else?'' she prodded.

"I didn't kill Vanessa.'' He handed Halliday the High Standard. The Colt and Baretta soon followed the first automatic into separate plastic bags.

Julia crossed her arms. "At this point, I find it hard to take your word about your relationship with Vanessa.''

"I told you the truth,'' Sloan said, securing the door on the weapons remaining in the case.

"Really?'' she asked, her voice edged with disbelief. "Every morning for the past three months, Vanessa stopped at *Here's to Your Health*. There, she bought one carrot juice and one orange juice, to go. She bought the orange juice for you, didn't she? She brought it to the gym where you worked out together.''

"It's an employee gym. We happened to use it at the same time of day, as did several other members of my staff. But you're not interested in them, are you, Sergeant? You're wanting to know if my assistant and I spent our mornings soaking naked in the Jacuzzi. We didn't.''

"What else didn't you do?''

"Have a personal relationship. If someone says otherwise, they're lying.''

"Someone is saying that.''

"Who?'' Sloan asked evenly.

"Vanessa. Her appointment book's filled with all the evenings the two of you had drinks, dinner…spent the night—''

"That's what she wrote?'' he asked taking a step forward. "That she and I did those things?''

Had he not possessed an intimate knowledge of Julia's every reaction, he'd have missed the quick hesitation in her eyes.

"The information Vanessa entered leads to that conclusion," she said.

A sardonic smile curved his mouth. "Spare me the police jargon, Jules. It's obvious something Vanessa wrote has you *jumping* to conclusions."

The statement earned him a frigid stare. Sloan knew that look, as well—a touch of defiance, a hint of temper, a dose of annoyance.

"What did you and Vanessa fight about?"

His gut tightened in involuntary response to the question, yet he kept his face expressionless, his voice smooth. "Did we fight?"

"At the museum fund-raiser. Several people overheard you."

"If that's the case, you already know what we said."

"You tell me. That way, I won't jump to conclusions."

"We didn't fight. I made a business decision Vanessa disliked. She chose to air her opinion at the museum."

"What decision?"

"Remington Aerospace has developed a new wing design. It's called the HELD—high efficiency, low drag. We use new materials and fabrication techniques that reduce drag by sixty percent with no loss in lifting ability."

"That'll reduce fuel consumption," Halliday commented. "Save the airlines millions."

"The military, too," Sloan confirmed. "After the Pentagon reviewed the plans and test results, they kicked in funding on the R and D side to guarantee their access to the design. I hold the patent and reserve the right to sell the wing to the general aviation market. I'm spinning off a new wing company, which will have two divisions, one for GA, one for the military. I've held off announcing who I want to head those divisions. Vanessa had made it known that she wanted one of those jobs. She brought the subject up again at the museum. When I told her she wasn't in the running, she told me what she thought."

"And that was?"

"She'd worked hard and she deserved the job. If I didn't name her, she'd make me sorry."

"How?"

"She didn't give specifics."

"Had she calmed down by the time you took her home?"

Sloan paused. "I looked for her before I left the museum. She'd already gone."

"Who did she leave with?"

"I assumed she called a cab."

"She didn't."

"I see."

Julia's eyes hardened. "If you know who she left with, you need to tell us."

"I don't know. All I can tell you is that Vanessa had too much champagne that night. I hoped she'd feel different about things the next morning."

"Doesn't appear she did," Julia stated. "On her stop at the health store, she bought only carrot juice. Nothing for you."

"Hardly a surprise," Sloan said. "Vanessa dropped a person instantly if he or she failed in any way to meet her needs or expectations. My decision not to give her one of those positions was irrevocable and she knew that."

"Yesterday, you said you preferred to have Vanessa working for you rather than a competitor," Julia stated. "Surely you knew your decision not to promote her might prompt just that."

Sloan nodded. "Lately, I'd gotten numerous complaints on her from the staff...even clients. Vanessa's presence in the company had become a liability. Had she not been killed, she'd have either resigned, or I'd have fired her."

"Why didn't you tell us the truth from the beginning?"

"Because what happened between Vanessa and me at the museum isn't connected to her death. I know that for sure because I didn't kill her."

Julia pursed her lips. "Vanessa had all sorts of data concerning the HELD wing in her briefcase. Page after page is stamped 'confidential.' If she leaked that information, she could have cost you millions.''

''Murder due to a potential loss of money,'' Sloan said, locking his gaze with hers. ''An interesting theory.''

''A solid motive,'' Julia shot back.

''True. But I've lost money in business before and haven't resorted to murder.'' He leaned in, lowered his voice. ''Do you really think I'd kill over a deal gone sour, Julia?''

''Vanessa was cunning,'' Julia said, her dark, intense eyes boring into his. ''Her leaving could have done considerable damage to you and your portfolio. Maybe she pushed you over the line.''

Sloan flicked his eyes to her left hand. ''Some women,'' he began softly, ''are worth breaking the rules for. Vanessa wasn't one of them.''

He saw the snap in Julia's expression before she turned to Halliday.

''I'm done...for now,'' she said in a flat voice, then walked out of the small room.

Halliday remained behind to hand Sloan a receipt for the weapons. ''We'll let you know if you can claim your property.''

''My lawyer,'' Sloan said, cramming the receipt into the pocket of his slacks. ''Let him know. And if you and Sergeant Cruze have more questions for me, go through him.''

Halliday eyed him with grim assessment. ''When someone refuses to talk to us, we usually find out later they had something to hide.''

''When you accuse someone repeatedly of murder, you should expect a reaction, Sergeant. You just heard mine.''

Halliday shrugged, gathered up the plastic evidence bags and walked out the door.

Sloan followed the detective into the study, his gaze settling on Julia as she grabbed her purse off the desk. She paused for a brief moment, her eyes riveted on the closed drawer.

"Ready?" Halliday asked.

"Yes." She turned and walked out the door.

Sloan closed his eyes and sucked in a ragged breath. Damn her and damn himself for allowing her maddening scent to toss him back to a time he'd vowed to wipe from his mind.

He muttered a vicious oath, pulled the door to the gun room closed with steel-rattling force, then stalked across the study.

How the hell was he supposed to endure her presence when he couldn't think of her in any other way except as *his?* How in God's name could he keep seeing her and not reach for her? How did he expect to control his emotions, when just the sound of her footsteps moving away was absolute torture?

He stood at the desk, his fingers digging into the back of the chair where she'd sat. He wasn't used to this inner struggle, this warring between emotion and logic. Two years ago, fate had run recklessly over his life, and he'd taken the only action he could. He'd done the right thing, harbored no regret over the course he'd chosen.

But knowing he'd done the right thing hadn't lessened his insidious, damnable need for her. That, he knew—had always known—would be with him always.

Sloan leaned over the desk, jerked open the lap drawer and stared at its contents.

"Hell," he said, then shoved the drawer closed on a groan.

Chapter 6

"You want to tell me what just went on in there?" Halliday asked as he placed the evidence bags holding the handguns in the trunk of his cruiser.

Julia stabbed on her sunglasses against the rays of the afternoon sun. "I interviewed a homicide suspect," she said, and willed her heart to stop its uneven thudding.

The massive oaks lining the cobblestone driveway stood motionless, untouched by any breeze. The temperature hovered at blast-furnace level. Why, then, did she feel frozen on the inside?

"Interviewed?" Halliday countered, closing the trunk lid with a decided thud. "Sounded more like a sparring match." He pulled off his suit coat and hooked it with a finger over one shoulder.

"I got the job done," she said, jerking the recorder off her waistband. "Sloan's on tape, admitting Vanessa threatened to ruin him and his company. He knew she had both the information and the ability to carry out her threats."

She jammed the recorder into her purse. "Call it an interview, an inquisition…whatever you want. I did my job."

"Yeah, you did," Halliday agreed quietly. "You all right?"

The question had her temper spiking. "Why wouldn't I be?"

"Because you could've sliced the air with all the unresolved feelings between you and Remington."

"I harbor an intense dislike of the man." She dragged a less-than-steady hand through her hair. "What's unresolved about that?"

"Not a thing, if it's the truth."

"Dammit, Halliday, I'm tired of you second-guessing me where Sloan Remington's concerned."

Halliday sighed, walked the length of his cruiser and pulled open the driver's door. He tossed his coat onto the seat, then turned to stand in the wedge between the car and open door.

"Want to tell me what you found in that desk?"

She met his gaze. "Nothing important."

"Really? So, some unimportant something turned you as pale as the corpses I saw this morning at the M.E.'s office."

"Drop it."

"If whatever it is in that drawer relates to the case—"

"If it did, I would have bagged it." She took an aggressive step forward. "Just because Sloan and I had a relationship doesn't change things. He's a suspect, so I treat him like any suspect. If he's guilty, I'll take him down. You don't have to worry about me getting all sentimental and screwing up this case."

"I'm not worried about that." Halliday lifted his arm, swiped the back of his hand across his damp forehead. "I'm worried about you."

His voice, like his eyes, was full of concern. Julia looked away, her temper diffusing. In the distance, pale-pink roses clambered up a brick fence, lacing the air with a faint, rich scent.

"Don't worry about me," she said at length. "I can handle it."

"Yeah, but what's it going to cost you?"

She opened her mouth, but no words came. It had cost her a great deal to sit at Sloan's desk and stare down at the thick file of medical reports and cancer-clinic brochures in that drawer. She hadn't had time to check the dates on the reports, but their sheer number suggested a lengthy time span. As she sat there, it had torn her apart to imagine that he'd suffered. Ripped her to shreds to think that perhaps he'd known he was ill when they were still together, yet he'd thought so little of her, of what they'd shared, that he hadn't told her.

Halliday glanced up at a blue jay shouting ownership of the oak in which it perched. "I got to thinking about all this on the way over here," he said, squinting against the sun. "Tried to put myself in your shoes. Damn, if Pam and I split up, then two years later I had to face her across an interview table, I'm not sure how I'd handle it. I don't know that I *could* handle it."

Julia's lips curved. "Careful, Halliday. You say stuff like that, people might get the idea you're a sensitive guy."

He gave her a sheepish grin. "Maybe the idea that I'm about to become a father is messing with my macho side."

"Maybe." She expelled a slow breath and leaned back against the car. Heat from the metal seeped through her cotton blouse. "You and Pam are married. She's carrying your child. Sloan and I didn't have those kind of ties." But they would have, she thought, if he had loved her. She'd wanted to share his life, have his babies.

Halliday shrugged. "Well, as of a few minutes ago, we don't deal directly with Remington anymore—at least not until we get more evidence against him. That ought to be a relief to you."

Her eyes narrowed behind the tinted lenses. "What are you talking about?"

"While he and I were in the gun room, he told me to

go through his lawyer if we have any more questions to ask him.''

"I'm surprised he waited this long," she said mildly.

"Yeah, well, it sure as hell makes him look like he's got something to hide.''

"Sloan's a suspect, Halliday, but don't make the mistake of viewing him as a typical one. His erecting a legal road-block isn't necessarily a sign of guilt. For him, it's the usual routine. He's used to having control. He can change a sit-uation to his advantage in about as long as it takes to flick a wrist.'' She paused, knowing deep inside her that Sloan's action was more than just an attempt at control. It was an indication that he no longer cared to deal with her.

She set her jaw, hating that it wasn't just anger curling inside her chest but hurt. This, after all, was how Sloan operated. Two years ago he'd opted to disappear from her life. Now he'd erected a barrier of lawyers to keep her away.

Her brows slid together. What she'd found in that desk drawer had questions humming in her mind. Questions to which she wanted answers. Answers he *owed* her. Maybe Sloan could block her professionally—for the time be-ing—but he wasn't going to do that on a personal level, not this time.

"Remington's cool, all right,'' Halliday observed, rest-ing an arm across the top of the car door. "He gives the impression he could freeze molten lava.''

"Steel is putty compared with him,'' she said, and looked away. Beneath Sloan's cool persona was a man whose very touch had, on uncountable occasions, sent fire coursing through her, head to toe. The memory settled a dangerous kind of heat in her belly.

"I bet,'' Halliday continued, staring at the massive stone house at the end of the curved drive, "the guy has a fleet of lawyers. And they all wear three-piece suits that cost about as much as a car.''

"Remington Aerospace has its own legal division,'' she

answered evenly. "We'll be drawing pensions before Sloan runs out of lawyers."

"He's cut us off, Julia, and he has the connections to do it. If we try to contact him now, it'll take him one, maybe two phone calls, and we'll have grief and woe of biblical proportions down on our heads."

She'd had grief and woe dumped on her before, thanks to Sloan. She'd survived.

"Speaking of grief and woe," she said, "you heard what I said to Sloan. Vanessa didn't take a cab home from the museum. That means she hitched a ride with one of the other guests."

Halliday nodded glumly. "One of those guests being the mayor. Having to question the guy who signs our paychecks—how much better can this get?"

"Let's hope we don't find out," Julia commented. "We'd better get with the lieutenant in the morning. Ryan will probably want Chief McMillan to handle the mayor."

Halliday tugged a patch of sweat-stained shirt from beneath the strap of his shoulder holster. "Damn this heat. Whatever we do next, let's make sure it's around air-conditioning."

Julia's eyes widened. "God, I forgot," she said.

"What?"

"We've got to go to Vanessa's apartment."

"Why?"

"Because of something her secretary said when I interviewed her right before I came here." Julia wrapped the ends of her hair into a twist, holding the heavy coil off her heated neck. "Eve Nelson made no secret of the fact that she detested Vanessa."

"Detesting Vanessa," Halliday said dryly. "There's a novel concept."

"According to Eve, her boss kept things ultrasecret, did most of her own typing on whatever projects she had going. Vanessa relegated Eve to a glorified receptionist, and Eve resented her for that."

"Add to that Vanessa's looks, her body, her effect on men."

"Probably didn't help," Julia agreed. "Eve admitted to snooping in Vanessa's briefcase a few times. More than once, she found unlabeled computer disks."

"She look at what was on them?"

"She tried. Each time, the computer asked for a password."

Halliday lifted a brow. "We had no problem accessing everything on Vanessa's home computer. In fact, while I was waiting for the paperwork on this search warrant, I went to the lab and picked up the printout of everything Kelly copied off the hard drive."

"What'd you find?"

"Her appointment calendar—which has almost identical listings to the one we got out of her briefcase. Financial stuff," Halliday continued. "Vanessa invested heavily in blue-chip stocks, municipal bonds—stuff like that. From the looks of it, she had a nest egg worth six figures." He shrugged. "We didn't get any files that related to her job."

"Okay, so she didn't load the information onto her hard drive. We need to find the disks Eve Nelson saw."

"Right." Halliday checked his watch. "I'll book Remington's guns into the property room, then meet you there."

"Fine." Although she focused her gaze on the house's handsome stone facade, Julia's thoughts centered on the man inside. It was as if, over the past twenty-four hours, her mind had reattached itself to him. In a dark, secret place inside her, she knew her preoccupation with Sloan was due to more than just his heading their short list of suspects.

She pulled a deep breath of sun-scorched air into her lungs. "There's something I need to do." She pushed away from the car and faced Halliday. "While you're at the station, go by Records. I ordered a run of gun registrations on all the Remington employees I interviewed yesterday. The printout ought to be ready by now."

Halliday cocked his head toward the trunk of his cruiser. "You don't think we've got the murder weapon, do you?"

She glanced at the trunk. Vanessa's threats to Sloan were solid motive for murder, yet she could not imagine him a victim of those threats. The man she knew would view them as a challenge to overcome, not the promise of ruination.

"No, we don't have the murder weapon," she answered. "Sloan isn't stupid. If he shot Vanessa, he used an untraceable gun."

"Yeah," Halliday agreed as he climbed into the car. "But we'd be crazy not to check."

"Crazy," Julia agreed. It didn't seem to matter that it was crazy to even consider marching back up the driveway. Crazy to face Sloan and ask the questions she didn't know to ask two years ago.

Halliday twisted the ignition key, sparking the engine to life as he looked up through the open window. "You leaving?"

"In a minute. First, I'm going to get in my car and wrestle off these tight panty hose."

She turned, walked to her cruiser and pulled open the door. When the taillights of Halliday's car disappeared around a curve, she slammed the door, turned and headed up the cobblestone drive. Heels clicking like gunshots, she crossed the deep-shaded porch where neat shrubs sprouted from twin planters on either side of the massive front door.

She didn't question the wisdom of her decision to face Sloan. Didn't let her mind go past this moment. All she knew was that he owed her answers.

Without bothering to knock, she twisted the polished knob and shoved through the door.

She found him where she'd left him, in the study. He stood with his back to her, staring out a floor-to-ceiling window through which broad shafts of afternoon sunlight slanted into the room.

Julia paused beneath the arched doorway, her heart pounding, her breath coming as hard as if she'd chased down a suspect. Now that she was inside with Sloan in her sights, she wasn't at all sure why she was here. Had no idea what force had brought her back. Was at a loss to explain her consuming need to find out if he knew he was ill when he'd broken their engagement.

What did it matter? At this point, what could it possibly matter?

It couldn't…yet she had to know.

Her throat so dry she couldn't swallow, she tore her gaze from his still profile and examined her surroundings. She'd been here less than an hour ago, yet it was as a cop, and she hadn't allowed herself to view the room as a place that held meaning for her. Now she took it in, saw the vibrant colors of the massive Oriental rug, the familiar leather volumes on the built-in shelves, the polished brasses and pewters. The study had always been her favorite room in the house. Quiet and comfortable, it was a place where she and Sloan had curled up with books on the leather couch, spent winter evenings making love while greedy amber and gold flames leaped in the fireplace.

Julia's hand rose, pressing on her stomach where an answering, bittersweet tug of longing settled. God, had she really thought the passage of time could dull the memories?

As if suddenly sensing her presence, Sloan turned, his dark gaze meeting hers. If he was surprised to find her standing in his doorway, he hid it.

"What now, Sergeant Cruze?" he asked smoothly. "Did you suddenly realize your sweeping search of my property failed to include a check of my fillings for murder weapons?"

She ignored the jab. "We need to talk."

"That's exactly what we aren't going to do. I told your partner to contact my lawyer with any further questions. The same goes for you."

"We'll be sure and do that."

She stepped into the room, feeling his cool scrutiny as she walked to the couch and dropped her purse on the leather cushion. With hands that weren't quite steady, she tugged the gold badge and holstered automatic off her waistband and laid them beside the purse.

She turned and faced him. "I'm not here as a cop."

He crossed his arms over his chest. "As what, then?"

"Just...someone who wants to ask a question."

His mouth took on a sardonic curve. "That's all you've done the past two days. Shall I wait to answer until you turn on your recorder?"

"Dammit, Sloan, I told you, I'm not here as a cop." She moved to the desk, her hand gripping the back of the leather chair. "This is personal, between you and me."

"So you're off duty?"

"Yes."

"I was about to pour myself a Scotch. Would you like one?"

She blinked. "I thought you quit drinking."

"I thought I did, too." He went to the carved liquor cabinet and poured Scotch from a decanter into crystal tumblers.

"Well," he said, walking across the room to where she stood. "Ask your question." He handed her a tumbler, knocked back the contents of his own and sat it on the edge of the desk.

She raised her glass, sipped. The Scotch went down like liquid gold, yet did nothing to loosen the knot in her throat.

"Were you sick when you broke our engagement?"

He said nothing for a moment, his eyes on hers. "It upset me to do it, if that's what you mean."

"It's not, and you know it."

"Do I?"

Very deliberately she placed her glass on the desk, pulled open the top drawer and removed the thick file. "This is full of medical reports. On you." She laid the file aside, then reached into the drawer and pulled out a handful of brochures. "These all deal with cancer. All addressed to you."

His eyes stayed on hers. "True."

"I saw your scar. You had more than just exploratory surgery, didn't you?"

He cocked his head. "Did you become a doctor while I was away?"

"Don't try to get around this, Sloan. If you were sick, I had a right to know."

"I had a right not to tell you."

"So, you had cancer then? When you broke our engagement, you knew?"

"Yes."

"And because you didn't..." Her voice trailed off and she shifted her gaze to the dark fireplace.

"Didn't what?"

She forced her gaze back to his. "Because you suddenly discovered you didn't love me, you decided I had no need to know."

His chin rose imperceptibly. "Under the circumstances, a clean break was best."

"A clean break," she repeated coolly. "Maybe it was a clean break for you, Sloan, but I had no closure. You showed up, told me everything we'd shared had been a lie, then you walked out." Her hands clenched at her sides. "How do you think I felt the next morning when I went looking for you, and Rick told me you'd left town? I'd never begged in my life, but I did then. You'll be glad to know your security chief used the utmost politeness when he told me that where you'd gone was none of my business."

Sloan slid a hand into the pocket of his slacks. "If you'd known where to find me, what would you have done?"

"For starters, told you what a bastard you are."

"Now you've told me. Is that closure enough for you?"

His cool, impersonal expression stirred her temper.

Damn him, she hated that wall he so effortlessly maintained around himself.

"No, it's not enough." Turning, she began moving around the room, arms wrapped at her waist as if a chill had settled in. "Why didn't you tell me you were sick? I don't understand why you couldn't have at least told me."

"I was leaving. There was no point."

She shook her head. "No point." Her heels sounded, hollow echoes against the polished oak floor as she paced alongside the wall of bookcases. Antique decoys nested on the shelves; the leather volumes that filled the air with their aged scent shared space with gleaming silver candlesticks.

"No point," she repeated.

"Just as there's no point to our rehashing the past. We've both moved on, have...other interests."

His very remote, very polite tone had her gritting her teeth. He sounded as if she'd dropped by to discuss the weather.

She paused before a shelf crowded with a homey collection of family photographs in odd-shaped frames. Sloan's parents smiled out at her as they lounged on the deck of a yacht, a glinting blue sea in the background. She had never met them—both had died years ago. Another frame held a picture of a teenage Sloan and his sister on a beach, tossing a stick to a retriever that appeared as drenched as they.

Julia frowned as pieces of a puzzle shifted in her logical cop's brain. A vague image formed, then immediately drifted away like gray smoke.

She turned. Sloan had remained beside the desk, half a room away. "You talked to me only once about your parents' deaths," she said quietly. "You said your father died of lung cancer."

"What is the point of this?"

It was not lost on her that Sloan's voice had taken on an icy edge. She lifted the frame that held his parents' photograph. "And you lost your mother a few months later.

You said she died from a combination of grief and the sacrificing of her own health while caring for your father.''

"Julia, this isn't something I want to discuss.''

She stared at him, her stomach tightening as the piece of the puzzle she'd been so long without slid neatly into place. Even after Sloan left, a deep, secret corner in her heart had never fully accepted that he had not loved her. How could he have whispered soft words across a span of uncountable nights while their bodies throbbed with passion and feel no love? How could he share such *intimacies* with her and remain emotionally untouched?

Standing motionless with the frame gripped in her hand, Julia let the questions roll over her. Questions that she'd grieved over for endless hours, days. Months. Agonizing questions that had brought no answers...until now.

"My God...'' The tautness in her stomach turned into a fist, a hot, clenching fist that drained the blood from her face. "You had cancer. Did you think if you stayed with me that the same thing would happen to me as happened to your mother?''

"I told you the reason—''

"You didn't love me. That's what you said, then you disappeared, making sure I wouldn't know you were sick. Making sure I couldn't be with you. Couldn't take care of you...the way your mother took care of your father—''

"Let it go, Julia.''

"Let it go?'' she asked, her voice trembling. "You thought I'd be like your mother. You thought I might die if you stayed with me.'' She replaced the frame on the shelf, her hand shaking so badly that metal rattled against wood.

Turning, she stared into the impassive face that told her nothing. "Do you know how ridiculous that sounds?''

He lifted a dark brow. "Ridiculous?''

"*Ridiculous,*'' she shot back, feeling grim satisfaction at his reaction, however slight. "When we met, I was a patrol officer, riding a black and white in a district called the 'War

Zone.' I ran the risk of getting pounded, pummeled or shot every day.''

"You don't think I thought of that?"

"I don't know what the hell you thought then. Or what you're thinking now."

"And it doesn't matter," he countered. "Don't try to second-guess my decision. It was the right one."

"Right for whom?"

"Both of us."

"You decided to tear my life apart, yet you gave me no say in the matter? How was that right for me?"

"So right that I'd do it again."

The hard set of his jaw, the cool control in his eyes sent anger and resentment bubbling to the surface. "You just turned off your feelings." She walked toward him, stiff with anger. "And where I was concerned, opted for total amputation."

He sliced her a look. "It was the only fair thing to do."

"Fair?"

"Yes, fair."

She could almost feel him tense as she advanced on him, stopping when only inches separated their bodies. "It's all a matter of control for you, isn't it, Sloan?" Her arm rose, her hand settling against his chest, his heart. She felt its steady beat beneath her palm, the heat of the man. Her fingers splayed, moved. "You tell yourself not to feel, so you don't."

His hand shot out, gripping her wrist. The gesture, she knew, was not meant to pull her closer, but to maintain distance.

"What's done is done," he said, his voice toneless. "Let it go."

Every nerve inside her quivered with fury. She'd be damned before she let it go. The need to break through that aloof, reserved wall was overwhelming, more powerful than the anger boiling inside her, or even her common sense.

She stared up into dark, unfathomable eyes, her kneading fingers feeling the power in the sinewy, muscled contours of his chest. The action seemed to have too much influence on her own pulse, but she'd gone too far to back off. "Was my touch that easy to forget?"

His silence spurred her on, had her turning her body into his until no space separated them. "Did everything we shared mean nothing?" she hissed, her breasts grazing his chest. "Did my kiss mean nothing?"

His fingers tightened on her wrist. "This is a bad idea," he said, his eyes narrow, whiskey-colored slits. "Very bad."

"Did your damnable control ever slip during the past two years? Did you even for one minute hurt the way I did?" she persisted, her voice trembling. "Did you ever once feel broken inside?" She rose on tiptoes, her weight against him now, her mouth inches from his. "Did you spend just *one* sleepless night thinking you'd die from the knowledge we'd never be together again? Never make love?"

"Julia...don't."

His hand had come up to rest on her hip; beneath the fabric of her skirt his fingers felt like steel rods. Whether the gesture went deeper than just an attempt to steady her, she didn't know. Didn't care.

She lifted her chin, brushed her lips against his. "You loved me then, didn't you?" she asked, hating that her voice was nothing more than a shaky whisper. "But said you didn't, on the off chance I might die, along with you. I *wanted* to die when you left, Sloan. *Did die,* a hundred times."

He stared down at her, his silence slicing at her heart. Her body trembled with the agonizing knowledge that she no longer had the power to break through the emotional barrier around him. Could no longer elicit more than the smallest reaction.

What the hell had she expected? What the hell had she

been *thinking?* God, that was just it—she hadn't thought. She'd reacted to a mixture of hurt and anger. And now, with her body plastered against the one that had fit so perfectly with hers in another lifetime, she was so filled with shame she couldn't even look him in the eye.

Weak-kneed and furious, she started to step back but went nowhere when his hand tightened on her hip.

"Damn you, Julia," he said, his voice low and rough. His arms were suddenly around her, locking her body against his. Fingers shoved through her hair, gripping, arching her head back. "Damn both of us."

The immediate and familiar rightness of being held in Sloan's arms passed like a shock through her whole body. He lowered his mouth to hers, and she did nothing to stop him.

His kiss was as hard and demanding as the body pressed against hers. Air seared in her lungs. A small voice of reason had her lifting a hand to push against his shoulder. She might as well have tried to move a brick wall.

His kiss deepened. Her mouth opened to his, and all reason slid into aching need. Something between a whimper and a sigh rose in her throat. Her hand fisted against his shoulder, remained motionless, and she found it was herself she now fought.

She smelled the familiar mix of musky cologne and the man underneath, tasted the trace of smooth Scotch on his demanding lips. Each separate scent and taste merged, instilling a longing in her that had been with her forever, pulling her back to a time when she was completely his.

Her mouth moved eagerly on his, while searing need churned the blood in her veins. She couldn't breathe. Couldn't think. She was on fire, burning from the inside out, but she didn't want to put out the flames. Wanted them only to consume her, along with his kiss, his touch.

Her heart drummed heavily in her ears. The pulse between her legs quickened; she felt herself go wet. She was wrapped around him now, one arm circling his back, one hand against his chest, her fingers curled into his shirt.

His hand slid down her shoulder, downward to mold her breast beneath his palm. Fingers moved, caressed; his hungry touch transformed the nipple that strained against lace into a hard, tight peak.

A moan ripped up her throat. She wavered slightly as her legs turned to jelly.

The tempo of his kiss changed, intensified. Need hammered inside her. She felt his hard arousal against her thigh, felt his own need pulsing.

She gave herself up to the taste, the feel of him. She wanted only to sink onto the Oriental rug, pulling him with her, pulling his strong, hard body over hers, into hers.

Had she ever stopped wanting him? For so long she hadn't allowed herself to think about him, yet the sense of instant connection that had streaked through her body the first time he'd touched her was back, firing her blood. She'd been helpless to fight it then. Couldn't fight it now.

But she had to.

The man who was this instant kissing her as though he didn't give a damn about anything in the world but her had lied, torn her apart and walked away. She'd survived his leaving, made a new life for herself. A life that didn't include him—could never include him.

Battling for control, she stiffened her spine and pulled her mouth from his. "Sloan, stop."

When she turned her head, he merely tugged her face around and kissed her again, his tongue delving into her mouth.

Her hesitation lasted only a brief second before she put her palms against his chest and shoved away, gulping in shallow, ragged breaths. "This...I...can't do this."

"You were doing fine, believe me."

She stared up at him, one of her hands gripping the desk to steady herself, her dark hair falling down around her face, covering her shoulders. She struggled to find her voice. "I...shouldn't have..."

"No, you shouldn't have, but you did," he shot back. "Dammit, we both did."

She had never seen his control snap. Never before heard the hard mix of fury and frustration in his voice, never seen his temper flash, then wash across his face. When he stepped toward her, his eyes dark and reckless, her breath backed up in her lungs.

He captured her chin with a strong hand, forcing her gaze to his. "Would you like to know just how afraid I was for you?" he asked, his voice low and thick.

"Doesn't matter," she said, willing her legs to stop trembling so she could make it to the door without falling on her face. She wanted to be anywhere else but here, with this man who'd reduced her to a pool of quivering mush.

Pulling from his touch, she took a tentative step back. "Like you said, it's in the past. I shouldn't have come back here. Shouldn't have asked—"

"I was terrified when my parents died within months of each other," he said, as if she hadn't spoken. "And when the doctor told me I was in Stage III of Hodgkins disease and had a slim chance of survival, I was sick with fear. Cold-blooded fear. Not so much that I would die, but that I'd take you with me, just like my father took my mother."

"God..." Julia dragged in a breath. "You couldn't have known that would happen."

"I'll tell you what I *did* know," he said, his eyes flashing. "When my father got sick, my mother's world shrank to the size of his hospital room. Month after month went by, and she wouldn't leave him. He had private nurses around the clock, but she wouldn't leave him. Wouldn't let my sister or me take her to dinner, didn't sleep more than a few hours at a time. All she did was sit by his bed and hold his hand. In the end, the drugs they gave him couldn't touch his pain. Watching him suffer tore her apart, broke her into pieces...." His voice trailed off and he closed his eyes for a moment.

Heart clenching, Julia raised a hand to reach for him, then let it drop to her side. "You never told me." Her voice was shaking as bad as her knees. "Why didn't you ever tell me these things?"

"I see no sense in discussing something that dredges up those kinds of memories." He shoved a hand through his dark hair as he turned and walked back to the window where he'd been when she came in. He stood in silence as he gazed out the glass, his grim profile a mix of sunlight and shadows.

"I know your mind, Julia," he said finally. "Your heart. You're so much like my mother. You'd have sat by my bed, day after day. You'd have insisted on taking a leave of absence from your job, maybe even given up the career you love. It was in my power to prevent those things, to stop the same thing from happening to you as my mother. So I did."

She pushed her tangled hair away from her face. "You're not God, Sloan. You had no way of knowing what would happen. You had no right to make decisions without considering my feelings."

He turned. "Do you want to know what I learned about feelings?" he asked quietly. "I discovered you never know how much you love someone until that person becomes a matter of life and death to you. I couldn't do anything about the fact I might die, but I damn well wasn't going to take you with me."

Her lips trembled before she pressed them together. "And you think all these *'what-ifs'* justify your lie?"

"I don't feel the need to justify anything. I'm sorry I hurt you, Julia, but the truth might have hurt you a lot more. I took the only option open."

"No," she said through her teeth. "You could have stayed."

"And allowed a damn illness to shackle you to me? Let

it turn you into a young widow after you'd maybe sacrificed your career, your health? I don't think so. You deserved a future without some black hole at the end of it. I no longer had that to offer.''

"So you offered nothing. You just turned off your feelings and decided you could control everyone else's.''

"You found someone else who can offer you what I can't.''

"Which is what you wanted.''

"Yes.''

She shook her head, seeing with agonizing sharpness the chillingly thorough steps he'd taken to sever their lives. "How satisfied you must feel, knowing you controlled even that.''

His hands clenched, then unclenched. "If you have one shortcoming, Julia, it's that you view everything in black and white, right or wrong, innocence or guilt, stay or leave. There are no gray areas as far as you're concerned. But they exist. Believe me, I know.''

"You *knew* you were going to die. You didn't.''

"I was told to put my things in order. That's what I did.'' He walked back to the bar, sloshed Scotch into a tumbler. "I survived this bout. So did my father the first time cancer hit him. It came back a few years later and took him.''

"And you think you're due the same fate?''

His eyes cooled and he shrugged. She could almost see the emotional shields coming up around him again. "I have no idea.''

She nodded. "That's right, Sloan, you have no idea,'' she said, her voice low and bitter. "No idea what it is to love someone. You can't love someone and just banish them from your life, not for any reason.''

His gaze held hers for a long moment. "You're wrong about that, Jules. Very wrong,'' he added softly.

"If I'm so wrong, why didn't you come back after you'd recovered?'' She trembled inwardly. "If you'd loved me, you'd have come back.''

"I was sick for months," he answered, his voice as soft as smoke. "Weak as a kitten. After the chemo, it took a long time to get my body back in shape." He sipped his Scotch. "I've kept up with you, Jules. You've moved on, both in your career and your personal life. You didn't need me dragging you down."

Julia stared at him, a mix of anger and hurt clawing at her heart.

In the silence that followed, he lifted his chin, his gaze flicking across the room. "I think there's been sufficient closure for both of us today. When I complete the launch of the wing company, this house goes on the market. I'm relocating to D.C.—"

"Not if you're in a cell," she shot back, then inwardly trembled with the possibility that her statement might come true.

"I won't be." His mouth curved. "It has always intrigued me how you slide so effortlessly into your cop persona."

"That's who I am."

"Yes, I know." He emptied the contents of his glass, refilled it and leaned a shoulder negligently against the bar. "So, Jules, you'll marry your D.A., maybe become OCPD's first female police chief."

"You're right on both counts," she said. Clinging to the slippery edge of control, she went to the couch, grabbed her weapon and badge, then shoved them into her purse.

"What about you, Sloan?" The question lashed out like a whip. "Do you plan to sit around D.C., waiting to die?"

"Does it matter to you what I do?"

"Not a damn bit," she said, and surprised herself when she didn't stumble on her way to the door.

Chapter 7

By the time she'd navigated through rush-hour traffic and pulled her cruiser into the lot of Vanessa West's apartment building, Julia's head had stopped buzzing. Her breathing had evened. Black dots no longer whirled before her eyes as they had when she'd gunned the engine, leaving skid marks down the length of Sloan's cobblestone driveway.

Now all she saw was red.

Damn him. Damn Sloan Remington for what he'd done. And damn her for letting it get to her after all this time.

She should have shot him. Just pulled out her 9 mm Smith and blasted him square between the eyes. If she hadn't despised him before, she did now.

He had torn her apart, put her through two years of gut-wrenching hell...all because of some moronic, arrogant attempt to protect her. *Protect her!*

"Idiotic bastard!"

She jerked off her sunglasses and slung them onto the car's dashboard. Rage, fierce and hot, had her entire body trembling.

How could Sloan have done it? How could he have *loved* her, and just walked away? How could he have known he was ill—terribly ill—and banish the one person who would have done everything...*anything* to comfort, to help?

Julia's fingers tightened on the steering wheel. It didn't matter how he could do those things. What mattered was he'd done them...and with such blood-chilling deliberation.

Knowing what she did now didn't change a thing, not a damn thing. She felt the same way about Sloan as she had for the past two years. No, that was wrong. She *loathed* him now. Loathed everything about him—his icy self-confidence, his simmering aloofness, his...touch.

Groaning, she leaned her forehead against the steering wheel.

What had just happened between them was nothing more than pure and simple lust. Chemistry. Animal attraction. A volatile situation that, granted, she'd started, but Sloan had done his part to stoke the flames. Her heedless, mindless surrender to him meant nothing. *Nothing.*

Something stirred inside her, something she didn't dare name, something that had her body buzzing like a hormonal teenager's. Her heart kicked against her ribs. Her bruised lips tingled, as if Sloan's hot, demanding mouth had again taken possession of hers.

"No!" she said through gritted teeth as her stomach twisted into a knot.

She would not let herself want him. Not again, never. He hadn't just sent her world tilting when he walked out. He'd sent it crashing down around her. She'd learned a hard and bitter lesson, and she knew how to deal with this.

She'd bury herself in work—Lord knows she had enough of it. She'd find who murdered Vanessa West. If it was Sloan, fine. If it was somebody else, fine, too. She didn't care. She just wanted the damn case closed. In what spare time she had, she'd hit the streets and work on her other unsolved case. She'd get things back to normal, think about Bill instead of—

"Oh, my God," she muttered as guilt seeped through her anger. She had a fiancé, yet less than an hour ago she'd had her body willingly wrapped around another man's. So willingly that *she'd* come perilously close to pulling Sloan down onto his Oriental rug and having her way.

But she hadn't, she instantly countered. She'd stopped the madness, hadn't *allowed* things to go further.

Forcing her hands to unclench, Julia leaned and retrieved her sunglasses off the dash, then slid them on with slow deliberation. She was in control. She knew what she wanted. And that something wasn't to sleep with Sloan Remington, but to hammer him into dust.

Or at least lock him in a cell and let him rot.

Setting her jaw, she fought to pull her emotions under control. Halliday was already inside the building. She'd seen his cruiser when she pulled into the lot. She had to get out of her car, find her partner and search a dead woman's apartment for computer disks. She could not let what Sloan had done affect her, damn sure couldn't let it interfere with her job.

Pulling in a deep breath, Julia stared out the windshield, forcing herself to take in her surroundings. Well-maintained patches of lawn bordered the high-rise structure where planters spilled ivy and vibrant blooms over each apartment's scrolling ironwork balcony. Stone benches on either side of the gleaming glass entry doors baked in the afternoon sun. Julia closed her eyes. The quiet refinement of the place Vanessa West had called home did nothing to calm the storm raging inside her.

She hooked her holster and badge onto her waistband, then opened the car door and stepped into the skin-soaking heat. Eyes narrowed, she stared up at the looming building, wondering if she'd find evidence in Vanessa's apartment that would put Sloan in a cell.

She caught up with Halliday in the building's airy, brightly lit lobby.

"Traffic was hell," Julia said, thinking too late she should have checked her cruiser's rearview mirror to see if Sloan's mind-numbing kiss had left her lipstick smeared.

"No problem," Halliday said, his unconcerned look erasing that possibility. "I used the time to have another chat with the landlord." He punched the button for the elevator, then swept an arm in the direction of the lobby. "Get a load of this place."

Julia glanced at the comfortable-looking armchairs positioned against a wall streaked in beige and coral tones. A carved cherry armoire stood against another. Positioned in the center of a polished end table was a gilded urn overflowing with sprays of gladioli, snapdragons and baby's breath. The flowers' heavy scent reminded her of the cloying smell of a too-small florist's shop.

"Learn anything new from the landlord?" she asked as the elevator's doors slid open. She dropped her sunglasses into her purse, then stepped into the elevator, Halliday behind her.

"He reminded me that Vanessa was a lovely young woman," Halliday said, and jabbed a button on the control panel. "Very discreet." The doors closed; the elevator shot up soundlessly.

Julia arched a brow. "Discreet?"

"Yeah."

"How so?"

"If she ever brought a man home, the landlord never saw him." Halliday shrugged. "That doesn't mean much, considering the guy's in his seventies. If he's not in bed by eight, I bet he's catching z's in his recliner. Our Miss West could have hosted an orgy in the lobby and it's probable he'd have slept through it."

Dinner with S. Julia again pictured Vanessa's entries in the black leather appointment book. *Drinks with S. Spend night with S.*

The thought of all the nights Vanessa had spent with *S* put an unwelcome tightness in Julia's stomach. In the silent moment that followed, she realized how desperately she wanted *S* to be someone other than Sloan.

"Okay," she said, the thought drawing her brows together as she stared up at the floor numbers blipping on the elevator's panel. "Maybe Vanessa never brought a date here. She could have gone to the guy's place. That way, she'd avoid the hassle of having to nudge him out the door the next morning."

"You could be right," Halliday agreed.

Julia slicked her tongue across her tender lips. Having experienced innumerable nights of hot, searing sex with Sloan Remington, she doubted there was a woman alive who would toss him out the door the following morning.

But then, Vanessa West was no longer alive.

The elevator came to a smooth stop, the doors sliding open with a hushed sigh. Julia stepped into a white-carpeted corridor, as softly lit and silent as a new snowfall.

"Down there," Halliday said, gesturing toward a door at the far end of the hall.

As they walked, she rummaged in her purse for her latex gloves. "What did the lab print yesterday?"

"Phone, answering machine, toilet handles, doorknobs, TV remote," Halliday said as he pulled a pair of gloves out of his suit coat and began nudging them on. "The usual places you'd find a visitor's prints. The computer, too, before we turned it on."

"Have you heard back from the lab?"

"They got plenty of smudged partials. Anything identifiable belonged to Vanessa. Also, the hairs we found in the shower and the bed are hers. If she had recent visitors, there isn't any evidence to prove it."

At the door, Halliday slid the key into the lock, snapped open the dead bolt and swung the door open.

They stepped into elegance.

Julia stood motionless, her gaze performing a slow study of the high-ceilinged living room and spacious dining area beyond. Vanessa's taste ran to antique woods and classic fabrics, ultraconservative, cool colors. Having grown up working summers at her mother's interior decorating business, Julia instantly identified the muted-toned landscapes that hung on the pale living-room walls as original oils.

"Mother would love this place," she commented, thinking of Georgia Cruze's knack for combining furniture and fabrics that whispered of class and expense.

"Maybe she did the decorating."

"Not hardly. If Vanessa had chanced into Mother's shop, she'd have gotten chucked out the door the minute her employer's name came up. Mother carries a distinct grudge against anyone or anything connected with Remington Aerospace."

Pulling off his glasses, Halliday used the end of his paisley tie to polish the lenses. "Including its CEO, I bet."

"Especially Sloan."

Halliday nodded, then strolled across the room to a bar of crystal decanters tucked into an alcove. "I also had the lab fingerprint the liquor bottles. Only Vanessa's prints showed up."

Julia set her purse on a table beside a tufted couch done in soft beige. Everything was neat, tidy, organized. That was how the Remington staffers she interviewed the previous day had described Vanessa...in appearance and work habits. Her personality was the thing that had garnered harsh comments. *Mean minded. Into control. Bitch.*

"One thing that doesn't add up is this Scotch," Halliday said, holding up a bottle he'd pulled from a shelf beneath the bar. A fine dusting of black fingerprint powder covered the bottle and its label.

"Why?"

"The brand. You'd think someone with a six-figure income would buy decent booze."

"You'd think," Julia said against the stiffening of her spine. She pictured Sloan, his dark eyes cool and assessing as he leaned negligently against the bar in his study, a crystal tumbler of Scotch in hand.

"This brand's rotgut," Halliday announced, and twisted off the cap to take a sniff. "Je-sus! Stuff is strong enough to cause a nosebleed."

Julia walked across the room to join him, her heels sinking into carpet so thick it would muffle the sound of a jackhammer. Halliday handed her the bottle, adding, "Bet it goes down as rough as it smells."

She took a whiff and grimaced. The Scotch had a decidedly unrefined aroma—a definite contrast to the heady, liquid gold she'd sipped earlier.

"It's not Sloan's brand." Privately, she conceded the relief that settled inside her.

Halliday met her gaze. "Maybe it didn't used to be his brand. His tastes could have changed over the past two years."

But not the past hour, Julia thought. "Trust me on this, Halliday," she said, handing him the bottle. "It's not Sloan's brand."

She caught her partner's assessing look before she turned and headed toward a set of French doors hung with white lace panels. Glancing out, she took in the sunbathers sprawled on towels around a glistening swimming pool.

"You take this room, the kitchen and dining room," she said, turning back to face him. "I'll do the others. Look behind picture frames, under corners of the carpet, inside sofas—anywhere big enough to hide a computer disk."

"Got it." Halliday replaced the Scotch bottle, then reached and checked the label on another before closing the cabinet door.

Julia headed down the hallway, then stepped into an enormous bedroom where sunlight spilled through curtains of dotted Swiss voile. A massive four-poster covered with a white eiderdown quilt angled from one corner. One wall was done completely in mirrors, making the room seem enormous. On the wall opposite the bed, a marble-topped dresser displayed a framed photograph of Vanessa West. A collection of crystal perfume decanters sat beside the frame.

Julia scowled as she walked across the room. What the hell kind of woman kept her own picture on display?

A gorgeous one, she decided, taking in Vanessa's flawless porcelain skin, light-blue eyes and blond shining hair. From all reports, the woman had used her beauty and her body to get what and where she wanted. Chances were, that same blind-sided ambition was the thing that had gotten her killed.

Julia dropped her gaze and pulled open the dresser's top drawer. A heady fragrance rose invitingly from delicate pieces of silk and lace. Her fingers paused amid the meticulously folded lingerie as her mind again returned to the appointment book, its pages carrying the same soft scent. Vanessa's scent.

A vague, hazy realization drifted through Julia's thoughts, tightening her mouth. She turned her head and stared at the eiderdown-covered bed. She could not picture Sloan there, lying on quilted softness in Vanessa's arms. Could not visualize him pouring himself a Scotch at her bar, couldn't even envision him stepping off the elevator and walking along the silent, snow-white corridor.

Following on the heels of that realization came an intense punch of doubt over his guilt.

"Get a grip," she muttered, then pulled the drawer out to check for disks taped to its bottom, back and sides. Finding nothing, she shoved the drawer closed and checked the next one, while reminding herself that just because she couldn't *picture* Sloan here didn't mean he hadn't spent untold hours jumping Vanessa's bones in this very room. Didn't mean he hadn't swilled her cheap Scotch, or strode down the building's pristine white hallway.

Julia closed her eyes, her gloved fingertips resting on the dresser's cool marble top. In every homicide case she'd worked, she'd had no trouble visualizing even the shakiest of suspects committing the crime. Even if a person hadn't done it, she could at least *imagine* him or her as the perp. Not Sloan. She couldn't picture him pulling the trigger.

And why not? He was capable of cold, calculating emotional murder because that was what he'd done to her. Yet physical murder? No, she couldn't see it.

Lifting a hand, she rubbed at the furrows that had settled across her forehead. She could feel her body coming off the adrenaline-charged rush that had overtaken her when she'd left Sloan's. Now all she wanted to do was curl up in her *Arabian Nights* bed and think. Let the knowledge seep through her numbed senses that Sloan had loved her when he walked out.

She hesitated only a moment, then squared her shoulders. No, she wouldn't think about it. *Couldn't.* If she thought about what he'd done and why, she'd go crazy.

Just do your job, she commanded, then took a deep breath and slid open another drawer.

She'd made him remember what he'd spent two years trying to forget.

With the fiery July wind blasting against his face, Sloan set his jaw, punched his Porsche 911 convertible into high gear and let the tires eat up the interstate.

Several miles back, he'd given up hope that speed would banish Julia from his mind. Flashes of the taste of her, of the weight of her breast beneath his palm, of the tangled silk of her hair sliding between his fingers, churned in his head.

How many nights had he dreamed of holding her again, kissing her? How many hours had he spent picturing every detail of her face, every curve and dip of her luscious body, when all he could do was lie in bed, as sick as a dog from the chemo?

Too many to count.

Other times, he'd imagined her naked beneath him, shuddering and quivering while he slowly took her, possessed her, restaked his claim.

But none of his imaginings had brought on the ravenous need that had overtaken him barely an hour ago—need that still curled like a fist in his gut. Even now, he could *feel* her in his arms, her body a mix of toughness and softness, all perfume and silken hair, her skin almost incandescent in the shadowy light of his study.

God, she was beautiful. And for a few brief moments, she'd been his.

He felt again the maddening graze of her lips against his, the scorching current that ran through her kiss. It had been the aching need for that kiss that had had him discard reason for instinct. He'd wanted that kiss for the past two years. Wanted *her*.

So, he'd taken what he wanted. And made one hell of a big mistake.

"Dammit!"

He steered the Porsche off the next exit, then turned west, narrowing his eyes against the low rays of the afternoon sun. Taking advantage of the absence of traffic on the road that edged Lake Hefner's shoreline, Sloan stepped on the gas, sending the speedometer needle quivering where it had seldom been.

Why the hell had he let business bring him back to Oklahoma? Granted, it would have been less convenient to oversee the details of forming the wing company from a distance, but it was possible. Why hadn't he just stayed away?

Because he'd *needed* to be at the corporate office to make sure things ran smoothly, he answered silently. Because there had been no way in hell to predict Vanessa's murder. No way to know that deed would bring Julia back into his life, and with her the reminder of all he'd given up.

Julia, who made him want to make promises he couldn't keep. Julia, who wasn't just any woman. She was the only woman.

And now, because his maddening want of her had snapped his control like a thin rubber band, she knew the truth. Knew he'd loved her when he walked out, knew the real reason for his leaving. Fine, so she knew. Sloan's mouth tightened as he pictured the mix of fire and challenge…and hurt that had leaped into her eyes.

Maybe after all this time it was best. Maybe someday she would develop a grudging understanding of why he'd purposely destroyed her love for him.

Maybe she wouldn't hate him for the rest of her life.

"Doesn't matter," he muttered. He'd be in D.C., not here to see if her feelings changed. Sure as hell not here when she walked down the aisle with another man.

Scowling, Sloan fought the urge to just keep heading west and wind up wherever the road took him. He'd worry about the consequences later. Consequences, he thought with a grim set to his mouth, such as dropping the ball with millions of dollars of defense contracts at stake. And what repercussions did a murder suspect face if he left town without advising the police?

He knew if he took off this time, Julia would follow. And it sure as hell wouldn't be out of love. But she *would* follow.

An interesting prospect, Sloan mused, and increased the pressure on the gas pedal. Julia following him. Julia *finding* him. Just the two of them, off somewhere. Together. Julia lying in his arms while he spent slow, uncountable hours indulging in the familiar taste of her skin. Hours together while he discovered her all over again, fit together every piece that comprised the woman.

Need, as scorching as the wind blasting against his face, fisted inside him.

His hands tightened on the steering wheel. He couldn't act on that need. Couldn't ponder a future with Julia when none existed. Her tomorrows lay with another man, and even if he could change that, he wouldn't. At this point, his illness was in remission, but he had no guarantee how long that would last. In turn, he could offer her no guarantee. No future.

His shoulders stiffened as he stared unseeingly out the

windshield. She wasn't his—hadn't been for two years. Yet in this fleeting pause in time, he could feel her slipping through his fingers again.

All he wanted to do was grab hold.

"No future, dammit," he reminded himself fiercely.

With silent regret, Sloan eased the pressure on the gas pedal, steered the Porsche off the lake road and turned back toward town.

An hour after she'd begun, Julia had searched every inch of Vanessa's bedroom and adjoining closet. She'd checked under, in and behind every piece of furniture; had felt inside seemingly endless rows of purses, shoes and boots. Her fingers had prodded every pocket in the color-coordinated rows of dresses and power suits. All she'd come up with were three paper clips and seventy-five cents in change.

"Find anything?" Halliday asked from the doorway. He'd taken off his suit coat and rolled up his sleeves; the latex gloves gave his hands and wrists a chalky sheen. His starched shirt looked hopelessly wrinkled beneath the straps of his shoulder holster.

"Nothing," she said, closing the mirrored doors of the walk-in closet behind her. "How about you?"

"Not one computer disk in the frozen entrées. And all that's in the fridge are low-fat cream cheese, bagels and carrot juice. Which, according to the autopsy report, are the foods consistent with the contents of Vanessa's stomach."

Julia sent him a bland look. "I live to hear stuff like that."

"Another perk of the job," Halliday observed with a wry smile, then glanced back down the hallway. "No disks taped on top of the ceiling fan's blades. Nothing in the washing machine—only towels and a bath mat in the dryer. I've gone through both bathrooms and the guest bedroom. There's nothing out of the ordinary in the medicine cabinets. No Baggies full of disks taped inside the tanks of the johns. Not one loose corner anywhere in the carpet, nothing hidden between the mattress and box springs.''

''That's the only room left,'' Julia said, gesturing in the direction of a small sitting room off the bedroom.

The room reflected more of Vanessa's expensive taste, Julia saw as she stepped through the door. The floor was bleached oak, the area rug a tasteful floral petit point. A slate blue couch spanned one wall. Tucked into a corner was an antique writing desk on which a computer monitor and keyboard sat.

Halliday inclined his head toward the desk. ''That's the computer we copied the files off.''

''Then we don't need to check it,'' Julia said as she settled onto the chair behind the desk and began searching drawers. ''Nothing,'' she said after a few moments.

She rose, moved across the room to a bookcase that held recent bestsellers and neat piles of financial magazines. She slid out a book, checked the empty space behind it, held the book by its spine and leafed the pages, then replaced it on the shelf.

Halliday lifted a cushion off the couch, then poked a hand down to search its depths. ''What we know,'' he began, ''is that if there was a special man in Vanessa's life, there's no sign of him in this place.''

''Remember what Rick Fox said at the scene?'' As she spoke, Julia continued pulling books from the shelf, peering behind them, fanning pages. ''Vanessa didn't share. Not her space, not anything.''

''I bet she shared that body of hers when it suited her purposes.''

''Probably.'' Julia moved to the second shelf and pulled out a book. She continued the process until she'd searched to the end of the row.

Expelling a breath, she propped her hands on her hips and did a slow scan of the room. ''Vanessa was smart. Calculating. She had some kind of information that was so sensitive she kept it off her computer's hard drive and put it on disks with a security access code. What's on those disks?''

Halliday crouched and peered at the underside of the table next to the couch. "Secret information on the HELD wing," he suggested. "And on Remington himself. Remember, at the museum she threatened to ruin both his company and him."

Julia stared at the desk where the computer monitor sat, dark and silent. Again, she tried to imagine Sloan as a victim of Vanessa's threats. The image simply wouldn't come.

She curled her hands against her thighs. "Whatever was on those disks, Vanessa had a reason to keep them hidden. But where?"

"Someplace readily available," Halliday answered as he levered up from the table. "But not where someone else could get their hands on them." He glanced at his watch, then scowled. "We went through Vanessa's bank statements and credit-card receipts yesterday. There's nothing to show she has a safe-deposit box. And after this search, we can rule out a hidden safe in this place."

"Okay. We know where she *didn't* keep the disks. We need to figure out where she *kept* them."

"Maybe she came home after her fight with Remington, deleted the access codes and mailed the disks to his competitors."

Julia shook her head. "I don't think so. The feeling I get about Vanessa is that she thrived on confrontation. After all, she went into work the morning after she threatened to ruin Sloan. She probably planned to quit, and throw a reminder in his face that she had the information and ability to put his company, if not him, in a world of hurt."

"Vanessa's secretary saw the disks in her briefcase. Remington might have seen them there, too," Halliday said. "He also knew how her mind worked. Maybe he cornered her in the garage and tried to reason with her. When he saw he couldn't, he shot her, then got the disks from her briefcase."

"No," Julia said. "Vanessa locked the briefcase with combination latches—the techs had to pry them open when they got back to the lab. The only fingerprints on the locks were hers."

Halliday checked his watch for the second time. "So she didn't have the disks in her briefcase." Giving his head a disgusted shake, he plopped down on the couch. "Looks like we struck out."

Julia stared up at the ceiling. "They're somewhere. Vanessa put those damn disks somewhere."

"Yeah, but—"

"Holy hell!" Julia turned to face him, her mouth set in an annoyed line. "Halliday, if I'm right, we've had them all along."

"All right, Cruze, I'll bite." He leaned forward, forearms propped on his knees. "What are you talking about?"

"Vanessa had a sack of disks on the back seat of her Jag."

"I read the report. The sack's from the office supply store where she bought the disks. The receipt was in the bag—"

"I didn't check the date on it," Julia said. "What I *did* do was look inside the box. It's full of disks…with no labels." Julia shoved a hand through her hair. "That must be what Eve Nelson meant when she said she saw some unlabeled disks in the briefcase. I assumed they had no file names written on their labels."

Halliday nodded slowly. "She could have meant disks with no labels."

"Right. I've got Eve's number in my car. I'll call her and clarify." Julia scowled, disgusted that it had taken her this long to figure out. "Just because a disk isn't labeled doesn't mean there's no data on it."

Halliday pushed off the couch, his mouth set in an appreciative curve. "You've got to hand it to Vanessa. She hid the things in plain sight."

"And made us look like idiots," Julia said. "Let's go

check the disks out of the property room. If an 'access denied' message comes up when we check them, we'll call Kelly in to see if he can figure out the code.''

Halliday frowned. "Damn," he said softly.

"What?" Julia asked.

"Nothing."

"What?"

"I need to call Pam. Tonight's our last childbirth class. We can maybe reschedule."

"Your baby's due next week, Halliday. You think he's going to wait to make an appearance until you finish your class?" She tilted her head. "Go home. Now."

"We need to get the ball rolling on those disks."

"You think I can't do that?" Julia asked, then gave him a patient smile. "It's been a big day for you, Halliday. First you get all sensitive on me, and now you're taking your impending daddy duties seriously. Pretty impressive stuff."

He grinned. "You tell any of the guys about this, Cruze, and I'll make you attend the next autopsy."

"Nothing I can't handle," she shot back. "Let's get out of here."

"What about you?" he asked as he followed her into the bedroom.

"What about me?"

"You seeing Bill tonight?"

"I…yes. For dinner."

Julia kept her gaze diverted from Halliday's as they walked side-by-side down the length of the hallway. She needed to see Bill. *Wanted* to see him.

Squaring her shoulders, she began peeling off her latex gloves. She was not into self-deception. What happened earlier between her and Sloan was her fault, and she accepted full blame. For one logic-erasing moment, she had succumbed to the heat of him, the taste of him…the touch of a man she'd once loved beyond all reason.

As she walked, the heady sensation of Sloan's kiss swept over her, kicking up her heartbeat. *Closure*, Julia decided, swallowing around the tightness in her throat. Best to view what had happened between them as the closure Sloan had denied her. And despite the deep, dark churning inside her that had made her forget both the past and future and just go with the moment, it didn't change the fact that Sloan belonged to her past.

And that was exactly where she intended he stay.

Chapter 8

Four days after Vanessa West's murder, Julia stood in the morning sun outside Fairhaven Memorial Chapel, still uncertain who had ended the woman's life and why. She had a mangled bullet, but not the weapon that fired it. Computer disks, but so far no access code with which to read the information they held. A request pending for a warrant to get the list of guests who'd attended the museum fundraiser, but due to political rumblings, no list.

From behind the tinted lenses of her sunglasses, Julia checked for Halliday's cruiser among the cars entering the parking lot beside the resplendent marble chapel. Seconds later, she expelled a frustrated breath at her partner's lateness. She shifted her gaze to the front of the building where a hearse sat, looking as sleek and glossy black as a panther. Parked behind it was a florist's van with its back doors gaping. The driver, his arms overflowing with baskets of bloodred roses, dashed up the granite steps, then disappeared through the chapel's carved doors.

A group of somberly clad men and women, some whom

Julia recognized as Remington staffers she'd interviewed the day of the murder, stood on the sidewalk, talking quietly among themselves. All wore expressions befitting the grimness of the impending ceremony. Only one of them, Julia recalled, had said anything remotely kind about their murdered co-worker. That someone was Don Smithson, Remington's personnel director. The man who'd turned green after finding Vanessa's body now looked pale and ashen as he stood amid the group.

Raising a hand, Julia lifted her thick hair off the back of her neck. The sun beat down with blazing intensity; the pavement around her seemed to exhale heat. She considered waiting for Halliday in her cruiser's air-conditioned confines, but didn't have the energy to retrace her steps to the parking lot. The dull headache that woke her before dawn had, only moments ago, transformed into a full-fledged hammering. Cursing silently, she dug into her purse, then washed down two aspirin with the dregs of her convenience store coffee. She stared into the empty foam cup, trying to think past the thrumming pain and get a fix on when she'd last eaten a decent meal.

The remains of the candy bar she'd unearthed from the bottom of her purse around lunchtime yesterday didn't count. Neither did the endless cups of caffeine-laced coffee she'd consumed throughout the past two nights while poring over reports on her and Halliday's other unsolved case. And, although she'd met Bill for dinner both evenings before hitting the paperwork, the guilt roiling inside her from the kiss she and Sloan had shared made it impossible to do anything more than pick at her food.

A lump formed in her throat. Had she imagined the strained silence that seemed to have settled between her and Bill? Had the wariness she'd sensed in him been nothing but a by-product of her own raw nerves? She didn't know. All she knew was that every time she'd looked up, she found him watching her steadily. He was a perceptive man—did he see the inner turmoil she so carefully tried to hide? Did he suspect the truth—that her thoughts were maddeningly centered not on him, but Sloan?

The rational part of her, the part that was pure professional, struggled to figure out what was going on inside her. She shouldn't think about Sloan, not in any context other than the investigation. She shouldn't. But she did. For the past two days—from the moment he'd taken her in his arms and feasted on her mouth—she'd thought of him constantly. Only him.

"Damn," she said, her voice an unsteady whisper.

Although he stood only inches from her, Sloan wasn't sure if Julia had spoken...or merely expelled a soft moan.

He remained silent, studying the intriguing lines of her profile while she stared into the depths of a foam cup as if every answer she'd ever sought were inside. After a moment, she crushed the cup beneath her fingers and gazed out at the chapel's parking lot, looking defeated and miserable...and gorgeous.

He dragged in a slow breath. There wasn't a man alive who could have resisted the sight of her at this instant— the way the morning sunlight glistened against the sleek fall of dark hair, the way cool shadows lengthened the elegant curve of her throat, the way she looked unaccountably soft and fragile in her trim, black coatdress.

Her hand rose, swiped back an errant curl off a cheek that seemed too pale.

Sloan narrowed his gaze. Despite her sunglasses, he could see the smudged shadows and small lines of fatigue at the corners of her eyes.

Because he wanted to touch her, soothe her, he dipped his hands into the pockets of his slacks before stepping forward.

"'Morning, Julia," he said quietly.

She swung around, her thick, dark hair swirling with the movement. The impression of fragility vanished as she stared up at him, her mouth tight. Annoyance, he judged, from his having come so close without her hearing.

"Sloan," she said, then dropped the remnants of the cup into her purse.

He gave the crushed foam a glance before lifting his eyes back to hers. "Do you attend the funeral of all your murder victims?"

"I go where the job takes me."

His lips curved. "I was thinking that very thing about you the other day. Wondering, actually, if a murder suspect left town, would you follow him?"

Her shoulders stiffened. "If you leave, I'll send Halliday after you."

"I'll stay put then," he said easily.

She stared at him for a long moment. "Wise decision," she said, then looked back at the parking lot that had filled to near capacity.

Sloan followed her gaze. "Waiting for someone?"

"My partner."

"Speaking of Halliday, my lawyer said he called yesterday. I understand I can pick up my guns."

Again, she raised a hand, this time to rub at her right temple. "None of them is the murder weapon."

"I know." He cocked his head. "You knew that, too, before you raided my house."

"It wasn't a raid. And I doubt you'd have shot Vanessa with a gun registered to yourself."

"I didn't shoot her."

"Not with any of the guns you turned over. Are there others, Sloan?" she asked, turning to face him. "Do you own any unregistered .22s?"

"No. You look exhausted, Julia. Have you been up all night?"

"I'm working two unsolved homicides. They take time."

He took a step closer, breathed in the warm scent of *Obsession* that rose from her sun-heated skin. The fatigue in her eyes, the weary curve of her shoulders pulled at him.

"Has it once crossed your mind that I'm as interested as you in finding the person who killed Vanessa?"

"That's either you or one of your employees."

"An employee." Anger, deep and dark, stirred inside him over the fact she considered him capable of murder. He paused, using well-honed control to bank down on the emotion.

"I'm aware that one of my employees pulled the trigger," he continued in an even voice. "The rest of my staff knows it, too. Try to imagine five hundred people working in the same building, all eyeing one another with suspicion. Doesn't promote a serene environment." Again he paused, took in the small lines of weariness at the corners of her mouth. "Not knowing the killer's identity obviously doesn't do anything for your peace of mind, either."

Her expression sharpened. "You want to help ease my peace of mind, Sloan?"

"There's nothing I'd like better."

"Use your connections. Get a copy of the guest list from the museum fund-raiser you and Vanessa attended."

His brows rose. "You can't get it?"

"I will, eventually. Certain…people think our upper-crust citizens will take offense if the police ask if they gave a woman a ride hours before her murder."

"Imagine that," Sloan said mildly. "I'll see what I can do."

"Fine," she said, her lips giving a bitter twist of a smile. "You get the list, maybe I'll nominate you for a crime-stopper's award."

The hard edge to her voice touched someplace deep inside him. For reasons he hadn't wanted to examine, it had become very important that she not spend the rest of her life hating him.

He leaned in. "Julia, what happened between us the other day—"

"Was a mistake," she shot back.

"I agree."

He caught her elbow before she could turn away, then waited until those dark-as-midnight eyes came back to his. "A pleasurable mistake," he amended softly. He felt her stiffen and he tightened his fingers to keep her where she was until he'd had his say. "One I'll always remember. For the rest of my life, I'll remember everything about you. About us."

"Sloan, don't—"

"You were too young to be a widow, Jules. Too good a cop to sacrifice your career." His hand gentled its hold on her arm. "Too full of life to die. I hope someday you'll understand that I did what I believed was right."

She closed her eyes, and he could guess all too well the images playing through her mind. Of him telling her he'd lied when he said he loved her. Of the agonized tears she'd shed on his best friend's shoulder. Of the bitter betrayal she'd surely felt. Still felt.

His jaw set. He wanted so much more than just to pull her into his arms and taste that luscious mouth again. He wanted to tell her that without her, he was less than complete. Tell her he would never be fulfilled with her gone from his life. Tell her how much he had, and still did, cherish her.

Burned to tell her he loved her.

A vicious case of frustration had him balling his free hand into a fist. "Julia—"

A sharp blast on a horn brought his gaze up and had Julia turning toward the parking lot. Sloan saw the detective's cruiser parked against the curb, took in Halliday's sharp, assessing expression as he stood in the vee of the car's open door.

"Sloan, let go." Her voice trembled. "Just let go."

This time when she stiffened her arm, he let her pull away.

"One more thing, Jules."

She hesitated before lifting her eyes to his. "What?"

"Get some sleep," he said softly.

* * *

The minute she slid into the passenger seat beside Halliday, Julia's stomach muscles began to tremble.

"What the hell's going on with you and Remington?"

"Nothing," she said, thankful the weakness that had overtaken her entire body didn't sound in her voice. She leaned and aimed the vent so that cold air blasted her heated face.

"It looked like something," Halliday insisted. "It looked like…" He scowled. "Hell, I don't know."

Refusing to meet his gaze, she glanced across her shoulder into the back seat. "I just took two aspirin on an empty stomach. Where's the bakery bag?"

"Pam ate everything. Have you forgotten that your ex-fiancé is a murder suspect?"

"Not for a damn minute."

"Then why the hell don't you act like it?"

Julia winced. The question stung. Especially since there was some truth to it. "Save the lecture, Halliday," she shot back. "We come to these things to observe whoever shows up—"

"*Observe*, Cruze. Not stand around while a suspect clamps a hand on your elbow and—"

"If you hadn't been late, I wouldn't have been standing on the sidewalk when Sloan…"

She held up a hand that wasn't quite steady and took a firm grip on her composure. "I'm sorry. I've got a headache that could make an elephant scream. I spent most of last night poring over reports on our other case—"

"You should have called me. I'd have burned the midnight oil with you."

"Sure thing. Pam will go into labor any time, and you want to spend the night sitting around the station, reading reports with me. Get real, Halliday."

"Yeah," he muttered. His eyes widened behind his wire-rim glasses. "Look, I'm late because Kelly caught me right when I was leaving the station. He broke through the access code on Vanessa's disks.''

Julia's instincts came up like radar. ''It's about time,'' she said, shoving her hair across her shoulders. ''What's on them?''

''Personnel records,'' Halliday said, pulling a printout from the briefcase that sat on the seat between them.

''Personnel records?''

''Of every Remington employee in this city.'' He pulled two additional printouts from the briefcase's depths. ''Also every employee in Houston, and the ones in San Francisco.''

''Personnel records,'' Julia repeated as she began leafing through pages. ''From all three Remington offices where Vanessa worked.''

''Suppose she was into blackmail?'' Halliday asked.

''From what we know of her, I wouldn't doubt it. Once you've got someone's birth date and social security number, they're yours.'' Julia paused. ''Halliday, do you think it's just a coincidence that Don Smithson, the head of personnel, found Vanessa's body?''

He stretched his arm across the top of the seat. ''I don't believe much in coincidence.''

''Me, either.''

''You need to remember something, Julia.''

''What?''

''There's another person who has full access to the company's personnel records.''

She lifted her gaze from the printout. ''Sloan.''

''Yeah. For whatever reason, Remington could have given her access to the information.''

''That wouldn't have been smart.''

''Murder isn't smart. People do it anyway.''

Julia pulled off her sunglasses, rubbed at the persistent ache in her temple. ''I don't think Sloan killed her.''

''You don't think he killed her,'' Halliday repeated quietly. "Or you don't want your former fiancé to wind up behind bars?"

Her chin came up. "My past with Sloan has nothing to do with my beliefs about the case."

"Is that right?"

"Right."

"Okay, Julia, let's look at what we've got on Remington. He was in that parking garage the same time as Vanessa. He's an excellent shot—you said so yourself. The night before she died, she threatened to ruin him and his company. That gives Remington the opportunity, the means and the motive for murder."

"I agree. But my instincts tell me he's innocent."

"You can't know that."

"I do."

"Maybe you do," he said carefully. "A cop's instinct alone has solved more than one case. But you sure as hell can't *prove* Remington's innocent, and that's what matters."

She turned her head and stared out the passenger window. Sloan was still on the sidewalk where she'd left him, talking now to a man and woman clad in black. Could any other man brush accusations of murder off like dust and still look so in control, so completely confident? Julia wondered. Sloan's impeccable black silk suit and sedate tie lent a distinguished air, but the aura of strength came from the man himself. It showed in those dark, unfathomable eyes, in the firm line of his mouth, in the assured set of his broad shoulders. While she watched, a gust of wind whipped his dark hair into his eyes. Lifting a hand, Sloan smoothed his hair in an achingly familiar gesture that put a knot in her chest.

She closed her eyes. Emotionally, she was in trouble. Terrible trouble. Why else would she have asked him to get the museum's guest list? Doing so had been inappropriate for all sorts of reasons. But, dammit, the mayor had sent orders that blocked their obtaining a warrant to serve on the art museum. She *had* to do something to knock the investigation off high center. Had to find proof of Sloan's innocence.

The thought had her groaning inwardly. She was more than just in trouble. She was lost.

"Julia, you going to stare out that window all day?" Halliday asked.

"I can't prove Sloan's innocence," she said, looking back at her partner. "I also can't prove his guilt. Can you?"

Halliday expelled a slow breath. "You know I can't."

She lifted the printout. "Vanessa had personnel records. The director of personnel claims he discovered her dead in the garage. We found a personnel service pin at the crime scene. Vanessa was seeing someone she identified by the initial 'S.' I don't know about you, but I'm *itching* for the funeral to be over so we can talk to Mr. Smithson."

Halliday's mouth quirked up on one side as his gaze swept the parking lot. "Nothing like starting the day by screwing up some citizen's schedule. Have you seen Smithson?"

Julia nodded, her gaze following his out the windshield. "Earlier," she said, surveying the sidewalk. "He was in front of the chapel. I don't see him now."

"He must be inside."

"We'll get him just as soon as the service ends," she said, then shoved open the car door.

"My plane just got in," Rick Fox said as he approached Sloan on the sidewalk and offered his hand. "I wasn't sure I'd get here in time. Too bad the corporate jet is down for maintenance."

Sloan nodded. "Is the problem in San Francisco taken care of?"

"I think so. I've ordered more security cameras for our production facility and new badging procedures. If we don't nab our thief that way, I'll put a man undercover on the inside."

"Fine." Sloan turned his gaze back to the parking lot, his mind veering from business as the doors to the detective cruiser swung open. A long length of black-stockinged leg appeared, then Julia stepped into the sunlight. Halliday came around the car to join her. As they spoke, she hooked her badge onto the belt of her black dress. Turning in unison, they headed toward the chapel.

Rick's gaze tracked them. "I don't have to ask what your mind's on."

Sloan's mood darkened. "I think about her all the time."

"You might want to tell her that."

"It's too late."

"She's not married yet."

Sloan watched as Julia's light steps took her up the granite steps, then through the chapel's carved doors. "Whether she's married or not isn't the point."

"Right, your health is." Rick slanted him a look. "You look healthy to me, Sloan. The doc said so himself after your last checkup. Hell, you'll probably outlive us all."

The echo of an unwelcome memory settled around Sloan, stirring glimpses of nondescript exam rooms and grim-faced doctors detailing even grimmer odds for his survival. Too many doctors...too few odds. No, he shouldn't—*wouldn't*—question the decision he'd made two years ago. He'd walked away to keep Julia safe, to spare her grief. And he'd stayed away after he recovered because she'd gotten on with her life and sure as hell didn't need him dragging her down. Walking away—and staying away—had been the right thing.

Let go, he told himself. *Just let go.*

He looked at Rick. "Now that you're back, I've got a question for you."

"Ask away."

"Do you know how Vanessa got home from the art museum?"

Rick blinked. "To tell you the truth, I never thought

about it. I guess I figured she cooled off after she let you have it, then you gave her a ride home.''

"I didn't. I looked for her when I was ready to go, but she'd left. So had you, for that matter. I thought maybe you'd given her a lift."

Rick gave a short laugh and slid a hand into the pocket of his slacks. "C'mon, Sloan, you know I couldn't stand Vanessa."

"That doesn't mean you didn't drive her home."

"Guess not. Actually, I took off about half an hour after the two of you had your run-in. I looked for you to tell you I was leaving—found you, in fact. You were in the middle of a conversation with a good-looking brunette wearing red sequins."

Sloan thought back. "The museum director's wife." He frowned. He had no idea what time he'd talked to the woman.

"Whoever she was, I didn't want to interrupt." Rick raised a shoulder. "Vanessa probably called a cab."

"The police say she didn't."

"The police, meaning Julia?"

"Yes." Sloan rubbed at the knotted muscles in the back of his neck. "Julia."

Rick nodded. "Interesting, isn't it, how everything circles back to her?"

Julia's senses sharpened like a lens coming into focus when Halliday escorted Remington's personnel director into the plush carpeted, velvet-draped waiting room the chapel staff had made available.

Although he was pale and wary eyed, little resemblance remained to the trembling, green-complected man she'd interviewed in the parking garage four days ago. Now Don Smithson stood before her tall and erect, his carefully brushed iron-gray hair a striking frame for his strong, square jaw.

"Mr. Smithson, we need to ask you a few questions."

"I'm planning on attending the grave-side service." He gave a sharp look across his shoulder when Halliday closed the door behind them. "Can't your questions wait?"

"No," Julia answered. Although several comfortable-looking chairs dotted the room, she'd chosen to remain standing beside the small, cherry-wood writing desk. "But if you cooperate," she added, "you should make it to the cemetery in time."

"I told you all I know the day of the murder, Sergeant Cruze. I'd like to leave for the cemetery now."

"Fine, you can do that. Then, when the grave-side service is over, we'll all go downtown and chat in a grubby interview room. Your choice."

A muscle in his cheek jerked as his gaze shifted, taking in the room's soft colors, plush, upholstered chairs and bouquets of fresh flowers. "I'd be a fool to choose that setting over this. What is it you want?"

"The truth," she said simply. "Have a seat, Mr. Smithson."

She gestured to a padded, straight-backed chair a few feet from the desk. "I'm taping this conversation," she advised, then clicked on her recorder and placed it on the table beside the chair into which he'd settled.

He eyed the recorder steadily. "The truth about what?"

"Your relationship with Vanessa West."

His gaze lifted slowly. "We were co-workers."

Halliday propped a shoulder against a bookcase that held several books of inspiration surrounded by brass and silver accent pieces. "What about the other aspect of your relationship?"

"Other aspect?"

Halliday nodded. "Yeah. Like, what compelled you to give her a truckload of classified files?"

Julia held her breath as Smithson's spine went rigid against the chair's back. One well-molded hand clenched in a tight grip against his thigh. *Got you*, she thought. They'd only guessed the man had been Vanessa's source for confidential personnel files. By the way Smithson's already pale face had gone dead white, she saw they'd guessed right.

"Classified files?" he asked.

She took a step forward. "Mr. Smithson, you need to understand something. If you hold back information, if you lie to us, we will charge you."

His chin came up. "With what?"

"Interfering With Official Process. You'll wind up spending time in a cell with some not very nice people."

"Perhaps I should call my attorney."

"That's your right." Julia flicked a hand toward the desk, where a phone sat beside an azalea heavy with pink blooms. "When you get him on the line, tell him to meet us downtown."

Smithson shot a look at the closed door. "Some of my co-workers are still here. *Mr. Remington* may still be here. Do you know what it will do to my reputation if you march me out of here like a common criminal?"

"Nothing positive is my guess," Halliday stated dryly. "So why not talk to us here and avoid the embarrassment?"

Jaw tense, Smithson stared at the phone, his eyes hard marbles of blue under silver brows. "All right," he said after a moment. He looked back and gestured toward the recorder. "I'd like your assurances that what I say will be kept confidential."

"We can't make any promises," Julia said. "But if what you tell us in no way relates to the homicide, then there should be no reason for us to disclose it."

He raised a hand, then let it drop. "I imagine you know a lot about Vanessa by now. About the kind of woman she was."

Halliday pursed his mouth. "Remind us."

"She was beautiful. Tall, elegant and stunning." He paused to stare at a blank spot on the wall, while thoughtfully rubbing his index finger up and down the bridge of his nose.

"We're listening," Julia said quietly.

Smithson expelled a slow breath. "About a month after Vanessa transferred here, we began a joint project of evaluating Remington's risk management policies. We had a deadline that required our working evenings and weekends. At that time I...admired Vanessa, was flattered when she turned her attention toward me."

"Did you have a physical relationship?" Julia asked.

"Yes." His face tightened. "The longer we worked on the project, the more...fascinated I became with her. I believed she was as attracted to me as I to her. She certainly acted that way." He shook his head, closed his eyes for a brief moment. "Since then, I've learned Vanessa could dispense considerable charm if it suited her purpose. With me, she was infinitely charming. I don't think I could have resisted her if I'd tried."

"Did you try?" Julia asked.

"No," he admitted. "My wife..." Smithson's voice shook. "In the twenty-five years we've been married, I never looked at another woman, until... She'll be terribly hurt if she finds out."

Instinct told Julia the remorse she saw in his eyes, heard in his voice, was real. But she knew that even some killers felt remorse. "Mr. Smithson, did you give Vanessa access to Remington Aerospace's personnel files?"

"I...no, I didn't give her the files directly. I wouldn't do a thing like that."

"You didn't give them to her directly," Julia repeated. "But she did gain access through you?"

He let out a breath. "Yes. On one of our evenings together, Vanessa brought a bottle of wine she said she wanted me to try. I drank too much. At one point she mentioned a concern she had that someone had breached our computer system. Before I knew it, I'd outlined the security measures we had in place."

"Security measures," Halliday repeated. "Such as access codes?"

Smithson put a hand over his eyes, then lowered it. "I woke up the next morning in a haze. It took me a while to remember our conversation, but when I did, it appalled me to think what I'd told her. Appalled and shamed me. I got to work before any of my staff and checked the computer. Someone had accessed every personnel file. I went to Vanessa's office. When I saw her sitting at her desk, her computer going, I got sick to my stomach. I told her I knew she'd accessed the files."

"What did she say?" Julia asked.

"She told me all I had to do was keep my mouth shut and no one would have to know I'd given her the codes. And...my wife wouldn't learn about our relationship."

Julia tilted her head. "How did you respond to that?"

"Like a fool. I asked Vanessa how she could do that after what we'd shared. She just laughed. Said I was crazy if I thought what had happened between us meant anything. She said that all along she'd been seeing someone else in the organization. Someone in a position to further her career."

Julia's heart stopped. "Did Miss West say who that someone was?"

"No. I assumed it was..." He looked away.

"You assumed it was who, Mr. Smithson?"

"Sloan. Mr. Remington."

Her gaze slipped to Halliday. She registered the grim set of his mouth before forcing her attention back to Smithson. He was leaning forward in his chair now, his elbows propped on his knees, his face in his hands.

"Did Miss West tell you she was involved with Mr. Remington?" Julia asked, her voice steady and calm. "Or did you assume it was him?"

Smithson raised his head. "I assumed it."

"You must have observed them together at the office, in meetings, and on many occasions," Julia persisted. "By the way Mr. Remington and Miss West interacted, did you get the impression they were personally involved?''

"No. Sloan treated her as he does everyone.''

A small thing, Julia thought, but it was in Sloan's favor. She allowed herself a moment to feel the spring release of tension that came with relief.

Halliday pushed away from the bookcase. "Okay, you screwed up and gave Vanessa the access codes to confidential files, then you came to your senses. What did you do about it?''

"What could I do?'' Smithson asked stiffly. "As I told you, Vanessa was already in her office when I arrived at work that morning. She'd downloaded the files before I got there.''

"That was a breach of security,'' Julia said. "Did you report it to Rick Fox?''

"How would I have explained what I'd done?'' he asked fiercely. "How could I have faced Sloan? My wife?''

"Vanessa laughed at you,'' Julia said, forcing back her growing dislike for the man so she could concentrate on her job. "She threw another lover in your face. She threatened to tell all to your wife. How did that make you feel?''

"Angry. Helpless.'' Smithson raised his gaze to hers, his face bloodless now. "You can't imagine the remorse I've felt over this. The pain.''

"Enough to make you shoot her in the back?''

His eyes widened. "God, no. I... No, I didn't kill her. You've got to believe me.''

Julia scowled. Dammit, for some reason she did.

"Vanessa had the data in everyone's personnel file,'' she said. "Did she give you any indication of what she intended to do with that information?''

"No.'' Smithson shoved a trembling hand through his silver hair. "Thinking about the possibilities made me sick. I...'' He took a shaky breath.

"You what?'' Halliday prodded.

"I thought endlessly about going to Sloan and telling him what I'd done.''

"Why didn't you?" Julia asked.

"I told you, it was possible his and Vanessa's relationship went beyond business."

"You've stated that was an assumption on your part," Julia reminded him. "On the other hand, you *knew* your files had been breached. You *knew* who'd done it. Yet you chose not to go to Mr. Remington—"

"I couldn't chance it," Smithson said, his voice shaking. "Sloan and Vanessa spent two years working together at the Houston office. When Sloan came back three months ago, Vanessa transferred here. I know they were both involved in the new wing project, and that could have been the sole reason for Vanessa's presence. But, I couldn't be sure."

"Sloan…" Julia stood motionless while the blood drained from her face. "Mr. Remington spent the past two years in Houston? Working with Vanessa?"

"That's right." Smithson nodded miserably. "Sloan is a fair man. He treats the workers on the production line with the same respect as his managers. But Vanessa had a way of making a man forget everything but her. I just thought…if she had her claws in Sloan…"

Julia remained silent, her thoughts engaged in fierce debate.

"I'm not proud of my behavior," Smithson continued, his voice thick and low. "I was a fool to get involved with Vanessa. And a coward because I couldn't bring myself to own up to what I'd done."

Julia cleared her face of all expression before meeting Halliday's gaze. He stood motionless for a long moment before giving her a slight nod, a familiar silent message that showed he believed the man had told them the truth about his involvement with Vanessa.

Julia agreed.

Stiffly, she turned back to Smithson. "Do you keep track of the names of the employees issued service pins?"

He blinked, giving her a puzzled look. "Yes, we have a list. Why?"

"What about lost pins? Would people notify your office with that information?"

"My department or security."

"Do you know if anyone has reported their pin lost recently?"

He shook his head, looking convincingly blank. "I'd have to check. I can phone you with the information."

"I'll expect your call. You can go now."

"You're not holding me?"

She narrowed her eyes. "Do you think we should?"

"No." He pushed out of his chair. "Of course not." He was out the door in less than two seconds.

"Julia—"

"I know what you're thinking, Halliday," she said as she snapped off her recorder. "That while they were in Houston, Sloan and Vanessa carried on a personal relationship."

"Did Remington ever once tell you he'd spent the past two years in Houston working with Vanessa?"

"No." That day in Sloan's study, she hadn't thought to ask where he'd gone after he left town, *couldn't think* while she stood in his arms, her body trembling with need for him. She pictured again the cancer-related brochures she'd seen in the desk drawer. She hadn't noticed a return address, just the center's name: *M. D. Anderson.* In her emotional state, she hadn't made the connection that the cancer center was in the same city where Vanessa West had worked.

"I never knew where Sloan went when he…"

"Walked out on you," Halliday finished. "Sounds like Remington made a beeline for Houston, where Vanessa *happened* to work. Think about it, Cruze. They're together there for two years. He comes back here, brings her with him. Things blow up and she publicly threatens to ruin him. The next morning she winds up dead. Remember what you said earlier about coincidence? You don't believe in it."

"That's right, I don't." She took a step toward him.

"Halliday, listen to me. Sloan didn't leave me because of Vanessa. He left because he was sick."

Halliday frowned. "What are you talking about?"

With fatigue pressing down on her like a lead weight, Julia dropped into the nearest chair. Her headache had transformed into a slow, persistent throb behind her eyes; the aspirin she'd swallowed had burned a nice, neat hole in her stomach. "Sloan had cancer," she said, then related what she'd found out three days ago.

"Remington walked out on you because he thought…" Halliday shook his head. "Damn. I don't know whether to pat the guy on the back or slug him."

"Sloan must have stayed in Houston to be near his doctors," Julia said quietly.

Halliday walked to the room's single window. Eyes narrowed against the rays of the sun, he stared out in silence. Finally he turned and said, "It doesn't matter why he was there. What matters is he *was* there, working with Vanessa. He brought her back here with him. That's a connection that has to be checked out. We need to go to the company's Houston office, find out what went on between the boss and his assistant while they worked there."

"Or what didn't go on," Julia added.

"Or didn't," Halliday agreed, his voice going quiet. "Julia, I hope you're right. I hope for your sake Remington didn't kill her."

"For my sake?"

"Yeah." He walked to her, placed a hand on her shoulder and squeezed. "I figure this case isn't the only reason you look like you've given up on sleep, partner."

She shook her head. "Sloan didn't kill her, Halliday. I know he didn't."

A dim beep sounded. Halliday pulled the pager off his belt. "Oh, my God," he said, staring wide-eyed at the display.

"What?" Julia asked, rising.

"It's the code Pam and I came up with. Jesus, Cruze, she's in labor."

Chapter 9

"What are you waiting for, Halliday?" Julia asked as she swung open the door of the chapel waiting room. "Go pick up your wife before she has the baby at home."

"Right." Eyes wide, he stood unmoving, as if someone had glued his shoes to the carpet. "Cruze, I'm about to become a father. What the hell do I do?"

"Why do men always fall apart under pressure?" Laughing, Julia grabbed his arm and tugged. "Go get Pam, hotshot. I'll meet you at the hospital."

"Right."

The instant they stepped into the hallway, Julia's gaze locked with Rick Fox's. Remington Aerospace's security director had settled in a plush leather chair across from the waiting room, his long legs stretched out in front of him, a cigarette dangling from fingers with neat, trimmed nails.

"'Morning, Julia." An engaging smile curved his lips.

"I'll see you at the hospital," she said to Halliday's retreating form before turning her full attention to Rick.

"Somebody sick?" he asked, his gaze tracking Halliday.

"No." The crystal ashtray on the table beside his chair held four cigarette butts, all unfiltered, as was the cigarette between his fingers. With a seemingly casual glance, Julia checked the pearl-gray carpet in front of the waiting-room door. A few dark ashes had dropped there. The possibility that Rick had eavesdropped on the interview with Don Smithson grated on her already raw nerves.

Mouth tight, she crossed the short expanse of hallway, halting to one side of his chair. "Engaging in a little listening at closed doors this morning, Rick?"

He put a hand to his chest. "Julia, I'm crushed you'd even suggest that."

"I'm sure," she said coolly. She knew it was of great pride to Rick Fox that people considered him Sloan's eyes and ears. Little went on at Remington Aerospace that its security director didn't know. Had Rick been aware of Vanessa's affair with Don Smithson? Julia wondered. Of the woman's unauthorized access of the corporation's personnel files? Of any other nasty tricks Vanessa might have had up her sleeve?

"How long have you been sitting here?"

"Long enough to see Smithson come out of that room looking like Satan himself had gotten hold of him. What did you do to the poor guy? Accuse him of murder?"

Julia ignored the question. "Aren't you going to the cemetery to pay your respects to the deceased?"

"I didn't respect Vanessa. My acting ability takes me only so far."

"How far is that?"

He blew out a stream of smoke, regarded her through the haze. "You look tired, Julia. I guess this case has you working all sorts of hours."

"If you didn't respect Vanessa, why are you here?"

"Sloan issued a memo urging everyone to attend the service. When the boss speaks, I listen. That explains the presence of ninety-nine percent of the people you saw in the chapel. Vanessa's mother, stepfather and grandparents make up the other one percent.''

Julia tilted her head. ''If everyone disliked Vanessa, why did Sloan keep her on the payroll?''

He drew in smoke again. ''Ask him.''

''I'm asking you.''

''Sorry, I don't know the answer.''

''Was it because of their personal relationship?''

''Personal relationship?''

''You know, Rick, how Sloan and Vanessa interacted outside the office.''

''If they had a personal relationship, I didn't know about it.'' He stubbed out his cigarette thoughtfully. ''As far as I know, Sloan's only had one woman on his mind the past couple of years. That would be you.''

Julia did her best to ignore the quick fluttering in her stomach. ''Of course, you've been in Oklahoma City the past two years,'' she continued. ''You weren't in Houston to watch Sloan and Vanessa interact.''

Rick's blue eyes sharpened beneath his blond brows. ''True.''

''But I imagine you made quite a few trips there to see Sloan. Surely you observed him and Vanessa together.''

''Whenever I saw them together, they were working.''

Julia glanced back at the sprinkling of ashes in front of the waiting-room door. Rick didn't seem surprised she knew Sloan had gone to Houston. Yet after he'd walked out, she'd begged Rick to tell her Sloan's whereabouts. Rick had guarded that information like a dog with a meaty bone.

''Are you seeing anyone these days, Rick?''

''You know me, Julia. Confirmed bachelor.''

''Confirmed bachelors are known to date.''

''Yeah. The lucky lady is a bank vice president. I'll introduce you sometime.''

She took an intentional step forward, invading his personal space. ''Did you date Vanessa?''

He leaned minutely away, sliding his fingertips down his dark, paisley tie. "Is this an interrogation?"

"I ask the same questions of everyone. Nothing personal."

When he remained silent, she leaned in. "It's a simple question, Rick," she said, locking her gaze with his. "Did you ever date Vanessa?"

"She wasn't my type."

"I didn't ask what type she was. I asked if you dated her."

"No," he said. "I didn't date her."

"Why not? She was a gorgeous woman—"

"She was a heartless bitch," he countered. The muscles in his jaw worked. "Into control and power. Some men like that in a woman. I don't." The edges of his mouth lifted. "Give me a break, Julia. I was a cop for ten years. I know what's going on."

"Meaning?"

"First you insist that Sloan and Vanessa had something going. Now you're asking about some nonexistent relationship between her and me. No telling what you accused Smithson of. This is a high-profile case. Sounds like you're pretty desperate to pin Vanessa's murder on somebody."

"Not somebody," she countered, her words cool, biting. "The person who pulled the trigger."

"If you're thinking it was me, you've got the wrong guy."

"How many .22-caliber handguns do you own?"

He pulled a cigarette and gold lighter out of his pocket. "None," he said, then ignited the lighter with a sharp thumb flick. "But then, I imagine you've run a check on everyone who had access to the parking garage, so you already know what guns I own." He touched the flame to the cigarette and inhaled deeply.

"I know what guns are registered to you," she countered, blinking against the thin, acrid smoke that made her already gritty eyes burn. "I'm asking if you have any unregistered .22s."

"Not a one."

"I've left several messages on your voice mail over the past two days. Why haven't you returned my calls?"

He leaned back, his complacent smile returning. "I've been in San Francisco—just flew back in this morning. I spent the last two days setting up security measures to keep the workers in our production facility there from stealing us blind." He lifted a negligent shoulder as he studied the glowing tip of his cigarette. "I didn't have time to check my messages. Is there something I can help you with?"

"I tried to view the tapes we confiscated from the cameras at the entrance to the parking garage and the door into the building. The tapes won't play on our machine."

"Sorry, I should have mentioned that the day you viewed the tapes in my office," he commented. "I've added a safety measure on all our cameras. There's a security code programmed into our video equipment, which imprints a code onto the tape. The tape can only be played back on a machine with the same code."

"Why did you do that?"

"Did Sloan ever talk to you about how competitive the aerospace industry is?"

He had. "What about it?"

"Suppose a rival got their hands on some of our production tapes? They'd find out a whole lot about our operation and product development that we don't want to get out."

"The tapes I have are evidence. I need to view them again."

"No problem," he said. "Come by my office anytime and use my machine. The coffeepot's always on."

"Fine." She glanced at her watch, doing a quick calculation of how long it would take her to get to the hospital. She wanted to be there to give her quivering partner support.

"In fact, why don't we go there now?" Rick leaned toward the table, tamped out his cigarette. "I'd sure as hell rather hang with you than spend the next hour standing in the sun at the cemetery."

"I don't have the tapes we booked into evidence with me."

"What you have are copies off our master system. I can call up the date and times you want, and you can view whatever you need off our network."

"I'll have to get back to you about a time."

"Suit yourself."

She hiked her purse strap higher on her shoulder. She knew the vague, nervous habits Rick had exhibited could have been an attempt at deception. On the other hand, maybe Rick was right. Maybe her own determined desire that someone—*anyone*—other than Sloan had killed Vanessa had her grasping at straws.

Rick rose. "One thing, Julia," he said, his expression turning solemn.

"What's that?"

"I meant what I said about Sloan. His mind's been on you for the past two years. It still is."

By the time Julia parked her cruiser in the lot of her apartment complex, she'd been awake nearly twenty-four hours. She'd paced with Halliday during the long hours of Pam's labor, then held his hand while surgeons performed an emergency C-section. Dylan Carter Halliday had come into this world red faced and wailing...and perfectly healthy.

Muscles twitching and aching from fatigue, Julia walked through the shadowy courtyard that led to her apartment. Off to one side, the barely discernible shapes of massive oaks stood like still, silent sentries. Humidity hung in the night air, giving it a thick, gauzy feel against her skin. Her black dress had a rumpled, slept-in look; exhaustion pressed down on her like a lead weight. All she wanted was a long, steamy shower, then to crawl into bed and die.

For a couple of hours anyway, she thought wearily. Lieutenant Ryan had okayed her request to take an early flight to Houston. There, she would make a surprise visit to Remington staffers who'd worked with Sloan and Vanessa over the past two years. Julia frowned as she walked. The fact that Sloan had failed to mention he'd worked with Vanessa in Houston was not a fact in his favor. Still, she hadn't specifically asked him how long he'd known Vanessa, so he hadn't lied to her. Nor had he been forthcoming—something a murderer rarely was. And yet, for reasons she couldn't quite fathom, she believed he'd been truthful about his relationship with Vanessa.

Depending on what she found out in Houston, that belief could go up in smoke. Then what?

Julia's frown turned into a scowl. She was only making herself crazy thinking about it. So she wouldn't, not for the rest of the night—what was left of it. She'd clear her mind of all thoughts of the case, of Sloan. She'd get some much-needed sleep, then jump back in with both feet and get the damn case solved.

Gripping her key ring, she rounded a corner to take the sidewalk that veered toward her apartment, and stepped into a world of gray and black shadows.

Julia halted midstride. Her stomach lurched to her throat. The darkness was wrong. All wrong. Last week she'd replaced the bulb in her porch light, which a sensor always switched on at dusk and off at dawn. Always. Either the sensor had failed or someone had unscrewed the bulb.

Clenching her keys to keep them from jangling, she slid them into her pocket. Her right hand went down; bracing herself, she drew her automatic from the holster she'd clipped to the flap on her purse.

The stainless-steel Smith & Wesson felt hard and powerful against her palm as she thumbed the safety off.

Body stiff, gun ready, she stood in the center of the sidewalk, silent and unmoving, waiting for her eyes to adjust to the dark.

The faint hum of an air conditioner drifted on the air. A cricket chirped, then stilled. Somewhere in the distance, a car door slammed.

Julia swallowed past the knot in her throat.

The only source of light came from a New Orleans–style gas lamp at the far end of the sidewalk. The weak, flickering flame heightened the shadows, transformed the corner of her porch where a lawn chair and potted plant sat into an inky web.

A faint scraping sound drifted on the still air, a familiar sound that tightened Julia's already taut muscles. Someone had moved the lawn chair, scraping the legs against concrete. Someone was either sitting or standing in the shadows of her porch. Waiting.

Finger poised on the trigger, she took a silent step sideways, then another, halting when she felt the sidewalk give way to soft grass. She crouched in the building's shadow, knowing if someone took a shot at her, chances were they'd aim at chest height.

"Police!" she shouted. "Put your hands up and step off the porch."

"Good God, you'll wake the dead if you keep that up." Sloan stepped out of the porch's blackness into the dim, gray shadows. "Do I really have to put my hands up, Jules?"

Her breath whooshed out. She pushed up from her crouching position, her legs not quite steady. "What the hell are you doing here?"

"Waiting for you."

"Maybe I didn't plan on coming home tonight."

"Then I would have had a long wait."

She took an aggressive step forward. "Why is my porch light off?"

"Bugs," he answered easily. "I unscrewed the bulb." He turned and disappeared into the porch's dark depths.

Seconds later, amber light flooded the sidewalk. He regarded her thoughtfully. "That better?"

Dressed in black shorts and a tan polo shirt, he looked cool and comfortable...and not one bit concerned that he'd come close to getting shot.

"Unscrewing that bulb almost got you blown away," she said with ferocity.

His gaze slicked to the automatic clenched in her hand. "I appreciate your restraint."

His complacent expression spiked her temper. "How the hell did you find out where I live?"

"Rick. Julia, do you plan to shoot me?"

"How?"

"Pulling the trigger makes a gun—"

"I'm not in the phone book," she said through her teeth. "How did Rick get my address?"

Sloan's mouth curved. "I didn't ask."

"I wouldn't be smiling if I were you, Remington. You're trespassing. I still might shoot you."

"Think of the paperwork you'd have to deal with," he noted as he crossed his arms over his chest. "I recall that's the one thing you hate about police work."

"Shooting you just might take the unpleasantness out of the task."

"Do you really think so?"

She remained silent, taking deep, long breaths to settle her nerves. Reverting to coolness, she clicked on the safety and slowly holstered her weapon. Flexing her rigid fingers, she stepped onto the porch. "What do you want?"

He leaned, pulled a manila envelope from beneath the chair. "You asked me to get the list of guests from the art museum. Here it is."

Julia held back the urge to snatch the envelope out of his hand. "That didn't take long."

"Like you said, I have connections. Just don't mention my name when you grill people. If you do, I might never get invited to another cocktail party," he added with a grin.

The grin sent a bolt of reaction right into her midsection. Heart clenching, Julia looked away. The first time she'd seen that grin she'd been on duty, assigned to the governor's security detail at his inaugural ball. While standing behind stage listening to droning, mind-numbing speeches, she glanced up and saw Sloan Remington walking toward her. Dressed in a tuxedo, he carried a champagne flute in his hand…and he'd had that grin on his face.

"Julia?"

His voice jerked her back to the present. Brows knitted, she took a deep breath. "Since Rick knows my address, you could have had him deliver the list."

"Consider this my attempt to show how fully I'm cooperating with your investigation."

"Consider me shown," she said, wondering if he would be as willing if he knew about her upcoming trip to Houston. Pulling her keys out of her pocket, she stepped into the pool of amber light and held out her hand. "If you'll give me the envelope—"

Eyes narrowing, Sloan took a quick step toward her, his hand shooting out to cup her chin.

"Don't!" She jerked back, but his fingers held firm, tilting her face to his.

"Dammit, Jules, you're exhausted."

She grabbed his wrist. "I've had it with people telling me I look tired—"

"And pale." Sloan frowned. If he didn't know her so well, didn't know the passion and dedication she put into each case, he might have missed the vulnerability beneath her combative facade. Might not have realized how close to the edge she was. But he did know her. Just as he was expert at sensing her storm fronts, he also knew when she'd pushed herself to the brink of physical depletion.

Knowing that she was precariously close to reaching that point undermined his own grim intention to just hand over the envelope and leave. Walk away. He stared down into her face, his fingers tightening on the soft curve of her jaw.

The shadows of fatigue gave her eyes a bruised, waiflike appearance; lines of utter weariness etched the corners of her mouth. Two years ago, he'd walked away from her because it was the wisest thing to do. Leaving now would still be the wisest thing, he knew. But he also knew it was time to stay…for a while, anyway.

"When was the last time you ate?"

"At the hospital. Two hours ago."

"Hospital?"

She knocked his hand away. "Halliday's wife had a baby tonight. I ate at the hospital."

"Chips and coffee from a vending machine, right?"

She glared up at him, showing her displeasure that he'd guessed right. "Give me the list, Sloan. Then take off."

He whisked the envelope out of her reach when she grabbed for it. "I'm not leaving until you eat a decent meal."

Her shoulders stiffened. "You're leaving—"

"After I get some food in you," he said, sweeping the keys from her grip before her fatigued senses could react.

"Get off my porch."

"That's the plan." He slid the key into the lock and pushed open the door. "After you," he said, his hand doing a wide sweep toward her entry hall.

She remained on the porch, still and unmoving.

"All right," she said after a moment. "I'll fix myself something to eat. You have my word."

He cocked his head. "That's hardly reassuring, unless you've learned to cook in the past two years. Have you?"

"None of your business."

"I thought not. What I think is that you plan to go in and crawl into bed, right?"

"Wrong. I plan to take a shower first."

"Fine. You shower while I cook—"

"Over my dead body."

"That's a possibility," he agreed. "You may not make it through the night unless you eat something nourishing."

"This coming from a man who used to live on hamburgers and greasy fries," she countered.

"Since I got sick, I've cleaned up my act. I know all about vitamins, minerals and proteins. I could teach a nutrition class."

"Sounds scary," she muttered.

"I'll tell you what's scary. If you drop in your tracks from poor nutrition, you can't solve this case. And I want it solved."

"It'll get solved, whether I eat tonight or not," she shot back. "I know my limits. I know just how much I can take."

He held up the manila envelope. "You don't get this unless you eat."

"I thought you wanted me to solve the case."

"That won't happen if you're a member of the walking dead."

"Look, Sloan, I just..." She lifted a hand, pressed her fingers to her eyes in a gesture that personified exhaustion. After a moment she dropped her hand and met his gaze, her eyes dark, rich pools beneath the porch light. "I'm too tired to argue."

"Then don't."

Squaring her shoulders, she walked past him into the cool confines of her entry hall.

"Nice," he said, after she flicked on a light switch. He took a few steps forward, his gaze doing an intensive sweep of the living room awash in white linen, wicker and lustrous wood and brass accents. "Georgia's work, right?"

"Right."

He turned, meeting her gaze. "How are your parents?"

"Fine."

Thinking of Fred and Georgia Cruze sobered Sloan's thoughts. "I imagine I'm their least favorite person."

Julia gave a short laugh. "Let's put it this way. If you run into Mother, don't let her within arm's length. She's threatened more than once to break your neck."

"And your father?"

"You can expect stern words from Daddy."

"I'm sorry for that," he said quietly, regret curling into a hard knot in the pit of his stomach. "I like them both. They were always very good to me."

Julia hesitated, then looked away. "I...wasn't the only one who got hurt when you left, Sloan."

"I know," he said, his voice quiet. "I guess I won't drop by their house to pay my respects."

"I don't advise it."

He nodded and looked around, determined to get off a subject there was no sense pursuing. "Want to point me in the direction of the kitchen?"

"Around that corner," she said. "And just to get things clear, my bedroom is down the hallway behind you. Get within three feet of the door, Sloan, and I will shoot you, despite the paperwork."

Slowly, he turned, his eyes locking with hers. "If I ever step foot in another bedroom of yours, Julia, it will be because you invite me."

"I'm not inviting you."

"I know."

She looked distinctly uncomfortable as her fingers tightened on the purse strap. "Have fun cooking," she muttered, then turned and headed down the hallway.

Twenty minutes later, Julia opened her bedroom door to delicious, spicy smells that had her sighing. Dressed in shorts and a well-worn T-shirt from her police academy days, she padded barefoot down the hallway, then headed across the living room.

Though she knew he was there, the sight of Sloan standing in her kitchen amid the stark-white appliances and sparkling ceramic tiles slowed her steps. She tried not to notice how his thick, dark hair glistened beneath the bright lights, tried not to think about the hard, sinewy muscles beneath the tan polo shirt. Tried not to acknowledge how at home he looked, how familiar it seemed to have him standing there, pulling a plate out of her microwave. *How right.*

She pulled her bottom lip between her teeth. He had chosen to walk out on her, and here he was again, invading her life. She knew she should insist he leave, *force* him to go. But deep inside, where logic meant nothing, she knew she wanted him to stay.

The realization had her stomach knotting. She was engaged to another man, a man she loved and respected. A man who would keep his promises to her—something Sloan had not done.

As if sensing her scrutiny, he looked up, his mouth curving as his gaze met hers across the counter. "Feel better?"

She nodded, took a deep breath. "The hot water worked out most of the kinks." She slid onto one of the green-and-white upholstered wicker stools on the opposite side of the counter. It was best, she thought, to keep an immovable object between them.

"What smells so good?" she asked.

"Beef Stroganoff." He settled a plate in front of her.

Julia stared down at the delicate slices of beef in a cream sauce smooth as silk. A side serving of snow peas laced the plate's border. "What did you do, order takeout while I showered?"

"I looked in your freezer." The microwave sounded a ding. Sloan pulled open the door and plucked a muffin cradled in pink ruffled paper from its depths. "There're about ten entrées in your freezer," he said while buttering the muffin. "They all have 'Julia, you need to eat right' scribbled across the foil."

"Mother," Julia groaned. She lifted her fork, then sliced into the tender beef. "Every so often she goes on a cooking spree. She fills her freezer, then starts on mine."

Julia took a bite, almost moaning as the meat's savory taste invaded her senses. "I forgot all about her bringing that last batch over."

"It's her way of taking care of you," Sloan commented

as he handed the muffin across the counter. "Looks like someone needs to," he added quietly.

Julia aimed him a cool, level look.

"I know," he said. "I had my chance."

"And blew it."

She dropped her gaze and dug into her food. While she ate, she made a valiant attempt to ignore the way Sloan moved around the kitchen, tossing a paper towel into the trash, putting away the butter tub.

He closed the refrigerator door, amusement glittering in his eyes as he leaned comfortably against the counter. "Do you know you've got a piece of cheese in there that has a beard?"

"Mother mentioned it the last time she was here," Julia said, nibbling on a crispy snow pea. "It only needed a shave then."

He grinned. "As long as you know."

Frowning, she stared down at her plate, using her fork to toy with the remainder of the peas. Was this happening? Was she sitting at her kitchen counter, joking about hairy cheese with the man who had ripped her life apart?

Her appetite suddenly disappeared. She set her knife and fork beside her plate. It made no sense that Sloan was here, made no sense that she'd *allowed* him inside.

He gave her plate an appraising look. "Did I mention you don't get the guest list unless you eat everything?"

"Why are you here, Sloan?"

"I brought you the list," he said without missing a beat.

"You have people available who could have done that. Why are *you* here?"

He was watching her now, his eyes focused, cool.

"Why, Sloan?"

He came casually around the counter, settled onto the stool next to hers. "When I saw you at the chapel this morning, you looked more than just tired. You looked...unhappy. I felt compelled to check on you."

She lifted a shoulder. "I'm unhappy because I've got

two unsolved homicides working.'' That was part of it, anyway. ''I told you that.''

''I know about one case.'' He propped a foot on the rung of her stool, his tanned thigh, hardened by exercise, inches from her own bare one. ''Tell me about the other.''

She could feel the heat of his body, smell the subtle, warm scent of his cologne. ''It's an active case. I can't discuss it.''

His hand drifted onto the counter. If he flexed those lean, capable fingers, they'd settle over her own.

''Really?'' he asked. ''That hasn't stopped you from discussing your other case with me.''

She sliced him a look. ''Cops tend to discuss some aspects of a case with the suspect. That's usually how we get it solved.''

''So, you still view me as a suspect?'' The thread of anger in his voice sparked in his eyes. ''Do you honestly believe I killed Vanessa?''

''My beliefs don't matter. What matters is the evidence, the proof.''

He pulled the manila envelope across the counter and shoved it beneath her hand. ''Here's your list. Maybe the actual murderer's name is inside.''

''Maybe.'' She glanced at the envelope, looked back up. And because she couldn't help herself, she asked, ''When we've solved the case, if you're not…detained, you plan to leave for D.C., right?''

''I won't be detained. And I will leave.''

Her teeth set. She knew nothing short of a jail cell would keep him here once she'd cleared the case. He'd be as determined to get out of town as he'd been two years ago.

The thought of his leaving sent an incongruous mix of anger and hurt sweeping through her. It shouldn't matter if he packed his bags and disappeared, she told herself. Shouldn't mean a thing to her. But, dammit, it did.

It was as if the emotion she'd suppressed over the past two years had suddenly bubbled to the surface. It battered at her, made her pulse pound, her stomach clench with something akin to panic.

"You never answered my question," she said, her voice clipped. "You could have left the envelope in the door. Instead, you chose to wait on my porch. Why, Sloan? Dammit, why are you here?"

He studied her face for a long moment before he spoke. "The most obvious answer is that I wanted to see you."

She slid off her stool, found herself caged between the counter and his rock-hard thigh. She stared into his dark eyes, her breathing coming with an effort. "I don't want you here." Her unsteady hands gripped the edge of the counter behind her. "Dammit, you don't belong here."

He rose slowly, his eyes hot, gleaming coals as his lean body towered over hers. "You'll get no argument from me on that point."

"Fine—" Her heart jammed in her throat when his hands went on each side of her to rest on the counter, effectively caging her.

"I don't belong anywhere near you," he advised, his voice derisive, his breath a hot wash against her cheek. "In fact, I don't *want* to be here."

She remained motionless, her hips pinned against the counter, his arms surrounding, though not touching, her. If he leaned in, his mouth would be on hers. That potent, addicting mouth that could be both stunningly tender and ruthless. Her pulse hammered; the air had suddenly become too thick to breathe. Heat fed through her veins, like flame leaping along spilled gasoline.

"If…you don't want to be here, why are you?"

"Because I couldn't help myself," he said viciously. "Like a *fool*, I sat on your porch for hours, knowing you were probably with your fiancé. But that didn't matter. I just sat there, wondering what the hell I was doing."

"What the hell were you doing?" she asked weakly.

"Thinking," he shot back. "About you. About…" He shoved back, uttering a muffled curse. "I'm going to walk out of here—that's the easy part." His eyes went as hard as stone. "But I'm damned if I know how to make myself stop wanting you. *Needing* you."

She opened her mouth to speak, but no words came out.

"Finish your dinner, then get some sleep," he said quietly. He turned and walked away; seconds later, she heard the firm snap of the front door closing behind him.

Julia's legs felt like glass, ready to shatter. She sank onto the stool. Sloan hadn't even touched her, yet he'd reduced her to rubble.

She propped her elbows on the counter and buried her face in her hands. Five days ago, her life had been exactly what she wanted it to be, and now she felt as if she'd stepped off solid ground into a deep, dark hole. Things had changed too much and too fast.

No, she realized, in the next heartbeat. Nothing had changed, because she'd never rid herself completely of Sloan.

"Damn you, Remington," she said, her voice a raw whisper.

She had fooled herself into thinking she'd gotten him out of her system. She never had; she knew that now. He was a drug, she the addict. No matter what she did, she'd never be completely free of the need for him, the wanting.

She stared down at her engagement ring, the diamond's facets throwing out rosy fire beneath the kitchen's bright lights. It wasn't that she didn't love Bill. She did. But the deep, aching passion in her soul belonged to Sloan—had always belonged to him. Her needs, both physical and emotional, were not just to have a man, a lover and companion, but to have Sloan. He was the man she wanted. Needed. *Loved*.

She loved Sloan, had never stopped loving him. It was as simple and excruciating as that.

An errant tear rolled down her cheek. She swiped it away with the back of her hand, took a deep breath, then another, as she stared down at her ring. She could come up with all sorts of reasons to leave things as they were and just wait. Wait until she found Vanessa West's murderer. Wait until she caught up on her sleep, wait for the emotional roller coaster she'd stumbled onto to come to a stop.

Wait until after Sloan left for D.C., and see how she felt.

She closed her eyes. The fact that he would again walk away and leave her shattered didn't seem to matter. Nothing in the world mattered, because she knew with aching clarity what was in her heart. *Who* was in her heart.

And he'd be there whether he was grinning at her from across her front porch or living thousands of miles away.

With silent regret, her gaze returned to her ring. That she would no longer be a part of Bill's life brought a profound sadness.

She sighed, knowing nothing good would come from forestalling the inevitable. Leaning across the counter, she grabbed the phone with a trembling hand and stabbed in Bill's number.

Chapter 10

"Julia, dear, you look terrible."

"That's just what I need to hear, Mother," Julia commented as she edged into the small storeroom in the back of Georgia Cruze's interior-design shop. Knowing her mother's habit of arriving at work before dawn, Julia had detoured by the shop on her way to the airport. She'd been both relieved and filled with dread when she saw her mother's lemon yellow BMW parked in the alley behind the store.

Georgia settled a hand on the waist of her tailored, black-and-white checked gabardine suit and examined Julia closely. "Maybe you're coming down with something."

She placed a cool, deliberate palm against Julia's forehead, the gesture accompanied by the tinkling of the charms crowding her gold bracelet. "No fever," she announced.

"I'm not sick, Mother. I need to catch up on some sleep is all." Stepping farther into the cozy storeroom, Julia leaned a hip against the polished Louis Quatorze table that doubled as a desk. The pungent smell of cinnamon and pinecones scented the air; the smooth strains of Pachelbel's *Canon* drifted from the dark, outer shop.

Georgia tilted her head. The soft overhead lighting cast her expertly styled chignon with a copper glow as she gave Julia a narrow, measuring look. "Well, dear, you'd better get some rest before you drop in your tracks."

"I'm catching a flight to Houston this morning to check a lead on a case. I plan to sleep on the plane."

"Interesting," Georgia murmured. She walked to a small butler's table, where she poured coffee from a china pot into a delicate matching cup.

"So," she began, handing Julia the cup, "since it's not your habit to check in with me about your work, I imagine you've got something else on your mind."

"Right." Nerves shimmering, Julia sipped the savory, rich brew while concentrating on a shelf loaded with elaborate tassels and beribboned boxes. Beneath the shelf, a rainbow of carpet samples sat in an orderly stack. To her right, bolts of fabrics in springtime pastels sprouted from a humpbacked trunk.

Best get it over with, Julia decided, and took a deep breath. "I returned Bill's ring."

"You what?" Georgia's disbelieving voice filled the overflowing storeroom. "Why?"

"Bill and I aren't getting married." Julia downed the contents of the fragile cup, then set it aside.

Georgia's red-glossed mouth tightened. "Since you came by to tell me that, I assume you're planning to tell me why."

Julia had expected the shocked, dismayed look on her mother's face. Expected, too, her need for an explanation.

"Nothing specific happened," Julia said, diverting her gaze to a glass-doored breakfront that held a collection of antique silver goblets. "I just realized…" She jammed her hands into the pockets of her slim black slacks into which she'd tucked a man's starched tuxedo shirt. "Marrying Bill would have been a mistake."

"I see."

"Mother, I'm pressed for time. I just wanted to let you know—"

"Sloan Remington returns to town, and you call off your engagement," Georgia said quietly. "Are the two events related?"

That Julia had also anticipated the question didn't keep her stomach from knotting. "I didn't break up with Bill because of Sloan. I did it because of me. Mother, I just can't…" She lifted a shoulder. "It wouldn't have worked."

Georgia took a step closer. "Are you seeing Sloan?"

Only in regard to his being a murder suspect. Julia hid the wince that accompanied the thought. Maybe, just maybe, she'd find proof in Houston that would verify Sloan's claims that his relationship with Vanessa had been solely of a business nature.

"I've…seen Sloan, but not in the way you're thinking," she answered.

"But you have seen him," Georgia said, her voice low and bitter. "And he talked you into dumping poor Bill—"

"No. Like I said, it isn't Sloan. It's me." Julia stabbed her fingers through her hair, still damp from a hurried shower. "Sloan's moving out of state in a few weeks. He won't even be here—"

"So, he comes back to town long enough to get you stirred up, to confuse you, then he leaves *again*. Darling, lend me your gun so I can shoot the man."

Julia held up both palms in surrender. "Mother, I have to catch a plane. I just wanted to let you know."

"I appreciate that," Georgia replied, her dark eyes simmering. "Julia, I want you to think carefully about what you've done." She reached out, touched her daughter's cheek with soft fingertips. "Bill is a wonderful man—"

"I know." Julia's throat tightened with fresh regret at the memory of the raw hurt that had settled in Bill's eyes only hours before when she returned his ring.

"I love you, Julia," he'd said. *"But I don't want to be someone you settle for."*

She dragged in a ragged breath, checked her watch. "I've got to go. I'll come by the house soon and talk to you and Daddy about this."

"Julia—"

She gripped her mother's hand, placed a kiss on her unlined cheek. "Later, Mother. There will be plenty of time to talk later."

Rick Fox exited the elevator and made a beeline for Sloan's office. He barreled past Elizabeth's desk, ruffling the executive secretary's serenely efficient manner.

"Rick!"

"Emergency," he said over his shoulder. His palms hit hard against the carved double doors, throwing them open with enough force that they banged against the wall. "We've got one hell of a problem."

Brows arched, Sloan turned slowly from the floor-to-ceiling windows, where he'd spent the best part of the past hour surveying the city's skyline. If asked, he'd have been hard-pressed to describe the view. Nor could he have remarked on the way the sun's fierce rays pounded down on the noontime traffic, reflecting brilliantly off chrome and windshields. His thoughts had centered exclusively on the previous night. On Julia. On how she'd looked sitting across the kitchen counter from him, her eyes smudged with fatigue, her dark hair a shadow enfolding her face and shoulders.

"Sloan, did you hear me?" Rick asked. "I said—"

"What problem?"

Sloan caught the stern look Elizabeth gave Rick as the security chief shoved the doors closed behind him. "Guess who's nosing around our Houston office, asking questions?"

"I don't want to guess." Sloan walked back to his desk

and settled into his high-backed leather chair. "You tell me."

"Julia."

Sloan frowned. "Questions about what?"

"You and Vanessa. Your relationship."

"Julia's there now?"

"As we speak."

Sloan's jaw set. He knew the police department had a slow-as-sludge procurement system, so it followed that Julia had to have requested her tickets prior to last night for her to be in Houston today. Yet during the considerable time he'd spent at her apartment, she hadn't mentioned it.

He raised a hand, kneaded at the tension in the back of his neck. Julia didn't owe him an explanation; he knew that. In truth, what galled him was the possibility that her impending trip had been the thing foremost on her mind while he'd had her backed against the kitchen counter, battling the urge to rip off her clothes and take her right there on those gleaming ceramic tiles.

"You can block her." Pacing along the length of the big mahogany desk, Rick dipped his hand in the pocket of his slacks, jingled his change. "She's trespassing. Has no warrant. Legally, no one at our Houston office has to talk to her—"

"If people want to talk to Julia, they're free to."

A spark of contemptuous amusement settled in Rick's eyes. "Yeah, well, I've taken steps to make sure that's not quite what's happening down there."

Sloan steepled his fingers, his gaze following his friend's movement across the plush area rug to the far wall, then back again. "What steps?"

"The minute Houston's security head called to say Julia was there, I told him to put her in his office until I had a chance to talk to you." Rick glanced at his watch, his mouth curving. "We can keep her cooling her heels the rest of the day without her talking to another person."

"We can, but we won't," Sloan said evenly. "Blocking

Julia will make it look as if I have something to hide. I don't. Call Houston and tell them she's free to talk to whomever she likes—"

"It's the principle," Rick countered. "Hell, Sloan, she can't find anything here, so she goes down there, digging for dirt."

"Let her dig. Hell, give her a shovel. She won't find anything."

Giving up on pacing, Rick dropped into a chair in front of the desk, his eyes narrowing. "I told you the questions Julia asked me yesterday at the funeral chapel. It's like she's trying to invent some relationship between you and Vanessa that didn't exist."

"She won't get far—"

"Dammit, Sloan, this whole thing's turned personal," Rick countered, anger whipping color into his face. "Julia's like every other woman scorned. You humiliated her when you dumped her. Now it's payback time. She's got a chance to take you down for murder, and, by God, she'll do it. You're a fool if you don't call the mayor and have her jerked off this case."

"Which would only serve to humiliate her a second time," he noted flatly.

"At this point, who the hell cares?"

"I do!" Sloan's fingers bit into the arms of his leather chair. He dragged in a deep breath, then another, as he fought for control.

Rick was right, he told himself. He should think about his own neck. After all, at this very moment, Julia might be quietly fashioning a noose to go around it. He closed his eyes. Why the hell didn't that seem to matter? Nothing mattered, he thought. Nothing, except her. The image of how she'd looked last night settled in his brain. He'd never forget the sight of her standing in the curve of his arms as her breath shuddered in and out, sending heat rising from her invisibly. Without uttering a word, she'd taken him precariously close to begging.

"Hell," he muttered, then rose and walked around the desk, examining his security chief with grim assessment. "I don't like the fact that Julia's asking my staff questions about my personal life, but that's too bad. It's her job. I made sure I didn't interfere with her job two years ago, and I'm not going to start now. Neither are you."

Rick shook his head, propped one foot across his knee. The movement hiked up the cuff on his navy slacks, exposing the bottom edge of a leather ankle holster. "Look, Sloan, I just think you ought to watch your back."

"That's what I've got you around for," Sloan said, his gaze narrowing as he stared down at the holster.

Rick shoved out of his chair. "You don't want to keep Julia from doing her job, but that's exactly what you're doing to me."

"Wrong. I'm just not letting you get overzealous about it." Sloan leaned against the desk and crossed his arms. "Call Houston. Tell them to give Julia free rein to talk to whomever she wants."

"You're the boss," Rick muttered, then headed for the door. "Damn, I'll be glad when all of this is over and we head for D.C."

"You're not the only one," Sloan said, then turned back to the wall of windows.

Flicking on headlights, Julia steered her detective cruiser out of the airport parking lot and headed north on the interstate. North, in the direction of Sloan's house.

She had gone to Houston to find answers, and had returned with even more questions. All she knew for sure was that only two people knew the truth about Sloan and Vanessa's relationship, and one of those people was dead.

She glanced in the rearview mirror. The dim light from the dash emphasized the smudges beneath her eyes. She had managed to nap on both legs of her flight, but two hours of rest couldn't make up for the sleep she'd lost over the past few nights. Nor had she found any release from

the aching guilt that had settled inside her when she returned Bill's ring. She glanced at the steering wheel; her
hand looked eerily naked without the diamond solitaire.

Still, she knew she had done the right thing.

An exit lane that veered west toward her apartment came
into view, yet she bore down on the gas pedal and kept the
cruiser heading north. She could have waited until morning,
then called Sloan downtown to the station to answer questions. Even the greenest rookie knew it was standard text-
book procedure to question a suspect on the cop's home
turf. Dingy interview rooms and the sense of being detained
often loosened tongues.

Julia knew all the rules, yet they didn't seem to matter,
not with this case. She was close to having enough circumstantial evidence to charge Sloan with murder, yet it didn't
matter.

What mattered was that to her he was no longer a suspect. Not in her heart, anyway.

She rang the doorbell five times. Despite the lights burning gold behind several upstairs and downstairs windows,
she had almost accepted that Sloan wasn't home. Just as
she was about to climb back into her cruiser, she heard the
faint sound of the hot tub's bubbling jets. Silently, she
walked along the cobblestone path at the side of the house
and let herself through the high wooden gate. As she
walked, a light breeze rustled the branches of nearby oaks.

Pink and blue hydrangeas lining the flagstone terrace
glowed in the moonlight. The trim lawn and manicured
hedges had transformed into a dim wonderland of shapes
and shadows. Julia skirted the pool, her steps taking her to
the raised deck that held the hot tub, its lights glowing
softly in the still night.

Eyes closed, elbows propped on the tub's rim, Sloan sat
in the swirling, steamy water, giving the impression of a
man lazily recharging his batteries.

Julia stepped onto the deck, her throat tightening as her

gaze slid across his broad chest covered with a mat of softly curling dark hair that trailed downward. Visible through the clear, churning water were narrow hips and sinewy thighs unobscured by bathing trunks....

The instinctive lurch of her stomach was followed by her heart's slow throbbing against her ribs. A bittersweet, undeniable longing had her legs going weak.

"Enjoying the view, Jules?"

Her head sprang up as waves of heat rushed up her throat and into her face.

Sloan's mouth curved into a smile full of insolence and charm. "Isn't voyeurism against the law, Sergeant?"

"We...uh... We need to talk," she stammered as the heat in her cheeks went to blast-furnace level.

He cocked his head, his damnably infuriating smile only heightening her embarrassment. "Are we becoming a regular thing?" he asked. "I drop by your house one night. You pay me a visit the next."

Struggling to regain her composure, she dug into her purse and pulled out her tape recorder. "You have a choice, Sloan. Talk to me now, or come downtown in the morning."

"Now's as good a time as any," he drawled. "But I'm getting a crick in my neck, looking up at you." He rose off the underwater bench, exposing a good measure of lean, fit hips. "Why don't I just climb out and talk to you on the deck?"

Sucking in a breath, Julia diverted her gaze to search for a towel. There wasn't one. "I think you'd better stay where you are."

"Whatever." Settling back on the bench, he conducted a slow survey of her white tuxedo shirt and dark slacks. "You could peel off those clothes and slide in here with me, Jules."

"I could, but I won't."

"Well, if you've gotten shy, put on a suit." His gaze

slicked to the dark guest house across the expansive lawn. "There are a couple of your suits still in the bureau there."

"No, thanks. But I'll be sure and take them with me when I leave."

"You ought to reconsider." His gaze came back to hers, hardened. "After your trip to Houston, I imagine you could stand a relaxing soak."

She scowled. "My trip wouldn't have been such a pain if your security people hadn't put up roadblocks."

"If you'd told me you were going there, I'd have made sure that wouldn't have happened."

"I'd have been crazy to tell you."

"Crazy in that a cop doesn't tell a suspect the game plan?"

"Something like that," she said as she crouched and placed the recorder beside him on the tub's tiled rim. Jets bubbled; steam rose. The heat of the water wrapped around her like a velvet glove.

"So now you're back with your recorder," he observed, the edge in his voice sharpening.

"I have questions only you can answer."

"Or my attorney."

"You, Sloan," she said, shoving her hair behind her shoulders. "Every employee of yours I interviewed today assumes you and Vanessa were having an affair."

"I can't help what people assume."

"She *told* her secretary there that she was sleeping with you."

Eyeing her, he propped an elbow on the tub's rim. "What do you think, Julia?"

"It doesn't matter what I think. What matters is what I can prove."

"I see."

"No, you don't see," she shot back, trying to keep calm. "You don't understand how close you are to being charged with murder. You're in trouble, Sloan."

"Am I?"

"You don't have an alibi for the time of the shooting. You're an excellent marksman. It would have been nothing for you to take Vanessa out with one shot from a .22. Only hours before she died, she threatened to ruin you and your company—"

"Dammit, I didn't kill her," he said through his teeth.

"I know that!" Julia countered, her voice trembling. "I know," she repeated.

He stared at her for a long moment. "Are you saying you believe me?"

"Yes, but it doesn't matter a damn bit what I believe. Only what I can prove." She rubbed at her forehead, trying to think past the numbing fatigue that had settled in her brain. "You've got to help me, Sloan. Tell me how often you and Vanessa worked late, then went to dinner where people saw you together. Tell me if you ever dropped by her apartment to pick up a file. Tell me everything about your relationship with her."

"I have."

"That's not true. You never told me you went to Houston. You never even hinted that you spent the past two years there with her."

He shook his head slowly. "I didn't go there because of Vanessa. Granted, she worked for my company, but I hadn't even met her before I got there. I went to Houston because my doctor here referred me to *M. D. Anderson* for treatment. I was sick, Julia. After I recovered from surgery, the chemo treatments started. I mainly worked out of my apartment. There would be weeks I never went in to the office. My being in Houston had nothing to do with Vanessa."

That was something, Julia thought. But not nearly enough. "I need to know if she ever mentioned anything to you about other men—anything at all. Help me, Sloan, so I can help you."

He reached out, his hand curving over her wrist. "Why? Why do you suddenly believe me?"

She stared down at his long, powerful fingers, the breath backing up in her lungs. "I never..."

"Never what?"

"Never could see you doing it." She attempted to pull away, but his fingers only tightened their hold.

"Go on," he prodded.

She met his dark, waiting gaze. "All along, I've tried to picture you standing in that garage, aiming a .22 at Vanessa. It didn't work because I could never put your face on that shadowy figure. I know you had the means and the opportunity to kill her, but I keep stumbling when I get to motive. That's when everything falls apart because I know you. You would have viewed Vanessa's threat of ruination as a challenge."

His thumb moved, stroking the soft, inner skin of her wrist. "That's exactly how I saw it."

The gentle, erotic sweep of his thumb had her pulse throbbing hard and thick. "God, you're officially a suspect. I can't believe I'm telling you this. I can't believe..." Her voice shook. "This could cost me my badge."

"Only if it got out that you'd come here," Sloan said quietly. "It won't get out." His gaze dropped to her hand, his thumb suddenly going still. "Julia, where's your ring?"

"I came here to work, Sloan, not talk about myself." With her free hand she grabbed her recorder, clicked it on, then replaced it on the edge of the hot tub.

"Mr. Remington, I need to know everything about your relationship with Miss West."

"Like hell!" In the next instant, he grabbed the recorder and tossed it away.

Mouth gaping, Julia watched it sink like a piece of lead in the hot, bubbling water. "Dammit, Sloan—"

He rose, his hand clenching her wrist. With a sharp tug he pulled her in with him.

She came gulping to the surface, sputtering like a lit fuse. "You...you..."

He ducked a swing from her right fist, grabbed her wrists and jerked her forward. "Where the hell is your ring?"

"I…" She wrenched a hand free, dashed streams of water from her eyes. "I'm soaked!"

"Your ring, dammit!"

"I gave it back," she snapped.

"When?"

"Last night."

"You were wearing it last night."

"After you left. I went to see Bill."

For a moment Sloan simply looked at her, his eyes luminous in the moonlight. Then he reached out and stroked a fingertip down her cheek. "You were supposed to get some sleep after I left."

His soft touch dampened the fire in her. "I…had to see Bill. Had to…"

"So, you're not engaged anymore?"

"No."

"Why, Jules? Why?"

She shoved her drenched hair away from her face. "Because I… I couldn't…. It has nothing to do with you." Her voice broke and she looked away. "Dammit, Sloan, why did you come back? Why the hell did you have to come back?"

His hand slipped to her nape, easing her closer, degree by degree. "I've asked myself that same question a hundred times." He bent his head, his lips grazing hers in a whisperlike kiss.

Need curled its way down her spine. Heat suffused her flesh with a penetrating warmth that had nothing to do with the hot, steamy water and everything to do with his touch. "We can't. We shouldn't… You're a…"

"Suspect," he finished, his dark eyes glinting. "You're right. We shouldn't. For a whole hell of a lot of reasons. But we're going to."

The next instant he captured her mouth with his in a long, rough kiss, full of demanding need. She shuddered;

her lips parted beneath his as blood roared through her veins.

His mouth burned over hers, his tongue diving deep as his arms circled her trembling body.

"We have to talk," she gasped weakly against his neck.

"Later," he murmured, his impatient hands tugging her shirttail from her slacks. "We've got all night."

"Yes." Her mind was already hazy. She dragged in air that clogged thickly in her lungs.

His hands moved, fighting open buttons, shoving off her shirt, then her slacks and tossing the sodden garments onto the deck. Her lacy bra and panties followed.

She stood before him naked, steam rising, caressing her flesh as his eyes moved slowly down the entire length of her body. "I've thought about you like this," he said, his voice low. He pulled her back to him, one hand tight on her bare waist, the other plunging up through her wet hair to angle her head back. "Every night for the past two years, I've thought about you like this."

Greedily his mouth savaged her throat. "I love the smell of your skin." His voice was rough. Urgent. "Sweet. Fresh." He reclaimed her lips, feasting, tasting, filling her with a clawing ache.

She whispered his name over the churning of the water, gazed up into his dark eyes through the curling clouds of steam. Her hands glided over the hard, sinewy planes of his body, discovering him all over again. Her teeth nipped, scraped against his jaw as she sated her ageless hunger for the taste of this one man's flesh. His muscles rippled with wild, reckless energy at her touch; his heart hammered against hers.

Her hands went to his chest, hard and solid, her fingers curling in the tight, wet mat of dark hair. She trailed kisses along the scar, so much a symbol of what had torn them apart.

Her hand slid down the muscled planes of his stomach, down to his loins. She thrilled in the feel of his arousal thrusting hotly against her palm. Her fingers curved around him, stroking; a wave of pleasure filled her when he groaned her name.

She wrapped an arm around his neck as she lost herself to sensations—the wet heat of his body sliding against hers, the dark hair plastered across his chest, the familiar, longed-for taste of him in her mouth.

"Let me have you, Julia," he said, his voice hot velvet against her flesh. "Right here."

He dipped his head. His heated mouth burned with wet fire as he suckled one breast, then the other. Teeth closed softly, nipping, tasting until her nipples hardened and throbbed. All thought, all reason, skittered away.

His eyes locked with hers as he slid his hand between her legs, cupped her. Her eyes fluttered closed; her breath quickened, thickened. His fingers began a slow, erotic circular movement that ripped his name in a raw, sobbing moan from her throat.

His touch, along with the hot, swirling water that lapped against her flesh, wrapped her in layers of sensation. Her head lay heavy on his shoulder; the light, silky night breeze caressed her wet skin. Beneath the star-dotted heavens, her entire being felt open, unguarded, yielding.

Sloan continued the warm, relentless massage of her sensitive flesh. His magic, tormenting hands took her slowly up, up toward the peak of passion, then catapulted her over the edge. Her body curved against his as the climax ripped through her, pummeling her with fevered pleasure.

"I want you," she gasped, her hands flexing on his shoulders, urging him on. "Want you...."

"You've got me." He crushed the bruised flesh of her mouth with his ravenous kiss. "You've always had me. Will always have me."

He brought her to ecstasy a second time, whispering words that her dazed brain had no power to understand.

Breath burned in her throat. Her blood pounded in her head as he continued the rapid, reckless assault on her senses. She clutched at him helplessly, her nails digging into his muscled arms as her knees weakened and gave out.

Cupping her hips, he lifted her limp body until her face came even with his. "There hasn't been another woman since you." His eyes blazed into hers. "No one."

His breath was hot and quick, his touch possessive as he thrust himself inside her. Her fingers dived into his hair, pressing the body that fit so perfectly with hers closer, closer.

The stars in the dark sky above them shattered into a million pieces of light. Her lips trembled with each gasping breath. Sensation after staggering sensation swamped Julia, steeping her in pleasure as she gave herself in delirious surrender.

Later, with the lights in the guest house on low, Sloan watched her. She slept on one side, a limp bundle of utter fatigue. His hand reached out, stroked across the length of her shoulder. She didn't stir.

After they'd crawled out of the hot tub, sated and spent, he'd carried her naked across the dark lawn into the guest house. There, they'd sprawled on the pillow-covered bed and made love with quiet, restrained desperation.

His fingers went to her lips, tracing their sensuous curve, then moved along the soft line of her jaw. He thought about how beautiful she'd looked with her skin pale in the moonlight, her long hair gleaming, her eyes dark and wide. And later, lying against the smooth, white sheets, she'd looked irresistible, gazing up at him in the half dark.

He closed his eyes as a surge of love, painfully sharp, overwhelmed him. He wanted her with every fiber of his being, was desperately in love with her. But he couldn't promise her a future, so he couldn't have her, not the way he wanted.

He set his jaw, his thoughts in a war between logic and emotion. He had told himself he would never regret the decision he'd made two years ago when he cut her out of his life. Now, with her lying still and silent at his side, regret roiled inside him, twisting his gut into a tight knot. Dammit, he'd done the right thing…hadn't he?

He took her hand, linked his fingers with hers as he studied her profile, both angular and soft. She looked curiously innocent with her lashes fanned against her cheeks, her hair a glorious tangle of dark silk against the snow-white pillowcase. Their lives were linked—would always be linked—just as surely as their hands now were, yet he could guarantee her nothing, so he could offer her nothing.

Reality. It wasn't going to change just because he wanted it to. He settled down on his pillow and eased his arms around her. It was best, he thought, to move up his departure to D.C. Best to leave before he tore her life apart again.

Chapter 11

Julia woke slowly amid a sea of rumpled sheets and tangled pillows. Shoving her hair out of her face, she blinked against the sunlight spilling through white linen curtains.

Because she was groggy, it took her a moment to remember she was in the guest house off Sloan's pool, another for all that had happened between them last night to register. Her lips curved as she snuggled into the cozy nest of pillows. She felt alive. Replenished. Sore and swollen and wonderful.

Languid as a cat, she gave a little stretch. Her smile deepened at the minor aches that registered in her body. After a moment she slid her arm sideways, felt the coolness of the creamy white sheet on what had been Sloan's side of the bed.

Vaguely, she wondered how long he'd been gone…and how soon he'd be back.

She burrowed into the crisp linens, inhaling deeply of his clean, masculine scent. An instant shaft of heat streaked straight up her spine. God, it had been so long since she'd felt anything this intensely. Since she'd *wanted* so intensely.

Feeling more than a little decadent, she summoned the energy to prop her naked body up on a bank of pillows, then lazily surveyed her surroundings. The bedroom was as she remembered it from the few times she'd used the guest house in the past to change into a bathing suit. White-washed pine furniture and alabaster accents gave the room a light, airy feel. A sofa and matching chairs upholstered in a creamy fabric sat before a fieldstone fireplace. Off to her left was a white-tiled bathroom, its interior dark. Her purse, Julia noted, had wound up across the room on a tufted footstool.

Her clothes were nowhere in sight.

Probably still in a wet heap by the hot tub, she decided. Pursing her lips, she debated the quickest way to get a change of clothes for work.

Work. She frowned as reality set in. Job-wise, sleeping with Sloan had been an inappropriate act—there was no question about it. Still, she couldn't bring herself to regret what they'd shared. Last night, caught between common sense and feelings, she had stepped aside from Julia Cruze, the cop, and lost herself in an overpowering whirlpool of emotion.

For that reason alone, she should march into Lieutenant Ryan's office and take herself off the case. But with Halliday on a week's leave with Pam and their new son, Ryan would assign the investigation to another team. Julia knew she'd lose all control over the case.

And Sloan might wind up in a cell before the day was out.

She couldn't let that happen. Drawing her legs up, she planted her elbows on her knees and mentally reviewed the case. No, she thought after a few moments, it wasn't just her heart that had convinced her of Sloan's innocence. It was her head, her instincts—everything in her that made her a cop. Long before she'd plunged into that hot tub she had eliminated as a suspect the man she loved. Now she had to go back to the beginning, review every piece of evidence—do whatever it took to find Vanessa West's killer.

And by doing that, she would free Sloan to walk out of her life for a second time.

She swallowed past the tightness that settled in her throat. Dammit, she knew Sloan still loved her. He hadn't said the words last night as they lay sated and drowsy in each other's arms, but that didn't matter. She had felt the way his hands molded, possessed, her body; felt the hot, searing kisses that branded her skin and laid claim as no words could.

She didn't need him to tell her he loved her to know that he did.

But when it came to leaving, she knew in her heart that Sloan would give as much consideration to his feelings as he'd done two years ago. Then, he'd walked out, although he'd loved her. And because of his blind determination to protect her from something that might never happen, his resolve to leave now would be just as great.

Somehow, *some way*, she had to ease the fear of the unknown that seemed to haunt him.

Julia stared across the room into the dark depths of the fireplace. Knowing she might lose Sloan for a second time sent a skitter of panic up her spine. She breathed deeply, banking down her emotions so she could think. She couldn't, *wouldn't* let him go. The problem was, she had no idea how to convince him he belonged here. Belonged with her.

The sound of the door opening had her snatching the sheet up beneath her arms to shield her naked body.

"Don't cover up on my account." Eyes full of appreciation, Sloan stepped in, carrying two mugs of steaming coffee.

The sight of him in a pair of well-worn cutoffs and nothing more started her pulse skittering. He resembled a Greek god with his skin tanned to bronze, the black hair covering his broad chest, curving down the supple muscles of his stomach and streaking his long, muscle-hard thighs.

The quickening in her pulse transformed into an ache.

She pulled in a slow breath. "How long have you been up?" she asked, noting that his face looked freshly shaved and his dark hair was slicked back from a shower.

"Long enough to do fifty laps in the pool and make two calls to the Pentagon," he said, shoving the door closed with his bare foot. "Sleep well?"

"Like a stone," she said, attempting to finger-comb her long hair into submission. "What time is it?"

"A little after eight."

"Eight?" She grabbed the clock on the nightstand, twisted it her way. "Lord, I needed to be at the office an hour ago."

"You needed sleep more," Sloan said as he handed her a mug. "And food." Using his fingertips, he gently nudged her shoulder back against the pillow. "Hattie's cooking breakfast."

Julia sipped the hot, rich brew and sighed. "I don't eat breakfast."

"You don't eat, period." He settled onto the mattress beside her, lacing their fingers together as he cradled her hand in his. "Humor me, Jules," he said before placing a velvety kiss against her knuckles. "Let me take care of you."

Her lips curved as she met his solemn gaze. "You took care of me quite well last night...and early this morning."

He didn't answer her smile with one of his own. His dark eyes remained on hers, with no glint of amusement.

"Last night was..." He set his coffee on the nightstand, then cupped her cheek in his hand. "I was going to say 'incredible,' but it was more than that," he said, his voice almost a whisper. "Much more. There's not a word for how it felt to make love with you again."

Her heartbeat hitched. She moved her head so that it was

she who was caressing him with the soft skin of her cheek. "I feel the same way," she murmured against his warm palm. "Like I'm complete again. Like I've found the part of me that's been missing for the past two years."

She felt the slight stiffening of his fingers before he dropped his hand and shifted his gaze to the window. A slash of sunlight cut across the planes of his face like a saber. In that instant, Julia saw with diamond clarity the hard determination in his eyes. He had already started reining in his emotions in an attempt to pull away from her.

Pain spread from her stomach, settled in a tight band around her chest. He could try, she thought, setting her jaw. He could try.

Slowly, she slipped her fingers around his, brought his gaze back to hers. "I came here last night to talk about the case." The edge of the sheet that she'd pulled up around her when he walked in loosened, then slithered slowly down, baring her breasts. "We still need to talk, Sloan. I have to brief my boss this morning."

It was satisfying, very satisfying, to watch his gaze drop, to see him absorbing her with his eyes before they came back to hers.

"I'm listening," he said, then reached for his coffee.

Acknowledging the need—for the time being—to keep her own concentration and his on the case, Julia pulled the sheet up and anchored it beneath her arms.

"Vanessa made entries in her appointment book about spending time with someone who had the initial *S*," she began. "Do you recall her ever mentioning a man with that initial?"

"Other than me?" Sloan asked, his mouth taking on a sardonic twist.

Julia watched him over the rim of her mug. "If I thought her entries referred to you, I wouldn't be here right now. And last night wouldn't have happened," she added quietly.

"Sorry." He tightened his hand around hers, stroked his

thumb across her knuckles. "It's good to know you believe I'm innocent."

"Like I said, it doesn't matter what I believe. I need proof. So, tell me about the men in Vanessa's life."

"I wish I could. She never talked to me about whom she dated."

"She just told other people she was seeing you."

"Vanessa didn't seem to let the truth get in her way."

Julia scowled. "I've gone over the guest list from the art museum, but haven't had a chance to question anyone. Someone on that list gave Vanessa a ride home that night. Before you and she argued, did you notice her talking to any one man at length?"

"No. She had a knack for working the room at any social function. By the end of the evening, she'd have all the men beaming at her and all the women glaring. It was a game she enjoyed."

"Did she know anyone there well enough who she could have asked to leave early and take her home?"

"Rick, but for whatever reasons she didn't approach him."

Julia's ears pricked. "Rick? He was at the museum?"

"Yes. I assumed his name was on the list."

She slowly set her mug on the nightstand. "It wasn't."

Sloan shrugged. "I remember him saying something the day of the fund-raiser about not receiving an invitation. Elizabeth called the museum and they sent one over by courier. They obviously didn't bother updating their list."

Julia pursed her lips. "So, you asked Rick if he gave Vanessa a ride home that night?"

Sloan drained his mug, set it aside. When he leaned away, his fingers slid from her hold. "I asked him about it after you questioned me." He moved his hand back toward hers, then stopped short. His fingers curled against the sheet; Julia saw a muscle flinch in his jaw.

When he rose and moved away, her heart stopped.

Shoulders rigid, Sloan walked to the window. There, he

pushed aside one edge of the curtain and directed his narrow-eyed attention toward the pool. "Rick said he looked for Vanessa after our disagreement, but he never saw her."

Julia took a deep, controlling breath. She had to keep her mind on the case, not the emotions whirling inside her. Not the silent, inner battle Sloan seemed to be waging.

"Did you see Rick after Vanessa left?"

Sloan turned slowly. She watched him process the question, turn it over behind those dark eyes. "No. According to Rick, he looked for me when he was ready to leave. He said he saw me talking to the museum director's wife, and he decided not to disturb us."

"*Did* you have a conversation with the museum director's wife, Sloan?"

He remained silent for a long moment. "Do you suspect Rick?"

"It's my job to suspect everyone. Did you talk to the director's wife?"

"Yes."

"When?"

He looked away, a frown tightening his brow.

"Talk to me, Sloan," she said softly. "I'm not asking you to do anything but tell me the facts."

"The museum was packed—I probably spoke to a hundred people that night." He lifted a hand, rubbed his fingers across his chin. "I can't even tell you if I talked to the director's wife before or after Vanessa left."

"Did anyone see you leave? Was anyone in the parking lot who can verify that Vanessa didn't leave with you?"

Sloan's mouth curved. "Just the mayor. We left at the same time, walked to the parking lot together."

The sudden, strident tone of a pager made Julia start. She blinked. "Yours?" she asked.

"I don't have mine with me." Sloan walked across the room, snagged her purse off the tufted footstool, then returned to the bed.

She grabbed the pager off the flap of her purse, checked

the display and grimaced. "My office," she mumbled, then reached for the phone on the nightstand. Seconds later, she had Sam Rogers on the line.

"Who paged me, Sam?"

"I did, sweetheart," the veteran detective said. "Where the hell are you?"

She glanced up at Sloan, who'd settled back on the bed and was studying her with dark, unfathomable eyes. "I'm in the middle of an interview," she said. "What's up?"

"Ryan wants to see you."

Julia's fingers tightened on the phone. "About what?"

"He didn't say."

"Right," she muttered. "I'll be there as soon as I finish this interview."

Sloan lifted a dark brow when she slammed the receiver onto its cradle. "Problem?"

"Probably. My lieutenant doesn't usually call me to his office just to chat about the weather." She shoved her hair behind her shoulders. "Dammit! I've got to get a handle on this case."

Eyes somber, Sloan reached out and took her hand. "You put your heart in your job, Jules. That's what makes you such a good cop."

"When you get handed a case, you have to give it all you've got."

"It's not just the job," he said quietly. "You put all you've got into everything you do."

She stiffened, sensing what was coming next.

"Two years ago, if I had told you I was sick, you would have done what you're doing now, only to a greater degree. You would have worn yourself out, forgotten to eat, sacrificed your job and your own health while you cared for me." He glanced away, and when he looked back a curtain seemed to have dropped over his eyes. "I couldn't let you do that then. I can't now."

Here it is, Julia thought. *He isn't even going to wait until he leaves town to turn his back on me.* The old hurt, the bitterness, came crashing in.

"You're not sick," she said, forcing her voice to remain calm.

"My numbers are good," he agreed quietly. "For now."

"Maybe forever."

"Maybe. Maybe not."

The absolute lack of emotion in his eyes started a slow, molten anger burning inside her. "I suppose you view your walking out of my life as a gift you need to bestow on me every so often," she shot back, and jerked her hand from his. "No more gifts, Sloan. I don't think I can stand another one."

"We can't be together, Julia. You know that."

She closed her eyes while pain washed over her. "What I know is that after all we've been through…even after last night, you're still only willing to share scraps of your life with me."

"That's all I have to give—"

"All you're *willing* to give." She shoved aside the sheet and rose. "I need to go home and get some dry clothes. You said I have a couple of swimsuits here, right? I can wear one to drive—"

"Julia—"

"I want to get dressed," she snapped.

Tiny lines etched their way from the corners of Sloan's mouth as he stood. He walked to the pine dresser at the far side of the room, slid open the top drawer and pulled out a black tank suit. Slowly, he pushed the drawer closed, then turned to face her. "My leaving is for the best."

"Right, you're *protecting* me." Naked, she fisted her hands on her hips and faced him. His frustrating coolness fueled her temper. "You think you might get sick again, and you don't want what happened to your mother to happen to me."

"What happened to her *won't* happen to you."

"Dammit, I'm not fragile." Shoulders stiff, she walked

across the room and snatched the suit from his grasp. "Not weak. I can handle both the good and the bad. I would have thought you'd have figured that out by now."

His eyes flicked over her face, then slid down her body, betraying nothing. "I don't think you're weak."

"Damn right I'm not." She pulled on the suit, the black maillot molding to her curves. "I can take whatever happens, and then some. So why don't you just tell me you fell out of love with me over the past two years? Why don't you admit that now that you've had me again, you want nothing more to do with me?"

His hands curled against his thighs. "Because that would be a lie."

"Oh, so you *do* love me?" She walked back to the bed, jerked up her purse. "And you're not planning on tossing me aside and taking off for another state?"

He stared at her, his face set in stone. "My leaving has nothing to do with tossing you aside."

"Right, you think you're being noble."

"A realist," he cut in, taking a step toward her. "I'm being a realist."

"You're being an ignorant, flaming...*jackass!*"

His hands shot out with such speed she had no time to react, could only utter a gasp when he jerked her against his rock-solid body.

"Listen to me, dammit!" Fingers digging into her arms like shafts of steel, he leaned over her, his eyes glittering. "My father survived his cancer the first time it hit. A few years passed, and the doctors declared him cured. But he wasn't. It was still inside him and it came back with a vengeance. That time it killed him. It killed my mother, too. She shriveled up and died, right before my eyes. That's not going to happen to you."

"I'm a cop," Julia said with ferocity. "Do you think cops have the greatest life expectancy in the world?"

"That has nothing to do with this."

"It has *everything* to do with it," she countered, her

voice shaking. "Each day I walk out the door, I can't guarantee I'll come back in. But knowing that doesn't stop me from wanting to share my life—be it long or short—with you. I'm willing to take a chance, Sloan. I'm willing to try to beat the odds. I see now that you don't care enough about me to even try."

He uttered a ragged curse. "Why the hell won't you listen to reason?"

"Because I haven't heard any," she shot back, knowing with heartbreaking clarity there was no way to get through the wall he'd erected between them. "All I've heard are excuses," she continued, fisting her hands against his bare chest. "Earlier, before you came in, I fooled myself into thinking that what we shared last night had changed things. I thought somehow I could convince you to stay. I was wrong. It's obvious now all we had was a one-night stand with great sex—"

"It was a hell of a lot more than that!" His eyes darkened with the fury she heard in his voice.

"For me it was, because I'm still in love with you. It galls me, knowing that, but it's true. And because it's true, I want to spend my life with you...." Julia's voice faltered as razor-sharp pain surged through her. "But you won't let that happen because of some perverse idea that you have to protect me. I don't need your protection, Sloan. I don't want it."

His hand came up, gripping her jaw. "I can't offer you a future when I don't have one to offer."

"You don't know that. You don't know what will happen."

"I know what *might* happen." He ran a thumb over her lower lip. "What could very easily happen."

"Fine." She jerked from his hold, the need to get away from him so fierce it nearly strangled her. "You've made your decision. I'll be damned if I stand here and offer you what you don't want to take."

"God, Jules—" His voice broke and he dragged in a ragged breath. "Do you think this is easy for me?"

"Sorry, but I don't give a damn how you're feeling right now."

He reached for her, but she lurched back, evading his hands. "I don't want you to touch me ever again. I'm not weak, Sloan, but I'm not made of steel, either."

She took another step back, holding on to the slippery edge of control. "I'll contact your lawyer if I have questions regarding the case. Don't leave town until you're officially cleared. I'll send word when that happens."

Mouth tight, eyes bleak, Sloan took a step toward her, but made no move to touch her. "How can I make you understand?"

"I do understand," she rasped. "You've chosen to let *'what-ifs'* rule your life. I hope that makes you happy, because in the end that's all you'll have. A bunch of hollow, meaningless *'what-ifs.'*"

She pulled open the door, then shut it behind her with heart-wrenching finality.

An hour later, freshly showered and dressed in a starched shirt and stovepipe, suspendered trousers, Julia walked into the Homicide detail.

"Boss wants to see you." The message came from the division secretary, who had to raise her voice to be heard over the busy din of ringing telephones and conversation.

Lieutenant Ryan's desk was its usual clean sweep of wood. All that lay on top was an open file folder, the reports inside in perfect alignment. The dust-free credenza displayed framed photographs of his grinning teenage daughter and his wife, A.J., who ran the department's Crime Analysis unit. Sitting amid the calm orderliness, Lieutenant Michael Ryan locked his ice-blue stare on Julia as she lowered onto the edge of the chair he'd waved her into.

"According to your report, the night before Vanessa

West died she threatened to ruin Sloan Remington and his company. He was well aware that Miss West had the ability to do just that.''

"Correct," Julia said.

"The following morning he drove into the parking garage minutes after her arrival. Not too long after that, someone pumped a .22 slug into her back. Remington is an excellent marksman. He could have easily made an accurate hit with a .22.''

"He could have." Julia curled her hands in her lap. The evidence against Sloan was all circumstantial, but hearing it outlined in stark detail started her stomach churning.

"The man has no alibi for the time of the murder," Ryan said as he closed the file folder, then crossed his forearms. "He had the means to kill her, the opportunity and ample motive. Why haven't you charged him?''

"We have no witnesses to the crime," Julia said, forcing an evenness into her voice. "We can't tie Remington to the murder weapon. There's no physical evidence that links him to the scene." She waited a beat before adding, "He didn't kill Vanessa West.''

Ryan arched a dark brow. "You sound sure of yourself.''

"I am.''

"Can you prove it?''

"Not…yet.''

"Who killed her?''

"I don't know.''

"You're one of my best investigators, Cruze." Ryan leaned forward, his fingertips tapping against his desktop. "That's why I'm giving you twenty-four hours to eliminate Sloan Remington as a suspect. If you don't, book him.''

"Yes, sir.''

Julia walked back to her desk on weak legs, dropped into her chair and went to work.

Late that afternoon, Julia parked in a visitor's space near the entrance to Remington Aerospace's corporate office.

She walked through the sluggish heat, catching her breath at the sudden sweep of cool air that hit her when she shoved through the revolving door. The vast, wood-and-etched-glass lobby seemed to stretch forever. Hiking the straps of her leather tote higher on her shoulder, she walked along a marble bank of glossy-leafed plants and azaleas heavy with white blooms. She paused at the curved receptionist's desk that rose from dove-gray marble tiles.

"Sergeant Cruze to see Rick Fox." As she spoke, she flashed her badge at the woman in a sleek black suit. On the desk, a purse and set of car keys sat beside a computer's darkened monitor.

"Do you have an appointment, Sergeant?" the woman asked in a soothing, polite voice.

"No."

She nodded, giving a discreet glance at the clock on her desk that had just clicked on 4:59. "I'll see if Mr. Fox is in." She swiveled and punched a button on her phone. A moment later she replaced the receiver. "Please take the elevator to the top floor. Mr. Fox will meet you."

"Thanks." Reclipping the badge to her waistband, Julia headed for the far side of the lobby. There, she punched a button, then stepped into the cool confines of an elevator. Classical music drifted on the air; a small chandelier tinkled overhead as the cab began its smooth ascent.

Julia closed her eyes, grateful for a few moments of calm. After leaving Lieutenant Ryan's office, she had spent hours at her desk reviewing the case, going over evidence, looking for something—anything—that would shift the momentum of the investigation away from Sloan.

She'd found nothing.

The only pieces of evidence that had escaped her reexamination were the videotapes from the security cameras at the entrances to the parking garage and the building. Cursing that they'd been coded for playback only on the company's specialized equipment, she'd stuffed the cassettes into her leather tote and headed across town.

She raised a hand to massage her temple and leaned against the elevator's paneled wall. Since the moment she'd left Sloan standing in his guest house, she had not allowed herself to think about what had happened between them. Now she did.

She hadn't thought there was pain worse than that which she'd experienced two years ago when he told her he didn't love her, couldn't marry her. She'd been wrong. This morning, something inside her had shattered, and she knew she would never be whole again.

A soft chime sounded, announcing the elevator's arrival at the top floor. The doors parted. Rick Fox, dressed in a neat black blazer and gray slacks, met her when she stepped into the carpeted hallway.

"Julia, this is a surprise." Louisiana sounded in his warm greeting. "What can I do for you?"

"I brought the surveillance tapes we confiscated from your cameras the day of the homicide. I need to review them."

Rick's lips pulled back in a smile. "Fine."

From the corner of her eye, Julia caught him glancing at his watch as they walked the length of the paneled corridor.

"Is this a bad time?"

"I'm meeting someone for drinks in a little while."

"The bank vice president?" she ventured. They turned a corner and crossed the dim reception area where the secretary's desk sat empty.

Rick paused at his office door, a look of genuine confusion in his eyes. "Bank…?"

"At the funeral home you mentioned you were dating a bank vice president."

He flashed a quick grin. "Give me a break. That was a couple of days ago. I've moved on."

His office was large and roomy, the furniture leather and masculine. Julia glanced at the panel of monitors built into one wall. Their screens displayed separate, real-time images fed from security cameras located inside and outside the building. One screen showed a slow, sweeping panorama of the parking lot, where her detective cruiser sat near the front entrance. Another monitor displayed the main lobby and the now-vacant reception desk. Still another flashed the image of the basement, where massive pieces of machinery squatted amid yards of pipe.

"You must know everything that goes on around here." Julia crossed her arms and watched two men dressed in regulation corporate suits and ties chat as they walked along a corridor.

"That's my job."

Turning, she moved to a floor-to-ceiling bookshelf that displayed uniform hats from various law enforcement agencies. She touched an index finger to the rim of a bobby's helmet. "I didn't get a chance to look at these the day of the homicide when I was up here. You've added to your collection over the past two years."

"Yeah. You know, I still haven't managed to get one from OCPD. Think you can help me out?"

"Sure. I've got an extra uniform hat in my closet."

She watched him put the flame of his gold lighter against the end of a cigarette. A glance at the polished, dark-wood desk revealed a brass ashtray heaped with stubbed-out butts.

Rick pulled off his blazer and draped it across the back of his leather desk chair. Julia's eyes narrowed. "Do me a favor."

"What's that?"

"Stow your Glock in your desk while we talk."

"It's legal, Julia. I've got a permit to carry."

"I know." She shrugged. "No offense, but armed civilians make me nervous."

His gaze dropped to the Smith & Wesson holstered beside the badge on the waistband of her slacks. "I could say the same thing about cops." He smiled. "But since I used to be one, I won't."

With an air of casualness, he pulled the holstered automatic off his belt and placed it in a desk drawer. "Now what?"

"We watch the tapes."

"I'll cue them up from our network system," he said as he closed the thin blinds against the late-afternoon glare.

"No." Julia slid the tape cartridges out of her tote. "I want to view the copies we confiscated the day of the homicide."

He raised a brow. "Like you said, they're copies. The quality of the tape in our system makes for better viewing."

Julia held up the cassettes. "These are what we booked into evidence. They may get shown in court someday. These are the tapes I need to watch."

She almost missed the slight jerk of the muscle at the corner of his mouth. "Whatever you say."

He took the cassettes, walked to the wall of monitors, where a built-in shelf held a television, VCR and high-tech stereo. "Are you close to solving Vanessa's murder?" he asked while pushing buttons on the VCR.

"Maybe."

She reached into her tote, pulled out the small tape recorder she'd checked out of Supply before leaving the station. The quick image of her own recorder sinking into the steamy water of Sloan's hot tub shot through her brain. Squaring her shoulders, she forced away the thought. She was conducting an interview, she silently reprimanded herself. She had to keep her mind focused. Clicking on the recorder, she placed it on the edge of the desk.

"So I don't have to take notes," she explained when Rick glanced over his shoulder.

Expelling a stream of cigarette smoke, he slid the tape into the VCR. "Catch," he said, then tossed her a remote control. "Make yourself comfortable." He gestured in the direction of a pair of visitors' chairs.

"I think better on my feet."

"Suit yourself." He eased back in his chair, propped his

tasseled loafers up on the desk. "Hit the Play button when you're ready."

"One question before we start. That night at the art museum, did you witness the argument between Sloan and Vanessa?"

"No."

"Did you take Vanessa home?"

"That's two questions."

"Did you?"

He met her gaze with unwavering blue eyes. "Come on, Julia, I was a cop long enough to know when someone's fishing. The day Vanessa died, I had to call our personnel office to get her address. I wouldn't have needed to do that if I'd have known where she lived."

"True."

Julia clicked on the security tape, then watched in silence as the entrance gate to the parking garage appeared. The lower right corner of the screen showed the date and time of the recording. She held down the Fast Forward button until a white car appeared in the dusky dawn light.

"That's Zack Sheraton," Rick said, watching a darkly tanned man lean from the car's open window and swipe a laminated ID card through the security reader. Seconds later, the gate slid open.

"He opens the gym every morning, right?"

"Right," Rick confirmed.

Sheraton was one of the *S's* on Julia's list who could have been Vanessa's mystery lover. But the man's presence in the gym at the time of the murder had been verified by several witnesses.

"Zack usually gets here around 5 a.m.," Rick added.

"Early bird," Julia commented. "As I recall, you scanned your card at six that morning."

"Something like that."

She leaned a hip against the desk and again hit the Fast Forward button. "This is your car," she said when Rick's blue Lincoln drove into view.

"Six-oh-nine," he said, reading the time off the screen. "That means you probably entered the building about 6:13."

"Six-fourteen to be exact. I noted the time when you and I first viewed the video off the camera at the door."

He glanced over at the wall of monitors. "You planning on seeing Sloan while you're here?"

Julia followed his gaze. "No, why?"

"He's leaving the building."

Julia found Sloan's image on one of the screens, watched as he stepped onto an elevator, briefcase in hand. Seconds later, the doors slid closed on his image.

She set her jaw, ignoring the fist that had tightened around her heart.

Rick swung his feet off the desk. "It's after five," he said, stubbing out his cigarette in the overflowing ashtray. "Most everyone's out of the building by now. I've put in a full day and I expect you have, too."

He swiveled his chair, then opened a door on the polished credenza behind the desk and pulled out a sterling silver flask. He gave Julia a conspiratorial wink across his shoulder. "Care to join me in a Scotch?"

Her finger froze over the remote's Play button while her mind flashed to the bottle of cheap Scotch she and Halliday had found in Vanessa's apartment. Her inner radar went on alert.

"Thanks. It's been a hell of a week."

"Amen to that," Rick said, snaring glasses out of the credenza.

"Okay," Julia began, scanning through the tape until Vanessa's black Jaguar appeared. "You can see the cup of carrot juice sitting on the dash. It must have spilled when she drove down the ramp."

Saying nothing, Rick twisted off the lid of the flask.

The instant Vanessa leaned out the Jag's window to scan her card, Julia froze the image. Rays of early-morning sun highlighted Vanessa's flawless porcelain skin, transformed the hair that cascaded around her shoulders into an ocean of gold. A hardness shone in the almond-shaped blue eyes that stared at the card reader.

"Here's your Scotch," Rick said, offering a glass of gold liquid.

"Thanks." Julia leaned and accepted the glass.

He tossed back his drink, poured himself another, then reached for the pack of cigarettes in his shirt pocket.

Slowly, she raised the glass to her lips and took a deep breath. The Scotch's unrefined aroma assaulted her senses. *Rotgut,* Halliday had called it that day in Vanessa's apartment.

She closed her eyes for the length of a heartbeat. Just because Vanessa had a bottle of the same cheap Scotch didn't prove a connection between her and Rick. Still, it implied one.

Every nerve in Julia's body went on alert. Now magnified in her brain were Rick's attempts to have her view the tapes off the network system, instead of those confiscated into evidence less than an hour after the homicide. Had he somehow altered the network tape to show himself entering the building much earlier than he actually had?

She looked back at Rick, found him examining her with guarded eyes. His hand trembled slightly as he raised his cigarette to his lips. A single bead of sweat tracked slowly down his right temple.

Dammit, Halliday, I need you, she thought as a gut-level instinct told her to tread carefully. Hundreds of hours of training clicked in as Julia evaluated her options. She was essentially alone in the vast building with Rick, who, less than a week ago, had possibly shot a woman to death. And he had a 9 mm Glock in a drawer inches from his fingertips.

With pretended casualness, Julia set her untouched drink on the edge of the desk. When she got to her cruiser, she would radio for backup. If Rick left before reinforcements arrived, she'd tail him. A patrol unit could pick him up, transport him to the station, where she'd conduct an intense interrogation on her own turf.

Aiming the remote at Vanessa's frozen screen image, Julia stabbed the Off button. "Look, I just remembered I have an appointment across town," she said, and placed the remote beside her glass.

Rick shifted in his chair, crossed his ankle over his knee and rested his hand on the cuff of his slacks. "Is that so?"

Tension twisted her insides into a cold knot. She kept her eyes on his hands, feeling the surge of adrenaline that had her ready to draw the automatic holstered at her waist if he made a move for the desk drawer.

He remained motionless, watching her steadily, one hand resting on the ankle he'd crossed over one knee.

"I'll check back with you about watching the rest of the tape at another time," she added.

In one fluid movement, he was out of his chair, swinging his arm her way. "There won't be another time."

Instinct kicked in the second after Julia caught a glimpse of blue steel. Her fingers froze on her weapon as she stared into the dark barrel of the revolver he'd pulled from an ankle holster.

A *Walther,* she thought. Twenty-two. The same caliber weapon that killed Vanessa.

Her pulse thudded hard and thick at the base of her throat. "Rick, you don't want to do this," she said, forcing a calmness into her voice.

"What I don't want to do is go to jail." He took a step toward her, keeping the gun pointed at her heart. "Understand something, Julia. I don't want to shoot you. But if you don't do what I say, I will."

Chapter 12

"Take your weapon out, slow and easy, and lay it on the floor," Rick ordered.

Pushing away the ice-edged fear clawing at her brain, Julia kept her eyes fastened on the Walther's dull black barrel. Rick was too far away to make a lunge for the gun, yet close enough for the .22 automatic to blow a serious hole in her. She unholstered the Smith and laid it at her feet.

"Kick it over here." He waited until she did so, then cocked his head toward one of the chairs at the front of the desk. "Sit."

Heart thudding, she stayed where she was, the smell of fresh gun oil cloying in her lungs. She was the only barrier between him and the door. Between him and freedom. "Rick, you need to put the gun down and stay here so we can talk. We need to work this out."

"I don't think so."

"Things will only get worse if you run."

"Jail will be worse. I was a cop, Julia. Cops who go to

prison don't always walk out alive.'' He lowered the gun's barrel until it pointed at her leg. ''If I have to tell you to move again, I'll kneecap you. A .22 slug can maim you for life. I don't want to do it, but I will. Don't force me.''

Back as stiff as cardboard, she walked to the chair and lowered onto the edge of the seat. Adrenaline surged through her veins; she took deep breaths to hold back the sick feeling that rose from the pit of her stomach.

His blue eyes flicked to the panel of security monitors. ''We'll wait until the stragglers clear out, then you and I are taking a ride.''

''A ride?'' The only ride she intended to take with Rick Fox was one with him subdued and cuffed in the back of her cruiser.

''I need time to get my things and clear out. If I leave you here, the cleaning crew will find you in a couple of hours. You'll be comfortable enough cuffed and gagged at my place. When I'm away free and clear, I'll send word where you are. Your pals in uniform will come get you.''

Julia kept her eyes on the automatic while her thoughts skittered to her still-running recorder on the edge of the desk. ''Since we aren't leaving right away, do you mind clearing up some things for me?''

Rick shrugged. ''You mean you don't have it all figured out yet?''

''I'd just like you to verify some things.''

One-handed, he shook a cigarette out of the pack and lit it. ''Why not?'' He blew out a stream of acrid gray smoke, then tossed his gold lighter back onto the desk.

''You took Vanessa home from the museum,'' Julia hazarded. ''What happened when you got to her apartment?''

Outwardly, Rick's face remained impassive, his bearing calm. An act, Julia knew. She could smell the sourness of his sweat, see the uneven rise and fall of his chest beneath his starched shirt and paisley tie.

''You know, Julia,'' he began as he leaned and plucked the recorder off the edge of the desk. ''I don't mind us having a little one-on-one discussion. After all, I'm not planning on hanging around to face repercussions.'' He held up the recorder in his thick, square hand, then stabbed the Off button with his thumb. ''But I prefer to keep things between us. I'm sure you understand.''

''Completely,'' she said between her teeth.

''Vanessa was furious after her fight with Sloan.'' He slid the recorder into the pocket of his slacks. ''All the champagne she'd downed didn't help her mood. When she stormed out of the museum, I had one hell of a time coaxing her into my car.''

He took a drag off the cigarette, exhaled slowly. Smoke hung in a silent curl between them.

''All the way to her apartment Vanessa ranted and raved about how she'd get even with Sloan,'' Rick continued. ''When we pulled up at her building, I tried to get her to let me go upstairs. I figured I could talk some sense into her.'' The lines at the edges of his eyes deepened. ''She wouldn't let me come up.''

''Too bad,'' Julia said evenly. ''She could have offered you a glass of your favorite Scotch.''

He flicked a look at the silver flask on the desk as his mouth took on a sardonic curve. ''Funny, it's always the little things that trip people up.''

While her mind worked, Julia sat motionless, her body strung tight with tension. ''You couldn't get Vanessa to listen to you that night,'' she stated. ''I take it you waited for her in the parking garage the following morning.''

''Hell, we'd been sleeping together for months. I had the crazy idea I could make her see some reason. That's all I intended to do. Just talk.''

''Let me guess—she wasn't in the mood for conversation.''

''She was even more furious, if that was possible. To top things off, she'd spilled the damn carrot juice all over that red suit of hers and she was cussing a storm about that.'' Rick's free hand clenched, then unclenched. ''I tried to get her to calm down, to listen to me. I offered to help her patch things up with Sloan.''

As he spoke, Julia cast a look past his arm to the wall of monitors. Her chest tightened when she saw Sloan reenter the building through the revolving door and stride into the nearly deserted lobby. God, what if he'd spotted her cruiser in the parking lot and come back inside to find her?

Her breathing quickened, became a painful thumping in her ears. How desperate was Rick? What would he do if Sloan walked through the door?

With a dry mouth and galloping pulse, she fought to focus her thoughts. She had to get Rick to let his guard down, had to find an opening.

"What did Vanessa say when you offered to help mediate things between her and Sloan?"

"She told me to go to hell." His eyes narrowed with the memory. "She said she'd gotten her hands on my personnel file, and if I didn't stay out of her way, she'd tell Sloan about the black cloud hanging over my past."

"Black cloud?"

He stared at Julia for a long, considering moment. "What the hell, it'll come out after this," he said, lifting a shoulder. "She found out I quit the New Orleans PD to escape an indictment."

Julia blinked. "That was in your file?"

"Hell no. On the surface, there's nothing there to cause me trouble—I'd made sure of that. But Vanessa never accepted things at face value. She took my background information and started digging." He expelled a bitter laugh. "I can't even say it surprised me. Vanessa turned everything to her own advantage. She disregarded the rules and played the game her way." He raised his hand, let it drop. "I knew that about her from the start, but I didn't care. To me, that only made her more exciting. Only made me want her more. Dammit, Julia, she was like a drug. I was always looking for ways to boost the dose."

"What did the indictment charge?"

"Money skimming." He shrugged. "From the first day I worked the street, I saw cops skimming cash at crime scenes. You know how it is, Julia. You bust into some coke house and there's hundreds of thousands of dollars lying in plain sight. By the time the money gets booked into the property room, there's a hell of a lot less. I didn't do anything that half the cops on the department weren't doing. But I got a tight-assed rookie assigned to ride with me, and Mr. Law and Order turned me in."

The fact that Rick had dumped on his badge sent disgust creeping through Julia's fear. "Why weren't you indicted?"

"The department had just put one scandal to rest. A few people in high places figured their careers couldn't withstand another. I got offered a deal—quit and the indictment would disappear."

"Sloan knows nothing about this?"

"No. I told him I got a medical disability because of a bad back."

"Why wouldn't he believe you?" Julia asked evenly. "After all, you're his best friend. He *trusts* you."

Rick's eyes narrowed. "I couldn't tell him the truth. How long do you think a known thief would last as head of security for a national corporation? Friendship is one thing, business another. Sloan would have had to let me go. And I'd be lucky to get a job guarding a parking lot somewhere." His jaw tightened. "I'd have lost everything, thanks to Vanessa."

His eyes hardened as if remembering that morning in the garage. "I asked her how she got my personnel file. She gave me this cool look and said that Smithson had given her access to all the personnel files. Then she added that she'd been sleeping with him the whole time she'd been seeing me." Rick's voice shook. "I had no idea, no idea...." His eyes narrowed. "Then she turned her back on me. She just turned her back...."

He took a deep breath, blew it out. "I grabbed her. She shoved me back and started to walk away. Suddenly I had the gun from my ankle holster in my hand...." His gaze lowered. "*This* gun. I told her to stop. She looked across her shoulder, saw the gun, then laughed. She just laughed.... It was like something inside me snapped and I lost control. Not that it matters, but I don't remember squeezing the trigger."

Julia stared down the same lethal gun barrel as Vanessa had. Perspiration pooled at the small of her back. She took a deep breath. "What happened after that?"

"I panicked. If I'd been thinking straight, I wouldn't have entered the building and gotten myself on tape. But I heard a car and panicked. All I could think about was getting the hell out of there before someone saw me."

Julia's gaze darted past Rick to the monitors. Sloan was still in the lobby, standing now behind the reception desk. He bent his dark head over the computer and tapped keys. She knew the standard procedure for visitors to the building was for the receptionist to log each person's name and the staff member they had business with into the computer. Julia's thoughts flashed back to the moment she'd entered the lobby. The clock had just clicked to 4:59. The receptionist had already shut off the terminal. Her name hadn't gone into the system.

She cut her eyes back to Rick. "It was Sloan's car you heard entering the garage after you shot Vanessa." It took all she had to keep her voice low and calm.

"I know that now. I didn't then." Rick frowned. "I came up here, not sure what the hell to do. It wasn't long until one of my men called to tell me Smithson had found Vanessa dead in the garage and I needed to get down there fast."

Julia nodded, everything coming together now. "Vanessa had just thrown her affair with the personnel director in your face. Now he'd come along and found her body. I take it you planted the service pin near her car when you went back downstairs.''

Rick arched a brow and gave her a slight nod. ''Very good, Sergeant.'' His chest heaved with his labored breathing, but his gun hand remained stable.

''Where did you get the pin?''

''Someone found it on the floor in an elevator and handed it to me while I was in a meeting. I tossed the pin in my desk drawer and forgot it.'' He shrugged. ''By the time I got the call about Vanessa, my brain had started working again. I thought about our esteemed personnel director.'' Derision thickened Rick's voice. ''Thought about him sleeping with Vanessa, giving her access to my file....''

''So you took the pin out of your drawer,'' Julia prompted.

''I figured if I left it by the body, it would shift things Smithson's way.''

''But you still had a problem. You were on tape entering the building around seven o'clock, right after the homicide.''

''A big problem,'' he agreed. ''To doctor the tape, I had to get into our video room off the security area in the basement, but I couldn't. There were too many cops around, too much going on. I couldn't get in there until after you and your partner had come upstairs to Sloan's office.''

''And after I finished interviewing the staff, I came in here and you played me the tapes off the network. By then they showed you entering the building at 6:13, a few minutes after you drove into the garage.''

''Right.'' His eyes glinted dully. Sweat beaded his hairline. ''My problem was that the uniforms who first arrived had already confiscated cassettes of the original tapes. Since they're encrypted with our security code, I knew you couldn't view them on your own equipment.'' The gun made a small arc as he spoke. ''I just hoped to hell that the next time you showed up to watch the tapes, you wouldn't bring the cassettes with you. If you hadn't, I would have offered to run you sharper copies off the network system and told you to toss the ones you already had.''

"But that's not what happened," she said slowly.

"Unfortunately for both of us, you brought the cassettes." Color flared in his cheeks as he stared down at the Walther. "And that brings us back to the problem."

"You didn't plan to kill Vanessa," Julia said, keeping her voice even. Out of the corner of her eye she watched the surveillance camera track Sloan across the lobby to the bank of elevators. Every fiber in her body told her he was coming upstairs to look for her.

She curled her sweat-slicked palms in her lap. She had visions of Sloan walking through the door behind her, of Rick whipping around and squeezing off a few rounds. Of Sloan crumpling in a bloody heap on the floor. Her heart pounded hard enough to rock her body.

"You didn't mean to kill her," she repeated. "The murder wasn't premeditated. That's to your advantage, Rick. I give you my word that I'll talk to the D.A. for you—"

"Then maybe I'll get forty years instead of life," he countered as he pulled the Glock out of his desk drawer and shoved the holster onto his belt. "Thanks for the offer, but no thanks. A beach house in a country that has no extradition treaty with the U.S. sounds a hell of a lot better than a cell. Don't you agree?"

A sick feeling flooded through Julia. She fought to keep her expression neutral. Sloan was on his way. She would soon run out of time. She had to distract Rick, had to put him off guard so she could go for the gun—*guns* she corrected, her eyes dropping to the Glock now holstered at his waist.

"Clear something up for me," she said, hoping the desperation seeping through her didn't sound in her voice. "Vanessa made numerous notes in her appointment book about seeing someone with the initial *S*."

Rick gave her a smile brimming with irony. "Think

about it, Julia. My last name's Fox. Vanessa used to point out that foxes were sly. *Sly.* That's what she called me…in bed.''

Using his index finger, Rick hooked his black blazer off his chair. "Enough talk.'' He shrugged the blazer on one arm at a time, shifting the Walther in his hands. "It's time we get out of here.''

He walked to the chair beside hers, dug her handcuffs and keys from her leather tote. "Lock one cuff on your right wrist,'' he said, then tossed the handcuffs into her lap.

Julia stared down at the shiny metal bracelets linked by a short, thick chain.

"Do it." His voice lashed out.

She picked up the cuffs, circled her right wrist with cool, heavy steel. Metal crunched against metal as the mechanism locked into place.

"I know what you're thinking, Julia.''

Her gaze rose slowly, locked with his. "Do you?''

"Yes. You think you can get the drop on me. You can't.'' His eyes flattened. "Try, and I'll shoot you. I don't want to, but I assure you, I will.''

Her stomach began to churn as a different monitor displayed Sloan stepping off the elevator, only about fifty yards from where she sat.

"I get the message,'' she said.

Rick took a step forward, his gun arm rigid and steady. "I'm going to lock the other cuff around my left wrist. In a few minutes I'll flip a switch, causing a temporary outage of the security camera system. That way there won't be a record of us leaving together. Once that's done, you and I will walk out of here holding hands, so the cuffs won't show. If we run into anyone on our way to the garage, you'll lower your head so they can't see your face. And you'll keep quiet. Do you understand?''

"Yes.''

She knew the minute they walked out the door they would run into Sloan. There was no way he'd miss seeing the handcuffs, no way he'd believe whatever excuse Rick conjured for them. No way Sloan would just step aside and watch them walk away hand-in-hand without questioning what was going on.

Rick looked coldly dangerous now with his mouth set in a hard line and desperation glinting in his eyes. Sweat-streaked tendrils of blond hair plastered his forehead. His index finger stroked the trigger. Julia fully believed his threat that he'd shoot her. He had already killed—had little to lose. If cornered, he might shoot Sloan...and any other innocent civilian who tried to block his escape.

She stared into the automatic's single, black eye and knew she had to act now.

"Stand up," Rick commanded. "And remember what I said."

Julia's nerves shimmered. She pulled in a deep, steadying breath, then slid her fingers into the circle of the empty cuff. The arched metal looped over her hand, brass knuckle–style.

Cursing violently, Rick punched the Walther forward, the grips dark against his white knuckles. "I said stand up!"

Arm stiff, Julia bolted off the chair, using the force of her body to drive the cuff's metal curve into the underside of his nose.

Cartilage crunched. Blood spurted across the front of her blouse. Rick howled and swung.

The back of his hand connected with her cheek with stunning force. She saw a flash of stars as she turned instinctively with the blow, landing heavily against the back of the chair. The rusty taste of blood filled her mouth.

He lunged for her. She swiveled, ramming her elbow into his sternum, then grabbed for the Walther while the momentum of her body shoved him backward.

His free hand flailed out, catching the loose cuff that dangled from her arm. He was a big man; he had her on height and weight, and when he stumbled off balance, he dragged her across one corner of the desk. A brass lamp clattered to the floor. The ashtray flew across the polished surface, spreading cigarette butts and a gray cloud of ashes in its wake.

He regained his balance with catlike fluidity. His meaty fist tightened on the handcuff. He yanked her around to face him, nearly jerking her arm out of the socket.

Blood from his nose slicked her fingers, making it impossible to get a firm grip on the Walther, which seemed fused to his hand. Sucking in a breath, Julia clamped onto the wrist of his gun hand and drove her knee toward his groin.

At the last second, he twisted, deflecting the full force of the potentially debilitating blow.

Heart pumping against her ribs, she stiffened her fingers then went for his eyes.

Sloan's frown deepened as he walked briskly along the thick-carpeted corridor with spacious executive offices opening to either side. He turned a corner, his determined stride taking him down the brightly lit hallway that led to Rick's office.

He'd been on his way to find Julia, when he'd driven out of the garage and spotted her police cruiser parked near the front door. The receptionist had not logged her presence into the computer, but her car was here, and Sloan had no intention of leaving the building until he talked to her. Logic told him to start looking for her in Rick's office. If he didn't find her there, he had a good chance of spotting her on a security monitor.

Sloan's hands balled, while frustration rose inside him like floodwaters. Since the moment she walked out of the guest house that morning, he'd thought of nothing but her. Of the defiance that glittered in her dark eyes and whipped color into her face when she'd stood before him naked, her hair a beautiful mess from their night of lovemaking. Of the passion and energy that swirled around her. Of the soft curves and temptation. Of the way he'd felt himself going completely and quietly unglued by the raw hurt that had settled in her eyes.

Hurt he had put there. *Had* to put there.

He'd done the right thing. The *best* thing. At least that was what he'd told himself throughout the day while he sat at his desk, staring at an endless stream of paperwork, but seeing only Julia. Finally, he'd shoved the unread piles of documents and spreadsheets aside and reached for the phone. The message he'd left for her at her office had gone unreturned. As had the one on her home answering machine. Finally, his ability to wait had died out like an oxygen-deprived fire and he'd left his office, intent on tracking her down.

He had to see her. Had to talk to her; had to find some way to bring a sense of peace to their parting.

Dammit, how could she think he wanted to leave her? Didn't she know that just the thought of walking away again twisted his gut into hot, agonizing knots? Didn't she know that he still loved her—had always loved her—beyond all reason?

Hell, no, because you didn't bother telling her.

He clenched his jaw. He had thought he'd experienced the worst life had to dish out when he walked away from her two years ago. But the knowledge he was ill and facing surgery had fueled his determination to leave. Now doubt wavered inside him. Temptation ate at him to let his clawing need for a life with her override every logic-based decision he'd made.

His eyes narrowed as he looked back through time, picturing his mother's slow deterioration while she sat beside his father's hospital bed for unending days that transformed into weeks...then months. She'd died slowly on the inside, along with his father.

For Sloan, the memory was like a slash of a scalpel to his senses—but it served its purpose. It confirmed how right his decision to leave Julia had been, how right it still was.

He continued down the silent, paneled corridor. Dammit,

he had to talk to her, had to make her understand why he couldn't take a chance with her life. He had no idea how the hell to do that, but he'd worry about using the right words after he found her. Right now, he was more concerned about where she was.

Turning a corner, he stepped into the dim reception area outside Rick's office. He was just about to sidestep a grouping of padded chairs, when a crash, followed by a hard thud, brought his chin up. Less than a heartbeat later, a gunshot blasted through the air.

The force of the bullet slammed Julia back against Rick's desk. Instant, clenching pain seared her chest. Her lungs heaved once, then her legs crumbled beneath her and she went down hard on her back.

Eyes blazing with desperate fury, Rick stood over her, the Walther still aimed at her chest. "You made me do it," he yelled. "Dammit, you grabbed the gun—"

A vicious shout registered in Julia's brain a half second before Sloan sailed across her, catching Rick in a flying tackle. Their bodies crashed backward together, somewhere out of her range of vision.

Dazed, she lifted her right hand to her chest, wincing when the swinging end of the handcuff hit her jaw. She stared at her blood-smeared fingers. She knew she was hit, but wasn't sure where, wasn't sure if the blood belonged to Rick or her.

Seconds later the pain intensified, burning and tearing at her lungs. She knew then that the blood was hers, felt her blouse going damp with it.

A quick series of grunted curses filled the air; glass shattered somewhere around her. Sloan shouted, but she couldn't make out the words.

Her vision swam; the floor tilted crazily beneath her, touching off nausea. She retched. There was nothing in her stomach to come up. The part of her brain that shock had yet to reach told her to get up, subdue her suspect, then call for backup.

All she could do was lie on her back, drawing in torturous breaths with great spaces between them.

Minutes—or hours—passed. Suddenly Sloan's face, bloody and bruised, swam over her in wavy distortion, like a desert mirage.

"Jules? Sweet Jesus."

"Almost…had…him."

Sloan tore open her blouse. She caught the dark flicker of fear in his eyes as he ripped off his elegant silk tie and crumpled it against the place on her chest where fire burned. The pressure sent a dim, raspy moan up her throat.

"I'm sorry, baby. I have to stop the bleeding. You're going to be all right."

"Get…Rick?"

Sloan spared a glance across his shoulder. "He's out cold."

"Has…guns. Two…"

"They're in my pocket."

"Call…in."

The pain intensified, twisting her shoulder muscles into breath-stealing spasms. "Killed…Vanessa," she finally managed.

"I called. The police are coming. An ambulance is coming."

"Sloan…"

"Don't try to talk. Lie still."

A sweeping wave of darkness closed in. Her eyelids took on added weight and fluttered shut.

"Look at me, Jules." Even through the racking pain she heard the trembling in Sloan's voice as his fingertips patted her cheek. "Stay with me, baby. Try to stay awake."

She could feel herself shivering on the inside. Not from pain, but an insidious, rawboned cold that crept through her bones, making them feel as if they might snap from brittleness. Her chest was on fire, yet her body might as well be floating in ice water.

"Cold…"

Keeping pressure against her wound, Sloan worked his way out of his suit coat and spread it across her. "They'll have blankets in the ambulance. You're going to be okay. Do you hear me? You have to be okay."

Her head rolled weakly to one side.

"You've got to hold on." He tore off his vest, wadded it in his hand and compressed it against her chest. "Hold on. You can't—" His voice broke. "I love you. God, I love you, Jules. You've got to hold on."

As he spoke, his voice faded, came back, faded again, until all she heard was a persistent, gray hum. She felt herself slipping toward darkness. She tried in vain to move her arms, to raise her hands so she could hold on to him, but she was incapable now of even the tiniest movement. Fingers of fear crept through the shock when she realized she couldn't keep herself from falling into the inky pit.

"Don't…leave…me."

Her whispered, gasping words had the flames in her chest erupting with fiendish intensity. Tears clogged her throat, turning the effort of breathing into agony.

"I'm right here, Jules. I won't leave you. Just stay with me."

He cupped her cheek with a trembling hand, his palm a warm oasis against her icy flesh.

"Fight it. Dammit, you've got to fight. *You've got to hold on.*"

Her lips trembled open on a moan. A thick, suffocating cloud descended around her like a blanket of cotton. Seconds later, a black void opened beneath her.

Chapter 13

Sloan would have gotten on his knees and begged if he thought it would save her. He paced the corridor outside the hospital waiting room, praying, making deals with God to please, just let her live. Let her be all right.

Remembering how lifeless Julia had looked sprawled on the floor of Rick's office was like the stab of a knife through his brain. Her flesh had not only been pale as ice, it had *felt* like ice. She'd lost so much blood. *Too much.* Could someone lose that much blood and survive?

As he'd leaned over her, he'd known he would give his life if only he could take away her pain, ease her tormented breathing. *Save her.*

Instead, all he could do was stand helplessly aside when the grim-faced paramedics wheeled in their equipment-loaded gurney. In hushed tones, they exchanged a litany of medical jargon while sliding an IV needle into a vein, then positioning small, round electrodes across her blood-soaked chest. "Vitals?" one medic had asked. "Weak," the other replied.

Everything so efficient, so matter-of-fact. So *terrifying*.

As Sloan paced, he glanced into the small waiting room off the main corridor. The thin, red second hand of the wall clock swept soundlessly around the dial. Had it been only an hour since the medics had shoved Julia's gurney through the doors to the ER? A thick blanket had covered her motionless body; there had been no color to the part of her face that showed around the oxygen mask, no fluttering of the dark lashes that lay still—*too still*—against ashen, hollow cheeks.

If only he'd reached Rick's office a few seconds earlier, Sloan thought as he paced to the end of the hall. He turned to retrace his steps, sidestepping a wheeled cart that held some sort of instrument with an array of cords, dials and switches. Maybe if he'd been faster, he could have shoved Julia out of harm's way, taken the slug himself. Anything to have kept her safe. *Anything*.

But he'd been too late. And the bullet had crashed through her chest, doing damage he was afraid to even think about. Damage that made his stomach muscles tremble, turned his heart into a sledgehammer.

He stared down at his hands, still shaking as if no time had passed since he'd knelt over her, desperate to stop her bleeding. He'd had so much blood on him that when he rushed into the ER, a nurse had mistaken him for a patient and tried to hurry him into an examining room. After his terse explanation of why he was there, she directed him to a sink; he'd gotten the blood off his skin, but the cuffs of his white shirt were crimson.

He swallowed back the sick taste that rose in his parched throat. He'd known he had to stanch the flow of blood pouring from the bullet wound, but he had no idea if he'd gone about it the right way. What if he'd added to her injuries with the pressure he'd placed on her chest? What if he'd pushed broken cartilage—or a bone—through an already damaged lung? God, what if she died from his clumsy attempt to save her?

"Remington!"

Freezing in midstep, Sloan swiped his gaze to the far end of the fluorescent-lit corridor. For an instant the identity of the man clad in a green polo shirt and khaki shorts who'd rushed off the elevator eluded him.

"Julia's recorder?" the man asked into a cellular phone while his ground-eating stride brought him toward Sloan. "Fox had it in his pocket?"

Halliday, Sloan realized, recognizing the detective's voice.

"What was on the tape?" Halliday halted beside Sloan, his eyes grim marbles of blue behind his wire-rim glasses as he listened into the phone.

"That's not enough to pin the West homicide on him," Halliday said after a moment. "Is the bastard talking?"

The detective's gaze rose and locked with Sloan's. One side of his mouth lifted briefly, then resettled into a tight line. "That so? He's here. I'll tell him he's up for a good citizen award."

Halliday clicked off the phone, his face taut with concern. "How's my partner?" he asked, his voice less steady now.

"She's been in surgery about thirty minutes. I've asked, but can't get any information on her condition." Sloan sent a dark look at the stern-faced woman sitting behind the nurses' station. "I'm not family."

"Yeah, standard policy," Halliday said.

"Their policy is about to go to hell. My secretary's tracking down the hospital administrator. After we talk, I expect to have unlimited access to everything concerning Julia."

Halliday gave him an appraising look. "I bet you will," he said, then shifted his gaze to the waiting room. "What about Julia's parents? Have you called them?"

"I talked to Fred." Sloan tightened his jaw. He'd had to treat the receptionist who worked for Julia's father with blunt rudeness just to get her to put his call through after he'd identified himself. "Fred handled the news as well as expected, but we both knew that wouldn't be the case with Georgia. He said he'd pick her up at the decorating job she's doing somewhere north of the city. They ought to be here any time."

Halliday took in Sloan's blood-soaked cuffs. "Think maybe you should roll up your sleeves before they walk in?"

"I didn't even think...." Sloan scrubbed a hand across his face, wincing when he hit the welt that a well-aimed blow from Rick's fist had left on his right cheek.

His hands shook as he unhooked one gold cuff link, then the other. "All I can think about is Julia. About how much blood... By the time the ambulance got there, she could barely breathe."

"I guess it was pretty rough on you," Halliday said, watching him.

"A lot rougher on her."

"Yeah." Halliday flicked a look across the corridor at the nurse, then reached into his back pocket. "Maybe I can bridge the gap until you talk to the head of the hospital," he said, flipping open a leather case to display his gold shield. "This baby works like a crowbar when it comes to prying information out of people."

He turned, walked the few steps to the nurses' station and held the leather case across the counter.

Hot, frustrated anger built inside Sloan as he watched the woman nod, then pick up the phone and punch buttons. She spoke, listened for what seemed an interminable time, then hung up and began talking to Halliday. The detective listened, nodding intently.

Sloan turned, expelling a heated breath between his clenched teeth. He'd relinquished his claim on Julia once and removed himself from her life, had told her just that morning he intended to do the same thing again. Why, then, had the fact that the nurse treated him with the exact status he'd chosen tear his heart out by its roots?

"So far so good," Halliday said a few moments later

when he returned to Sloan's side. "Julia's pretty well holding her own."

Sloan turned, saw the guarded look in the man's eyes. "Pretty well? What the hell does that mean?"

"The bullet nicked a major vein. She lost a lot of blood before she got here. It'll take a while to get the bullet out, and she'll lose more blood. They're having a problem keeping her pressure stabilized. They've already pumped a couple of pints into her and will have to give her more." Halliday shoved an unsteady hand through his blond hair. "Hell."

A sickening combination of fear and remorse blasted through Sloan. The barrage of sensation nearly staggered him. He thought about their last moments together in the guest house when they'd fought, the things said...and those unsaid.

"I can at least give her some blood—"

Halliday caught Sloan's arm as he turned toward the nurses' station. "The hospital contacted the police chaplain. He's already called out the troops. The nurse says there's about a hundred cops downstairs waiting to donate."

The absolute feeling of helplessness had Sloan's hands balling at his sides.

"Word is Julia will be in surgery for a couple of hours total," Halliday added. "All we can do is wait."

Sloan stood silent, while the sterile scent of disinfectant thickened in his lungs. His inability to help Julia—to do *something*—edged control further and further from his grasp.

"Where the hell were you, Halliday?" he snapped. "Dammit, why weren't you with her?"

A muscle worked in the detective's jaw. "I should have been." He looked away for a long moment. "My wife had a baby two days ago. I'm on leave."

Sloan held up a hand, let it drop. "Sorry."

"Forget it," Halliday said. "I was upstairs in my wife's room when my pager went off. It was Sam Rogers, the lead detective at the scene. That's who I was talking to when I got down here. Sam gave me the rundown of what he thinks happened between Julia and Fox, based on the tape that was recovered. Something clued her to the fact that he killed Vanessa West. Julia used a forgotten appointment to try to get the hell out of there, but Fox didn't fall for it. He drew down on her."

Thinking about what Rick had done clouded Sloan's vision with a dull red haze of fury. "I went crazy when I saw him leaning over her. Dammit, he'd shot her and still had the gun aimed at her chest. I wanted to kill him."

Sloan flexed his right hand, only now feeling the bite of pain from swollen, bruised knuckles. "I think I would have killed him if I hadn't had to get to Julia."

"Sounds like you did okay," Halliday commented. "According to Sam, Fox has a broken nose, two black eyes and a busted lip—that's just the injury to his *face*. A couple of uniforms took him by the county hospital. They're on the way downtown now to book what's left of him. It will be my personal pleasure to make the bastard talk once I get him into interrogation."

The sudden rush of footsteps on the hard, polished floor had both men turning. Hands gripped, Fred and Georgia Cruze raced frantically down the corridor, both looking as if they'd entered their own private hell.

"Travis, how's my baby?" Georgia asked, her voice thin and desperate. The oversize white lapels on her tailored navy suit made her already pale skin seem ghostlike. "Where's my baby?"

"She's in surgery," Halliday said, sliding his arm around the woman's trembling shoulders. "I just talked to the nurse. She said Julia's doing fine. Just fine—"

"Fred said she's been shot." She clenched a hand sparkling with rings on Halliday's arm. "What happened? My God, where *was* she?"

"At my building," Sloan said quietly.

Two pairs of eyes slashed his way, one red-rimmed, one raw and dry-eyed.

"What was she doing there, Sloan?" Fred Cruze asked, his voice steady and low.

It was Halliday who answered. "Julia was following up a lead on a case—"

"Who shot her?" Georgia insisted.

"We've got a suspect by the name of Rick Fox in custody—"

"Rick Fox?" she asked, whipping her gaze back to Sloan. "Your *friend* Rick Fox?"

"Yes—"

"The man whose shoulder Julia cried on when you walked out on her?"

Sloan stared into eyes filled with a combination of antagonism and tears. "Yes."

Georgia lifted her chin. "You're responsible for this, aren't you?" Although delivered in a shaking voice, the question lashed out like a whip. "You're always responsible. Whenever you're around, Julia gets hurt. Just the other morning I warned her to stay away from you. And now, because of you, my baby might—"

"She's going to be fine," Sloan said, taking a quick step forward. *"She has to be all right."*

"Actually," Halliday interjected in a mild tone, "it was Mr. Remington who subdued Fox. Then he called for help and administered first aid to Julia until the ambulance arrived."

For the first time, Georgia seemed to take in Sloan's appearance. Her tear-filled eyes settled on his bruised cheek. Seconds passed, then her gaze lowered, taking in the rumpled white shirt that showed spatters of crimson on the pocket, the loose collar with no tie beneath it, the dark stains on his black slacks.

Her lips trembled; tears streamed down her pale cheeks as she turned to her husband. "We…need to call Bill. It doesn't matter that Julia broke off their engagement. I know she'll want him here when she wakes up.''

"Use this." Halliday slid the cellular phone from his pocket and handed it to Fred Cruze. "The waiting room is empty right now. You'll have some privacy if you call from in there. I need to check a few facts with Mr. Remington, then I'll be in."

Arms entwined, the couple leaned heavily on each other as they disappeared into the waiting room.

Sloan rubbed a hand across the knots in the back of his neck. "Hell," he mumbled.

"Did I hear Georgia right?" Halliday asked. "Julia broke her engagement?"

"There's nothing wrong with your hearing."

Halliday's eyes narrowed. "When?"

"Does it matter?"

"I'm just trying to get something clear in my mind."

"She told him sometime yesterday."

The detective nodded. "So, I figure you're the reason I couldn't get hold of Julia when I called her place until 2 a.m. this morning."

Sloan matched the detective's gaze and said nothing.

"Right." Halliday nodded as if he'd received confirmation. "Julia made her choice and I'll respect that. But it doesn't mean I'm not going to have my say," he added, lowering his voice as he leaned in. "From day one, I thought *you* murdered Vanessa West. My thinking didn't change until I got that call from Sam Rogers about twenty minutes ago."

Halliday paused while a gaunt, dark-haired man in a red-plaid bathrobe shuffled by at a snail's pace, leaning on his IV pole like a cane.

"What Julia thought about your guilt—or lack of—is a different matter," the detective continued. "I doubt she ever really believed you'd pulled the trigger. And because of that, she put up with a lot of grief from me." The hard lines etching the corners of Halliday's mouth eased slightly. "She told me why you walked out on her."

"Leaving was the right thing to do," Sloan said evenly.

"Yeah, well, you're entitled to an opinion, but I don't happen to agree."

"I don't care—"

"Let me clue you in on something, pal. You may have more money than the mint itself and own a house big enough to have its own zip code, but that doesn't make you smart. If you were smart, you wouldn't have left her then. And you damn sure wouldn't consider doing it again."

"Look, Halliday—"

"No, you look, Remington. Julia may be tough, but that doesn't mean she's invincible. In the six months we've been partners we've gotten so close we can damn near read each other's minds. She never mentioned your name in the whole time, never even said she had an ex-fiancé. Even so, I knew there was something there, some pain she carried around deep inside her. That pain is you, pal."

"Dammit, I left to keep her from getting hurt."

"Well, I don't like the idea that history may repeat itself. Maybe you haven't thought past right now, but that's exactly what you ought to do. Julia's going to be weak as a kitten for a while. In my mind, weak translates to vulnerable. What she'll need when she wakes up is support, not added misery from you. If you're still planning on taking off for D.C., I suggest you do it now and save her the goodbyes."

"When she was on that floor bleeding," Sloan began, forcing the words past the knot in his throat. "she asked me not to leave her. I promised I wouldn't. *I can't leave her now.*"

"You really think she was talking about things on a short-term basis?" Halliday asked as he slid his hands into the pockets of his shorts. "I've had my say. What you do is up to you. I'm going in to sit with Frank and Georgia. You coming?"

Sloan stared into the waiting room. Georgia had just finished her call and turned to her husband in the chair beside hers.

"Bill's out of town," she said, her knuckles white as she clutched the phone to her heart. A mix of despair and fear played in her face. In contrast, Fred's expression was bleak. Closed.

Sloan looked back at Halliday. "Later," he said. "I'll be in later."

The detective nodded, then walked into the waiting room. He settled into the empty chair beside Georgia, leaned forward and began talking to the couple in soft tones. At one point, Georgia glanced up; Sloan could feel the heat of her gaze boring through him.

I wasn't the only one who got hurt when you left.

The memory of Julia's words settled like lead weights on his shoulders. He knew he deserved her parents' recriminations. Had expected them. What he hadn't counted on was the pain that came with them.

None of it mattered, he reminded himself, then took a deep breath and walked into the waiting room. He settled into a chair near the door, rested his elbows on his knees, then pressed the heels of his hands hard against his eyes. Nothing mattered, as long as Julia survived. God, please let her live.

Two hours later, the small waiting room had filled to capacity. The police chaplain sat with the Cruzes, lending support with words of faith and cups of strong coffee. Julia's boss, Lieutenant Michael Ryan, and his wife, A.J., had joined in the seemingly endless waiting, along with a number of Homicide detectives and uniformed officers.

As he had every five minutes since he'd arrived at the hospital, Sloan checked the time. Julia had been in surgery almost three hours. *Three hours.* Thinking about all the blood she'd lost, the shocked paleness of her skin, her labored breathing, made his body ache with fear.

"I have a few things to say to you."

His chin jerked up. He had no idea Georgia had left her husband's side. No idea she'd settled, spine as stiff as a knife blade, into the chair beside his. Her unlined face was delicately pale. Now it was a reluctant understanding, rather than tears, that filled her reddened eyes.

Sloan straightened in his chair. He knew it had not been easy for her to cross the room to him. "I'm listening."

"I've spent the past two years despising you, Sloan Remington."

"I gave you good reason."

"When you left, you nearly destroyed my daughter. You hurt Fred and me. I hated you for what you'd done to my family. Sometimes, I wished you dead." Her breath shook as she let it out and drew in more. "I'd always thought you were crazy in love with Julia. And then you just left...." Her clenched palm opened to reveal a wad of white tissue. "I couldn't understand how you could do that. It was beyond my comprehension how we could have all been so wrong about you."

Wordlessly, Sloan stared into her shadowed, reddened eyes.

"Now I understand we weren't wrong." Georgia looked across the room to where Halliday sat. "Travis told Fred and me why you left. You were sick, and you wanted to protect Julia from the same fate as your mother."

"I'm not looking for redemption, Georgia. Under the circumstances, I did what I thought was the right thing. I won't apologize for that."

"I believe you had my daughter's best interests at heart." She stared down, fumbling with the gold watch on her wrist. "God, how much longer?"

"Soon," Sloan said quietly. "It has to be soon." He didn't tell her he'd asked himself the same question a hundred times since he settled into the chair by the door.

Georgia shuddered visibly. Sloan could feel her despair, thick and heavy. He had the urge to reach out and take her hand, then caught himself. He doubted the gesture would be welcomed.

"I don't agree that your cutting Julia out of your life was the best way to handle the situation," Georgia said, wadding the tissue tighter in her fist. "But I understand why you did it."

She paused to dab an errant tear from her cheek, then looked over at Sloan, the edges of her mouth lifting slightly. "I was delighted when Julia was born because I thought I had a little girl I could have tea parties with and dress in pink, frothy dresses. As it turned out, she preferred denim and a good game of cops and robbers."

Her voice broke, and she shook her head before going on. "Julia was tough from the start. She never let the class bully get away with picking on the weaker kids, and for that she sometimes came home all scraped and bruised. In that sense, she never needed protecting—never wanted it. My tough little girl grew into a strong young woman. I'm wondering if you realize just how much inner strength she has."

Sloan closed his eyes, fighting the pressing need to wrap his arms around Georgia in an attempt to give comfort as well as receive it. "My mother was a strong person, too, but in the end that strength didn't do her a bit of good," he said. "There's only so much a person can take—Julia's no exception. I couldn't chance her getting hurt. I just didn't want her…"

To die.

He dragged in a breath, unable to say the words for fear they might come true. "Today, I couldn't protect her. Couldn't do a damn thing for her."

"But you did." Georgia inclined her head toward a corner of the waiting room where a group of police officers were gathered, talking among themselves in soft tones. "The detective who worked the scene is here. The paramedics told him Julia would have bled to death if you hadn't done what you did. You kept her alive, Sloan. Fred and I thank you for that.''

"I don't want your thanks. I just want her to be okay."

The slap of crepe-soled shoes on tile brought both their heads up. A tall, lanky man dressed in sweat-drenched green scrubs stepped into the waiting room.

As they rose, Sloan placed a hand beneath Georgia's elbow to steady her. Fred Cruze hurried over to join them, accompanied by Travis Halliday. The quiet murmur of voices that had filled the room for the past hours ceased, replaced with a collective, breath-holding silence.

"Mr. and Mrs. Cruze, I'm Dr. Averey. Your daughter is out of surgery. She's stabilized, and her prognosis is good."

"Thank, God," Georgia said, her voice a raw whisper. The tissue she held to her mouth had deteriorated to a damp lump. "Thank, God."

"The bullet nicked the subclavian vein, which lies across the chest," Dr. Averey continued. "That's why she lost so much blood. The surgery was lengthy because we had a lot of tissue damage to repair. Her blood pressure dipped several times."

"But she's all right?" Georgia asked breathlessly. "She's all right?"

"She will be," the man said in a reassuring voice. "She'll experience quite a bit of pain at first, and she'll be weak—very weak—from the blood loss. We transfused her with three units. She may need more later. Your daughter is young, healthy and strong. A month from now, I expect her to be almost good as new."

Throughout the room, the silence transformed into sighs of relief.

"When can we see her?" Fred asked, his expression relaxing for the first time since he'd arrived.

"She's still in recovery. I'll tell the nurse to let you know when she's moved to her room. You can go in and stay five minutes, no more. I assure you, she won't know you're there. It's unlikely she'll wake until morning. The best thing you can do for your daughter is go home and get some rest. After she wakes up is when she's going to need you here.''

While Georgia and Fred asked the doctor a few more questions, Sloan expelled the breath he'd been holding. He was shaking, he realized. Trembling. Filled with relief that the first barrier had been crossed.

But only the first. He intended to be there to help Julia over each and every one.

Julia fumbled her way through the suffocating darkness, trying to find her way out. The air had the consistency of syrup, too thick to pull into her lungs. No, she thought as her head filled with the roaring sound of rushing water. It wasn't the air. She couldn't breathe because someone had dropped an anvil on her chest and left it there.

Her fingers flinched. In her half-lucid state, her fuzzy brain took a moment to send the message that an answering, steady hand had tightened around hers.

Sitting beside her in the dimly lit room, Sloan watched her eyelids flutter open, then close again. That and the faint flexing of her fingers were his first indication that she might regain consciousness—however briefly—hours before the doctor had predicted.

God, what if she'd woken up and he hadn't been here? He set his jaw, knowing now how right he'd been to make the call to the hospital administrator. It was the first time he'd ever used the power behind the Remington name to bring him special privileges, and he felt zero remorse.

Her hand twitched weakly in his.

"Jules, can you hear me?" he asked softly as he placed his other hand against her cheek. Paleness had wiped away her tan, giving her skin a thin, bone-china look that scared the hell out of him.

Her lashes fluttered again, then closed.

"Jules, try to stay with me for a minute. Just a minute."

Slowly her eyes opened, focused. "Sloan..."

Her voice was flat and far away, and the sound of it tightened the fist around his heart.

"I'm here, baby. Right here."

"Where am…?" She shifted minutely and a silvery flash of pain shot through her eyes. "Oh, God."

"You have to stay still. Very still."

"Rick shot me. In the…chest." She winced, as if each breath was a wheezing, hurting effort. "How…bad?"

"The doctor said you'll be good as new in no time. All you need to do is rest."

It nearly broke him to watch pain cloud her eyes. God, if only he could trade places with her. If only he could keep her from hurting. "I'm going to get the nurse, have her give you something."

Julia's hand moved in his. The flutter of a moth's wings would have had more strength.

"Don't…leave." Her eyes closed. "Don't…go."

"I won't. I'll stay right here. I swear to you, Jules, I'll stay."

Chapter 14

Halliday gathered up the newest photographs of his six-day-old son from the wheeled table that bridged Julia's bed. "Now that we've gotten the important stuff out of the way, let's talk a little more about the case."

"Okay." She saw the stain of baby slobber on his right lapel and smiled.

"Fox—or should I call him '*Sly*'?—sang like a church choir," Halliday said. He settled onto the edge of the bed, the mattress shifting with his weight.

Julia leaned, trying to find a comfortable position. Her smile faded and she gritted her teeth when the bandage tightened on her chest.

"You all right?"

"Fine," she said through clenched jaws.

In the four days since the shooting, the ache in her chest had gotten worse, not better, as shocked nerves began to regain their function. The doctor had assured her that was normal. God forbid she'd have to experience the abnormal, Julia thought, waiting for her muscles to unclench.

"So, you got Rick to confess," she stated when the pain turned from hideous into simply breathtaking.

"To every sin he'd committed since third grade." The smug look Halliday gave her transformed into a frown as he flapped a hand in her direction. "What's with all the lace and stuff, Cruze?"

She glanced down at the frothy peach robe with its row of tiny, shell-shaped pearl buttons that ran from throat to hem. "Mother brought it by this morning. The only way I could get her to agree to go back to work today was to promise to wear this thing. She says it's ghastly the way some patients walk the halls with their underwear hanging out the back of a tacky hospital gown."

Halliday grinned. "She should just be glad they're wearing underwear."

"I doubt that's occurred to Mother. She said she wants me to look elegant on my 'daily spins along the corridors.' Never mind that I'm so shaky by the time I make one lap that I've come close to crawling back to bed."

"At least if you pass out in that robe, you'll look good."

"I'll look like a damn Kewpie doll." It was Julia's turn to flap her hand in his face. "Get on it, Halliday. Tell me more about the case."

"We found a former employee of Remington Aerospace on who Vanessa used her sneaky tricks with the personnel files. A guy by the name of Tony England."

"What about him?"

"He and Vanessa worked at the San Francisco office a couple of years ago. They were both in the running for the same job. It meant prestige and a substantial promotion. All bets were that England had the job sewn up tight. It took everybody by surprise when he quit the day before the promotion was to be announced. Nobody knew why."

"I guess you found out."

Halliday nodded. "England's résumé listed an impressive educational background. Only problem was, he hadn't completed his MBA like he'd claimed. Vanessa found out and confronted him. All he had to do was quit and she'd keep her mouth shut about how he'd perpetrated a fraud on the company. That's what he did.''

"And she got the promotion," Julia added.

"Right. Talk about a woman with a dark side," Halliday commented as he slid off the bed. He stood quiet for a moment, taking in the lush, flowering bouquets that crowded every surface of the room. "Did Remington send all these?"

"Most of them." Julia extended her arm across the table to touch the crystal vase that held flawless, violet blue hydrangea blossoms. In her mind's eye she pictured the banks of blooms that had glowed in the moonlight while she and Sloan made love in the hot tub. It seemed like a lifetime ago, instead of just a week.

"Speaking of Remington, where'd he get off to?" Halliday asked. "I thought he'd taken up permanent residence here."

"He has." Julia pulled her bottom lip between her teeth. Although Sloan had been an almost constant presence since she'd regained consciousness, he'd said nothing about the night they'd spent in each other's arms. Nothing about the angry, seemingly final words that had passed between them the following morning.

Nothing about his plans to leave for D.C.

"Cruze?"

She frowned, scrambling to remember Halliday's question. "Sloan went to take a shower. They've given him unlimited use of the doctors' locker room."

Halliday chuckled. "I'll bet they have." He checked his watch. "I'd better get back to work—"

"He sleeps there, Halliday," Julia said quietly. "A nurse told me Sloan didn't leave this room for the first forty-eight hours after they brought me in."

"You gave him a hell of a scare. You gave us all—"

"The nurse says he comes back in here at night after I'm asleep. He just sits by the bed and holds my hand."

Halliday inclined his head, his expression softening. "The guy cares about you, Cruze. Don't tell me that comes as a surprise."

"I know he cares," she said, staring toward the window, where the morning sun streamed through the open blind. "But Sloan doesn't let his feelings rule him. He cared about me two years ago and he still walked out. A few hours before I got shot, he told me again he was leaving, moving to D.C." She paused. Hurt filled her, tightened her throat. Hurt that came with the knowledge that the hours they'd spent in each other's arms had done nothing to lessen Sloan's determination to walk out of her life a second time.

She dragged in a deep breath and raised her chin. "Now that the case is cleared, he's free to go. I reminded him of that yesterday."

A blond brow slid up Halliday's forehead. "What did he say?"

"Nothing. He just looked at me, then changed the subject." She raised an unsteady hand, toyed with the shell-shaped buttons at her throat. "I know him, Halliday. He had nothing to do with what happened, but he feels guilty because his best friend shot me. What if Sloan's staying here because of some misplaced sense of guilt?"

"Whoa, Cruze. You may have taken a bullet in the chest, but it's your brain that's not working right. Believe me, it wasn't guilt that had Remington pacing the wax off the tiles while you were in surgery."

"He was worried. Everyone was—"

"He called the hospital administrator and threatened to bulldoze the wing he'd just built on this place if he didn't have twenty-four-hour access to your room. I have to admit I like Remington's style."

Julia opened her mouth, closed it again. "Sloan threatened to tear down the building?"

"Just one wing. The guy's dealing with a lot of emotions where you're concerned, Cruze, but misplaced guilt isn't one of them."

She blinked back the swell of tears that had teetered on the brink of spilling ever since she'd regained full consciousness. To Julia, tears had always been a sign of weakness, as the ones she now fought were. The doctor had assured her the feeling of vulnerability that had settled over her was a temporary result of her injury, as were the disabling weakness and chronic fatigue that allowed her to perform only the most simple tasks. But knowing the symptoms would fade as she healed didn't make the constant threat of tears any easier to bear.

As he watched her, wariness settled in Halliday's eyes. Shoving his glasses higher on his nose, he took a step away from the bed. Then another. "You're not going to start crying, are you?"

"Back off, Halliday, I don't cry. Ever. I'm just…trying to figure out why Sloan won't tell me how he feels."

"How the hell do I know?" Halliday asked, easing his way farther toward the door. "He's a guy…you know how often we screw up when it comes to dealing with women."

Hair slicked back from his shower, Sloan walked into the sun-drenched room just as the nurse unwound the blood pressure cuff from Julia's arm.

Surrounded by a rainbow of lush blooms and dressed in the peach gown Georgia had brought that morning, Julia might be considered the picture of good health by the casual observer. Her long, dark hair tumbled past her shoulders, glistening from the recent shampoo Georgia had arranged. Blush tinted her cheeks; lipstick that matched the gown—another gift from her mother—slicked her full lips.

Sloan set his jaw. He was far from a casual observer. To him, no amount of makeup could camouflage the lack of color in her skin or disguise the hollow look around her eyes. The frailness that seemed to hang over her tightened the ever-present fist around his heart.

"Hello, Mr. Remington," the plump nurse said, smiling as she glanced across her shoulder.

"Agnes." Sloan set his shaving kit beside the small stainless-steel sink, then walked to the bed. Careful to avoid the IV tube suspended from the pole to Julia's arm, he leaned and placed a light kiss against her temple. He felt the warmth of her flesh beneath his lips, remembered the icy feel of her skin as she'd lain bleeding on the floor of Rick's office. She had come so close to dying. So close.

"How do you feel?" he managed after a moment.

She scowled. "The same way I felt two hours ago when someone else took my blood pressure."

Agnes gave a brisk nod as she jotted a note in Julia's chart. "We like it when our patients get testy. That means they're getting better."

"If that's the scale you use to judge things, then I'm fully recovered," Julia muttered. "Why don't you tell Dr. Averey how much *better* I'm feeling so he'll sign my release papers?"

"I'd hate to try to tell the doctor how to do his job." Agnes fluffed the pillows behind Julia before gathering up the chart and heading for the door in a rustling blur of starched cotton. "Give it a few more days, Sergeant Cruze. He'll probably consider letting you go."

"A few more days," Julia echoed hollowly, and sank against the pillows.

Sloan saw the sides of her mouth tighten and realized the movement must have jarred her incision. He turned and walked to the window. He couldn't handle the misery in her eyes.

"I knew staying here wouldn't be easy for you, Jules." He dipped his hands into the pockets of his slacks as he stared blindly out at the sun-drenched parking lot. "So I talked to Dr. Averey about releasing you now, setting you up with full-time nurses."

"What did he say?"

"That he'd reevaluate your condition in a couple of days and let me know." Sloan turned in time to see the glimmer of hope fade from her eyes. "I'm sorry." He crossed to the bed and took her hand. "You need to get some rest now."

"Do you know how many times a day someone tells me to rest?"

His lips curved. "I bet you're going to tell me."

"Too many." He saw her gaze sharpen on the bruise on his right cheek, which had transformed to healing shades of yellow gray and green. "Speaking of rest, when was the last time you slept through the night?"

"I get enough sleep." He raised their joined hands and placed a soft kiss against her knuckles. "We'll talk later—"

"Now, Sloan." She tugged her hand from his. "You haven't left this place in four days. And how come I never see you eat?"

"I eat while you're resting."

"I'm not an idiot. Don't treat me like one. I may be zonked out most of the time, but I know what you're doing. And you and I are going to talk about it."

His brow creased. "The doctor said you need to stay free of stress—"

"I'm going to explode if we don't talk this out. Right now."

He nodded slowly. "All right, talk."

"You're doing the exact thing you denied me—you know that, don't you? You walked away from me so I couldn't be with you while you were sick. You were afraid I'd stop eating. Afraid I'd let my career go down the tubes. Afraid I'd stop sleeping just like your mother did when she took care of your father. Like what you're doing now with me."

"It's not the same."

"I'm stuck in a hospital bed, the same as you were," she said. "Have you been to your office lately?"

Not since she'd been shot. "It's been a few days."

"Have you looked in the mirror?" she continued. "It'd

be hard to decide which one of us has the darkest circles under our eyes."

He reached, rubbed the pad of his thumb across her cheek. "The only way yours will go away is if you rest—"

"Don't you dare try to placate me, dammit." She batted his hand away, then sucked in a breath, pain settling in her eyes.

"God, Jules, don't talk." He gripped her hand. The tears that welled in her eyes, then streamed down her cheeks, nearly broke him. "We can discuss everything you want—for however long you want—after you get out of here. For now, you've got to build up your strength. And the only way to do that is rest."

"How can I rest when every time you walk through that door I look to see if you've got plane tickets sticking out of your pocket?" She grabbed a handful of tissues out of the box beside the vase of hydrangeas and dabbed at her eyes. "I don't cry. I hate to cry."

"I know—"

"You told me that morning at the guest house you were leaving. The case is closed. You're free to go." Her chest heaved. "Why prolong this, Sloan? Why the hell don't you just go?"

"The only way I'll leave is if you tell me you want me to go." He clenched his fist against his thigh and waited for her to do just that.

But she didn't say the words. She was crying too hard to say anything.

Mindful of the IV tube, he slid onto the edge of the bed and gathered her close. He closed his eyes as her sobs racked her body. "Don't cry," he said, placing a soft kiss against her hair. "Baby, please don't cry."

"I'm...not," she said, and sobbed harder.

In the four days since the shooting he had come to the knife edge of things. He had sat beside her bed, holding a hand he'd always thought delicate, but knew now was strong. Her slim body appeared fragile, but after unending hours of watching her—just watching—he'd come to the understanding that she possessed an inner strength and purpose that made her capable of dealing with whatever fate dealt her.

Why? he asked himself. Why had it taken him so long to see and fully understand all that she was?

He had planned to wait until she healed—both physically and emotionally—to tell her how he felt, tell her what she'd wanted to hear that morning in the guest house. Tell her that he would beg, crawl—do anything, as long as she gave him another chance and let him back into her life.

He stroked his hand down the silken fall of her hair and listened to her helpless sobs that made him want to weep himself. Now he realized he could no longer wait to tell her.

"I can't stand to see you hurt." He leaned away just far enough to place soft kisses against her wet cheeks. The briny tang of her tears flooded his mouth. "I can't stand it, Jules. Every time I picture you on that floor with your blood pumping out of you..." His own body quavered against hers. "I thought you were going to die in my arms. I thought you were going to die."

It was as if the desperate intensity in his voice stemmed the flow of her tears. "I'm...fine now." She used an unsteady hand to swipe the tissue at her swollen eyes. "I'm fine. You don't have to stay with me just because—"

"I love you, Julia. I love you so much that I can't bear to think about losing you."

She stared at him, her dark lashes spiked with tears. "You loved me before, and you still left."

He nodded. "I've done a lot of thinking over the past four days. And I came to realize a few things." He reached up, tucked a wave of unruly dark hair behind her ear. "When I came back three months ago, I had myself convinced it was because of the business with the new wing company. I know now I came back because of you."

"I'd just gotten engaged..."

"That's what brought me back—knowing you no longer belonged to me. That I'd lost you forever."

She blinked. "You didn't call. You'd been here three months, and you never called."

"I lost count of how many times I picked up the phone and started to dial your number. Eventually I would have let the phone ring." His mouth tightened. "Then Vanessa died, and fate ran us headlong into each other again. From that moment on, I was a goner."

An ingrained wariness crept into her eyes. "I can't do this again, Sloan. I can't go through this twice in one lifetime."

A knot of panic settled in his gut at the thought of her sending him away. "You have my word I won't walk away again," he said, tightening his hold on arms that seemed too thin. Paper-thin. "Seeing you hurt made me realize that our lives can change in the next instant. The next heartbeat. If you're willing to take me back, we have another chance at happiness. Another chance at love. I love you, Julia. I have since the first moment I saw you."

She stared up at him, her hair a dark, vivid frame against her pale skin. Her eyes flashed fire, despite the tears that still swam in them. "Another chance, Sloan? Does that mean you'll stay with me only as long as you're healthy? If it does, I'm not interested."

"That's not what I mean." He shifted onto one hip, slid a small box out of his pocket and placed it in her hand. "I want you for a lifetime, Julia. No matter what that lifetime brings. Marry me, Jules."

She remained motionless, staring at the box in her trembling hand.

Sloan reached and opened the lid. The enormous, pear-shaped diamond flashed in the morning sunlight.

"My ring." She looked up. "I mailed this back to your office after you left."

"It's been in the safe there all this time. I called Elizabeth and had her send it over." Sloan wanted to slip the ring on her finger, restake his claim. Instead, he reached over and stroked her hair with an unsteady hand.

She shook her head. "I don't know what to do."

"If you need time to think things through, I'll wait." He placed a soft kiss against her temple. "I'll wait as long as I have to. I'm all yours," he added, "whether you're wearing my ring or not."

"That's not what I mean," she said, her dark brows sliding together. "I don't know what to do about a wedding. How can I plan a wedding when I can barely stay awake two hours at a time?"

"Don't even consider it, Julia."

Julia and Sloan turned their heads in unison at the sound of Georgia's voice.

"Mother! How long have you been standing there?"

"Long enough to hear *everything.*" Georgia marched into the room. In her olive suit with brass buttons and gold braiding on the sleeves, she had the look of a general about to harangue the troops.

She stopped directly in front of Sloan, hands crammed on her hips. "My daughter should be resting."

"I agree." He turned back to Julia, plucked the ring out of its velvet nest. "I love you, Julia Cruze. Will you marry me?"

She nodded. Tears reappeared in her eyes as she held out a shaky hand.

"We're getting married," she managed after a moment, and flashed the ring her mother's way.

"No need to restate the obvious, dear," Georgia said as she stepped to the bed and dropped a kiss on Julia's forehead. The woman took a deep breath. When she raised her arm to pat at her expertly styled coiffure, the charms on her heavy gold bracelet jingled like Christmas bells.

"Well, Julia, you want a wedding, so that's what you'll get." Georgia reached, smoothed her hand over the sleeve of the coral robe. "You leave everything to me, dear." She then turned slowly to face Sloan. "I think it'd be best to get the unpleasantries out of the way first thing."

He remained on the edge of the bed, Julia's hand firmly ensconced in his own. "Have your say, Georgia."

"My family has gone through hell because of you, Sloan Remington. And now you're going to pay."

"Mother—"

"Quiet, darling." Georgia held out her palm toward Sloan and jiggled her fingers. "I hope your credit limit is in the clouds, because this is going to be one hell of a wedding."

The gleam of acceptance in Georgia's eyes curled around Sloan's heart as he rose and placed a kiss on her cheek. "You've got *carte blanche*." He pulled his wallet from his pocket and handed her a gold credit card. "Anything goes."

Julia's eyes widened. "Be careful, Sloan. I said the same thing to Mother once, and got a bedroom straight out of the *Arabian Nights*."

He looked down, gave her a quizzical smile. *"Arabian Nights?"*

Julia nodded and grabbed her mother's hand. "Nothing elaborate, Mother. I just want something simple—"

"We'll have the ceremony at Sloan's house," Georgia said. "Outdoors on the grounds. It's the perfect setting for a lovely little ceremony. Very quaint."

Julia gave her a wary look. "Little and quaint sounds fine."

"Just leave everything to me," Georgia said as Sloan's credit card disappeared into her pocket.

Epilogue

If Georgia Cruze knew the meaning of "little and quaint," she ignored it. Construction workers descended on Sloan's house, erecting an immense framework across the expanse of manicured lawn. Before the sawdust settled, a team of decorators moved in, using hundreds of yards of white silk to create a canopy that draped from the framework's center and waterfalled in soft folds down each side. Truckloads of white roses added their heady scent to the already vast, blooming gardens. Guests packed the tented wonderland, sitting on velvet-cushioned chairs swaddled in clouds of white netting. The soft, evening breeze fluttered the folds of white silk as the harpist switched to the wedding march.

Julia, clad in her mother's antique-lace bridal gown and exquisite veil, walked down the orchid-strewn aisle on her father's arm. As they moved, she acknowledged the fluttering in her stomach and trembling in her legs. She knew these latest symptoms weren't a result of her brush with mortality. The weakness that assailed her had begun when she first glimpsed Sloan standing at the altar, looking darkly handsome, as if he'd been born to wear the elegantly tailored tux.

The wedding march ended in the harp's soft, dreamy notes. Julia kissed her father's cheek, then turned and slid her hand into the crook of Sloan's arm. He stared down at her, his intimate gaze filled with love.

The police chaplain said a prayer, then began the ceremony.

Hours later, Julia's head was still spinning when Sloan carried her up the stairs of Remington Aerospace's corporate jet. Keeping her securely in his arms, he strode the forward part of the lush cabin.

"I can walk," she protested, but kept her hands looped firmly around his neck.

"Don't you know it's bad luck if a man fails to carry his bride over the threshold?" He settled her onto a plush sofa, then tucked her into the pillowed corner.

"I don't think the door to a plane counts as a threshold," she said. Glancing out the window, she caught sight of the last of their luggage being loaded into the plane's belly.

She looked back at Sloan. After leaving the reception with its tables laden with food and fountains of champagne, he had changed into a dark-gray suit and discreet tie. Julia glanced down, having no idea if the short black cocktail suit her mother had picked out for her was appropriate for their destination.

She reached for his hand. "You know, this is my honeymoon, too. Don't you think it's time you told me where we're going?"

"I have no idea."

Her eyes widened. "Who does?"

"Your mother and the pilot."

"You let Mother pick out where we're spending our honeymoon?"

Sloan nodded, pulled off his jacket and draped it across

one of the thick, upholstered chairs. "She asked me to let her do that as a favor. I said yes."

"Did she return your credit card?"

"No."

Julia leaned back on the cushions and groaned. "Pick out the most expensive spot in the world, and that's where we're going."

"If this is how Georgia thinks I should pay for my mistake, so be it." Smiling, he leaned and clicked the ends of Julia's seat belt together. "I don't mind," he said, placing a soft kiss on the tip of her nose, "as long as we're together." He settled beside her, fastened himself in, then leaned and flipped on an intercom. "Ready."

Julia sat silent during takeoff, wondering what it was that had suddenly begun nagging at her mind. Only when they were airborne did she figure it out.

"Wait a minute." After unlocking her seat beat, she scooted across the cushion onto Sloan's lap. "You said you're letting mother make you pay for your mistake."

He stared at her for a long moment. "So?"

"*Mistake.* You're admitting you made a mistake when you left me?"

His hands rose, framed her face. "The biggest one of my life. We lost two years that we'll never get back."

Julia smiled, her love for him blissfully overpowering. "Then we'd better start making up for lost time." She glanced around the cabin. "Are there any flight attendants lurking?"

"Not on this trip. I intend to wait on you hand and foot myself." He arched a dark brow as she leaned and nipped his bottom lip. "Don't you think you ought to—"

"Dammit, Sloan, I've been out of the hospital almost a month. If you so much as mention the word *rest,* I'll shove you out of this plane." She tugged at his tie, slipped it from beneath his collar and tossed it aside.

Her mouth took on a seductive curve as she attacked the buttons of his shirt. "Just because we don't know where we're going shouldn't stop us from starting our honey-moon.''

He smiled as his nimble fingers slid her jacket off her shoulders. ''Whatever you say, Sergeant.''

Later, as the jet streaked through the dark sky, Julia lay drowsy and sated in her husband's arms. She raised her head, gently stroked her fingers across the scar that sliced down his stomach. She had her own scar now, not yet fully healed. ''In sickness and in health,'' she murmured softly.

Sloan cupped her cheek, his thumb slowly tracing the curve of her lips. ''In sickness and in health.''

* * * * *

Available in February 1998

ANN MAJOR

CHILDREN OF DESTINY
When Passion and Fate Intertwine...

SECRET CHILD

Although everyone told Jack West that his wife,
Chantal—the woman who'd betrayed him and sent
him to prison for a crime he didn't commit—had
died, Jack knew she'd merely transformed herself
into supermodel Mischief Jones. But when he
finally captured the woman he'd been hunting,
she denied everything. Who was she really—
an angel or a cunningly brilliant counterfeit?"

"Want it all? Read Ann Major."
—Nora Roberts, *New York Times*
bestselling author

Don't miss this compelling story
available at your favorite retail outlet.
Only from Silhouette books.

Take 4 bestselling love stories FREE

Plus get a FREE surprise gift!

**Make a Valentine's date
for the premiere of**

◇ HARLEQUIN® **Movies**

starting February 14, 1998 with

Debbie Macomber's
This Matter of
Marriage

on the movie channel 🌐tmc

Just tune in to **The Movie Channel** the **second Saturday night** of every month at 9:00 p.m. EST to join us, and be swept away by the sheer thrill of romance brought to life. Watch for details of upcoming movies—in books, in your television viewing guide and in stores.

If you are not currently a subscriber to The Movie Channel, simply call your local cable or satellite provider for more details. Call today, and don't miss out on the romance!

*100% pure movies.
100% pure fun.*

◇ HARLEQUIN™
Makes any time special.™

Harlequin is a trademark of Harlequin Enterprises Limited. The Movie Channel is a trademark of Showtime Networks, Inc., a Viacom Company.

An Alliance Production   HMBPA298

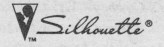

SANDRA STEFFEN

**Continues the
twelve-book series—
36 Hours—in February 1998
with Book Eight**

MARRIAGE BY CONTRACT

Nurse Bethany Kent could think of only one man who could
make her dream come true: Dr. Tony Petrocelli, the man who
had helped her save the life of the infant she desperately
wanted to adopt. As husband and wife, they could provide the
abandoned baby with a loving home. But could they provide
each other with more than just a convenient marriage?

For Tony and Bethany and *all* the residents of Grand Springs,
Colorado, the storm-induced blackout was just the beginning
of 36 Hours that changed *everything!* You won't want to miss a
single book.

Available at your favorite retail outlet.

Silhouette ®

BESTSELLING AUTHORS
IN THE SPOTLIGHT

.WE'RE SHINING THE SPOTLIGHT ON SIX OF OUR STARS!

Harlequin and Silhouette have selected stories from several of their bestselling authors to give you six sensational reads. These star-powered romances are bound to please!

THERE'S A PRICE TO PAY FOR STARDOM... AND IT'S LOW

$1.99 U.S.
$2.50 CAN.
Special Offer

As a special offer, these six outstanding books are available from Harlequin and Silhouette for only $1.99 in the U.S. and $2.50 in Canada. Watch for these titles:

At the Midnight Hour—Alicia Scott
Joshua and the Cowgirl—Sherryl Woods
Another Whirlwind Courtship—Barbara Boswell
Madeleine's Cowboy—Kristine Rolofson
Her Sister's Baby—Janice Kay Johnson
One and One Makes Three—Muriel Jensen

Available in March 1998
at your favorite retail outlet.

PBAIS

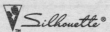

Return to the Towers!

In March
New York Times bestselling author

NORA ROBERTS

brings us to the Calhouns' fabulous
Maine coast mansion and reveals the
tragic secrets hidden there for generations.

For all his degrees, Professor Max Quartermain has a
lot to learn about love—and luscious Lilah Calhoun is
just the woman to teach him. Ex-cop Holt Bradford is
as prickly as a thornbush—until Suzanna Calhoun's
special touch makes love blossom in his heart.
And all of them are caught in the race to solve
the generations-old mystery of a priceless
lost necklace…and a timeless love.

Lilah and Suzanna
THE
Calhoun Women

**A special 2-in-1 edition containing
FOR THE LOVE OF LILAH and
SUZANNA'S SURRENDER**

Available at your favorite retail outlet.

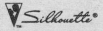